Simon Rowe grew up in small town New Zealand and big city Australia when orange Fanta came in glass bottles and AM radio was king. He now writes and teaches in the samurai castle town of Himeji in western Honshu. His stories have appeared in TIME Asia, the New York Times, the South China Morning Post and the Paris Review.

Short fiction by Simon Rowe also appears in:

Zawadi & other short stories (Ouen Press 2020)
The Best Asian Short Stories Anthology
(Kitaab International 2019)
Encounters with Kyoto: Writers in Kyoto Anthology 3
(Writers in Kyoto 2019)
Noir Nation: International Crime Fiction No. 7
(Noir Nation Books 2019)
Good Night Papa: Short Stories from Japan and Elsewhere
(Atlas Jones & Co. 2017)
Flesh: A Southeast Asian Urban Anthology (Fixi Novo 2016)
Another Time, Another Place
(Swinburne Anthology Group 2015)
Noir Nation: International Crime Fiction No. 3
(Noir Nation Books 2103)

PEARL CITY
Stories from Japan and Elsewhere

SIMON ROWE

Front cover: Jeremy Hannigan - www.jeremyhannigan.com
Layout: Claudia Rowe

ISBN 978-0-646-81935-8
Printed and bound in China by Imago.

For Masami, Marina, Aiden, Claudia, Joe, Ashley and Catherine

Family is true wealth.

ACKNOWLEDGEMENTS

A humongous thank you to my sister, Claudia Rowe, for readying Pearl City for publication; to Simone Ford for applying her copy editing magic, and to artist, Jeremy Hannigan, for bringing the Pearl City characters to life with his magnificent cover design. My sincere thanks also go to Writers in Kyoto (Japan), Ouen Press (U.K.), Noir Nation Books (U.S.), and Kitaab International (Singapore), for having deemed four of my tales worthy of their own publications.

Finally, to longtime friend, Kevin Ballou, for his generous contribution, and to the international band of backers who threw their support behind me —
a sumo-sized arigatō gozaimasu!

Tony Hall
Raymond Malone
Mark Bahlin
Greg Rouault
Jesse Pasley
John Gayed
Dimitri Van Beverloo
Greg Lund
Rob O'Keefe
Michele Tardini
Warwick Tiernan
Eugene Ridgley
Bergen O'Brien
David O'Hara

CONTENTS

Pearl City

Silhouetted against the noonday sky, the president of Tokai Pearls Limited stood at his suite window and surveyed the harbour. His gaze ranged from the shipyards and submarine docks of Kawasaki Heavy Industries to the Mosaic shopping mall and its slow-turning Ferris wheel, then to the Port Tower where tour boats came and went from the ferry terminal, and finally to the Rokko mountains which lifted the suburbs in a great pale wave above the sea.

'Do you know why they call this Pearl City?' he asked.

The three dark suits at the back of the room said nothing. Their collective gaze instead fell to the middle-aged woman in a blue pantsuit who sat on the leather sofa chair in front of them. She was generously built, wore her hair in a jet-black bob, and rested her manicured hands on a chestnut brown handbag in her lap.

'Because pearls are a Kobe girl's best friend?' she ventured.

The president's laughter rolled about the room like distant thunder. 'Good, good! I like it,' he said. Then, to the back of the room, 'Danno, make a note of that. We could use it in advertising.'

A slim young man with a fashionable hairstyle gave a curt 'Hai!', drew a pen from his breast pocket and scribbled into a notepad.

The president seated himself behind a desk of polished walnut, a pink conch shell paperweight to one side, a speed-dial phone to the other. He was a short man, heavy-set, with a cherubic face and a smooth, tanned pate that caught the sunlight at such an angle that it made him look almost angelic.

'I'll tell you why it's called Pearl City, Ms Suzuki,' he said. 'Because more pearls pass through this town than anywhere else in the world, and more pearls pass through this company than any other in this town. Our reputation, like our pearls, is unblemished.' He leaned forward. 'That is why we have asked you here today.'

Suzuki glanced about the room. She noted the reproductions of old photos showing pearl luggers, turn-of-the-century fishing villages and half-naked female divers—the famed 'sea women' of Mie prefecture. She noted the brass diving bell helmet set on the teakwood sideboard, the mounted staghorn of red coral, and the framed photo of the Empress of Japan, around whose neck gleamed three strands of fine Akoya pearls. Her gaze returned to the president.

'Someone is stealing from me and I want to know who,' he

said, then nodded towards the young man behind her. 'Danno here is my assistant.'

'Thank you for coming, Ms Suzuki,' Danno said, stepping lightly across the room to his boss's side. 'You come highly recommended.'

'Oh?' she said.

'You did some work for my wife's sister a few months ago—a Ms Deguchi?'

Suzuki's eyebrows arched. 'The underwear thief case?'

'She said you're a fast worker. "Very intuitive" were the words she used.'

'I had some help—'

'Nevertheless,' the president interrupted, 'there are one hundred and twelve staff at this company, nearly all of them female. We believe a female detective, such as yourself, stands a better chance of finding a thief than the city police. We are offering a fee of three hundred thousand yen, paid upfront, with another three hundred thousand paid to you for proof of the thief's identity.' He nodded at Danno, who reached into his breast pocket, produced a white envelope and passed it to her.

She felt the tight wad of crisp banknotes inside and drew a breath—more than a month's salary in her hands. She looked up and her gaze was arrested by the image of a solo free diver on the wall behind the president. She was full breasted and strong armed, wearing only a loincloth and a line tethered to her waist as she descended the depths on shafts of sunlight. Suzuki had heard that the 'sea women' of Mie could stay down longer than men; their extra body fat kept them from freezing. She wondered how much a woman like that had gotten paid for her time and efforts.

'Ms Suzuki?' said Danno. 'May we have your answer, please?'

Her gaze returned to the two men and she breathed out slowly.

***

The Tokai Pearls building stood at the end of the esplanade, a handsome six-storey monolith of sandstone and steel that had miraculously survived the American air raids of the Pacific War. The pearl-sorting rooms were located on the second and third floors. Their wide windows ran the length of the harbour-facing side, which, explained Danno, allowed the pearl graders to take full advantage of the natural light.

They stopped halfway along a corridor and Suzuki peered in through the porthole window of a door labelled 'B Section'. Dozens of women in powder blue uniforms and matching hats bearing the Tokai insignia hunched over their workstations, dexterously scooping pearls from small blue buckets and placing them on sorting mats. They held each pearl to the light with a set of digital calipers, rotated it slowly for a few moments, then placed it into one of several containers.

'Pearls are assessed for their size, colour, lustre, shape and surface,' said Danno.

'Are they paid well?'

'The graders? Two hundred and eighty thousand yen a month is their starting salary.'

'May I see one of the workstations?'

He glanced at his watch. 'D Section is on a tea break. Follow me.'

They took the stairwell to the third floor and stopped at a door identical to the first. Danno swiped his access card and they stepped inside. Clear, bright light bathed the room and the air smelled faintly of chemicals. It reminded Suzuki of a veterinarian clinic, or a school science lab.

She sat at a workstation near the window and examined the sorting trays, the caliper, tweezer and loupe stand, the rubber gloves and alcohol spray dispensers, all arranged neatly on the white table before her. She glanced up at the CCTV cameras on the ceiling, then down at the blue plastic bucket filled with pearls beside her. The set-up reminded her of a pachinko parlour, the kind that one passed in downtown alleys where patrons sat dumbly for hours amassing buckets of ball bearings, which they exchanged for cash at a mouse-hole window outside.

'May I?' she said.

'Be my guest,' Danno said.

She plunged her hand into the bucket, gathered a handful and held them to the light. Then she let them slip between her fingers, feeling their coolness, listening to the music they made as they tumbled back into the bucket.

'Where do they go from here?' she asked.

'To the pearl masters on the fifth floor. Six qualified gemmologists make the final selections.'

'And then?'

'Then the highest quality pearls are barcoded and given ID numbers. After that, they're threaded into strands for sale.'

'How do you know if any are missing?'

'Until they reach the pearl masters, we don't.'

'You don't?'

'Thousands of pearls move through here each week, too many to be counted individually.'

'And those that don't make the cut?'

'Sold at auctions. Mostly to local Chinese and Indian gem traders.'

Suzuki gazed out the window. Sighting the wavelike outline of the Oriental Hotel on the other side of the harbour, she glanced at her watch and gasped. 'Final question,' she said, gathering her bag and rising quickly from the workstation. 'To your knowledge, have any pearls ever been stolen before?'

'The president is a very suspicious man ...'

'Has he ever been proven right?'

Irritation flashed over Danno's face, but in a practised and professional tone he replied, 'In an uncertain world, Ms Suzuki, there are people who will pay for certainty.'

***

She took a taxi to the Oriental Hotel, in her purse the previous week's CCTV tapes of the sorting rooms and a memory stick containing personnel files of all the graders, including the gemmologists. It was a logical place to start, even if the assignment itself seemed illogical. For there to be a thief there must be a theft. When forty-three pairs of women's underwear disappeared from a neighbourhood's clothes lines, one could be sure it wasn't the sea breeze that had carried them off.

The hotel lobby clock chimed once as Suzuki slipped behind the reception desk and checked the guest register. Despite her growling stomach—the meeting at Tokai Pearls had consumed her entire lunch hour—she set to work with vigour. A cruise ship had arrived in port, disgorging several hundred tourists from Shanghai, and the afternoon passed quickly as she and her colleagues processed the guests and got them settled.

With her shift finished, she left the hotel and hurried along the esplanade. Passing beneath the hourglass-shaped Port Tower, where the hobby fishermen cast for rockling and horse mackerel, a voice called out, 'Oi, Suzuki-san!'

She turned to glimpse a man in his mid-fifties. He stood by himself with a fishing rod in his hands, smiling. Unlike the other old salts, he hadn't gone to seed; he was clean-shaven with a full head of hair and a strong, tanned face. She flashed him a smile and hurried on.

She took the subway train to Minatogawa station, collected her bicycle and made her way up the gentle slopes, through narrow streets of tight-packed neighbourhoods, to the Octopus's Kindergarten. There, she roused her four-year-old daughter who had been dozing peacefully under the watchful eye of the duty teacher, paid the monthly school fee for lunches and overtime care, and departed.

It was a skilful act carrying a sleepy child home by bicycle, and she had to ride the brake for most of the way. When the two of them reached the small apartment building, which stood on a knoll overlooking the city, the child's grandmother was waiting in the street.

'Okaerinasai,' she said, lifting the youngster from the bicycle. Then to Suzuki, 'How did it go?'

'Cruise ship chaos again,' Suzuki said. 'What's for dinner?'

The third-floor apartment smelled of steamed rice, seafood tempura and roasted green tea. Suzuki changed into tracksuit pants, took a low-malt beer from the fridge and collapsed into an old massage chair in front of the TV. She awoke to her mother's hand gentling rousing her, and with her daughter already fed and asleep in bed, she ate dinner hungrily. With dishes done, she set up her laptop on the kitchen table and inserted the USB containing the Tokai Pearls staff files.

The profile photos were mostly of young women with fresh faces and serious expressions. They hailed from rural villages with names like Taka, Tamba, Ono, Shiso and Sasayama, having traded rural oppression for urban crush, drawn to the bright lights and excitement that no boonie backwater could ever offer a young woman in her prime. Suzuki doubted any one of these youngsters would risk it all to pocket a pearl or two.

By eleven p.m., the apartment was quiet and still. Her mother had long since bathed and gone to bed. Suzuki took another beer from the fridge and turned to the internet, a notepad beside her. She trawled sites on pearl grading, gem trading, pearl markets, auction sites, dollar–yen exchange rates. She scribbled like a madwoman, stopping only to swig her beer and ponder the ever-diminishing likelihood that the president of Tokai Pearls was being ripped off by one of his employees.

And yet the size and lucrativeness of the pearl trade surprised her. No less than a dozen companies kept offices downtown, and many of these represented industry heavyweights like Tiffany & Co., Cartier, Harry Winston and Chow Tai Fook.

She drained her beer, thought about a third but stopped herself; thirds led to fourths. She took a few moments to view the CCTV footage on her MediaPlayer. The images, although fuzzy, showed nothing more than rows of women in identical uniforms performing a very mundane task. It made her wonder about the motive behind the investigation—was it one man's folly or a savvy businessman's intuition?

***

The Haru-ichiban blew off the harbour the following night. It brought with it the tang of the sea and wind gusts which set the red lanterns of Chinatown bobbing like fat jellyfish.

Suzuki turned off Nankin-machi Street and into a narrow laneway. The uneven flagstones made this no place for a woman in high heels, but she had been here many times and deftly navigated to the end of the alley where a neon sign announced the Bar Bon Voyage. She paused beneath its orange glow, adjusted her midnight blue one-piece—just a pinch too tight—and pushed on the door. The warm, smoky fug of a Tuesday night washed over her. A chorus of greetings from the staff followed as she stepped inside and made her way along a long, dark wooden counter. At the very end sat a man with a sake flask and a small cup in front of him. At her approach he looked up and there it was again—that smile.

'How come you never wave to me?' he said, pulling out her chair.

To the staff she said, 'A beer, please,' and in the same breath, 'You know it's nothing personal, Teizo.'

'So it's professional,' he said, returning to his sake cup and pouring it anew. 'How's the sleuthing business?'

'How's the fishing business?'

'Like you, I'm catching only small ones.'

Her beer arrived. 'Kampai,' she said, touching the lip of her vessel to his.

'A new case?' he asked.

'Can't talk about it—yet.'

'Can I help?'

'Maybe not.'

'I helped on the panty thief case.'

'You did.' She took a long draught of beer and wiped her lip.

'And I helped you catch the shoplifting granddad.'

'You did.'

'Well, what have you got for me this time?'

'This time I need to get inside a woman's head, not a man's.'

'You came here tonight ...'

She let a smile work its way to her lips and sighed. 'This time I might just be chasing fresh air on the wild hunch of a paranoid company president.'

'A man?'

'Yes.'

'I'm a man.'

'I've noticed.'

'Remember, a man fears things like a woman. Things that sometimes can't be explained—or proven. Some feel it, some don't.' He took a sip of sake, then another. 'Paranoia is just another word for fear.'

She raised the beer to her lips and in the bar mirror caught a glimpse of a middle-aged woman, full-faced, with gleaming black hair. Her eyes were quick, her red lips glistening.

'Do I look like a private eye?'

Most men would have taken advantage of the question to

let their gaze linger over her generous proportions, but Teizo looked her in the eye and said, 'No.'

'Good. Then tell me, what's all this "male fear" business? Did they teach you that at submarine school?'

'Didn't need to. When you're at sea for weeks, months even, you just learn it. You learn to smell fear above and below the surface.'

'You smelled an underwear thief.'

'What I'm saying is no man is born with instinct. He acquires it. And the faster he acquires it, the better his chances of survival. Maybe your pearl company president is such a man. Maybe he fears a thief will make him look bad and just needs you to prove there isn't one.' He drained his cup and ordered another flask.

'What do you know about pearls?' she asked.

'Submariners call them mermaid tears.'

'Interesting, but not useful.'

'Then fill me in.'

'Alright then.' She swivelled on her chair to face him. 'Why would a young woman, a high school graduate from a rural town, risk a good salary and her name to steal from the biggest pearl dealer in Asia?'

'Tokai Pearls?'

'Yes.'

The staff returned with fresh sake. Teizo waited for her to leave then said, 'Pearls aren't just pretty baubles, you know. They have practical uses. Medicine for one. The Chinese use pearl powder to treat skin problems. Chinese royalty used it as a beauty cream. In India it's used to treat stomach aches. There's also pearl tea, a health tonic ...'

Suzuki had taken a pen from her handbag and began to scribble busily on a bar napkin.

'Never really cared for pearls myself,' he said finally. 'They remind me of weddings and funerals.'

She put down her pen, raised her glass and said, 'I'll drink to that.'

***

To save the taxi fare she walked along Nankin-machi Street. The late-night ramen joints and the upstairs karaoke boxes resounded with drunken laughter, but the alleys that branched off it were sullen and cavernous with shadow.

She reached Sakaemachi Road, busy with westbound traffic, and feeling pensive, crossed over and continued south into the old financial precinct. Here the paving stones were wider, smoother, and the streets carried a whiff of the wealth and history they had accumulated from over a century of international trade. Sandstone and granite towered over her, corniced and classically hewn. Where no insurance company, bank or shipping office stood, an Armani, Porsche or Tiffany & Co. showroom glowed like a jewel in rock.

She pondered Teizo's words—not so much the 'male fear' part but the possibilities that pearls presented. She passed by Mikimoto, the boutique of the famed pearl merchant of Mie, stopped and retraced her steps. Peering in at the strands of gleaming Akoya pearls, earrings, brooches and rings, she couldn't help but repeat to herself Teizo's words, 'pretty baubles'. Ornaments like these were not the fashion statements of young women. They were certainly not the status symbols a pearl company employee would flash around, much less pitch on the open market. She caught herself, aware once more of the possibility that there might not even be a thief, that this could all be a sadistic scheme cooked up by a company president to project power and control over his staff—over her. On the other hand, who was she to complain? The advance would cover kindergarten lunches for six months. And if she did catch a thief, well, there was an extra three hundred thousand yen she could put towards her daughter's future.

She continued walking and her thoughts turned again to Teizo. Was theirs a professional relationship or was it just two lonely hearts sharing a drink in Chinatown on Tuesday nights? She'd paid their bar bill and asked for a receipt; information was a commodity and she valued his learned opinion. But the jury remained out on the true motive for their night-time meetings.

After a short while she looked up, startled to see the huge red hourglass structure of the Port Tower looming large against the night sky.

'Damn it,' she hissed.

Resigning herself to the extra cost to save her legs, she hailed a taxi at the next convenience store and slumped back, watching through heavy eyelids as the peckish, the lonely and the drunk did their best to keep the night alive.

***

She awoke around two a.m. with her daughter asleep beside her, and her own mother emitting a snore from the next-door room that vibrated softly throughout the apartment.

She rose and went to the bathroom, but once back in bed could only lie on her back and stare up at the faint but irritating glow of the ceiling 'bean' light. The more she stared at it, the more her mind churned.

That was it!

She leaped from bed and rushed to the kitchen. Turning on the hot water pot and opening her laptop, Suzuki drummed her fingers on the table until the Tokai Pearls staff files materialised before her. She scrolled downwards, searching the faces of the young women as steam billowed behind her. And there it was: a photo of a woman older than the others, with a gaze more measured and calmer than her fresh-faced colleagues. She had dyed-brown hair, wrapped in a tight, fashionable bun that said she took pride in her appearance. But on these details Suzuki didn't dwell; it was the redness covering the woman's cheeks, a hot and irritated-looking skin condition—acne perhaps—that held her attention. She scribbled onto her pad as the hot water pot screamed and the jar of Nescafé lay untouched.

***

'Reiko Ogino?' Danno said, reading the name slowly. 'She's a supervisor in D Section. She's been with us several years now.'

'May I see her at work?' Suzuki asked. Then added quickly, 'She's by no means a suspect.'

Danno smiled wryly. 'We're all suspects, Ms Suzuki. Just some more than others.'

They made their way to the third floor, stopping outside the grading room Suzuki had inspected the previous day.

'Reiko Ogino is the one standing in the corner,' said Danno.

Suzuki peered in through the porthole window and saw a woman speaking with one of the graders seated beside a window on the far side of the room. She strained to see Ogino's face; the angle at which she stood gave away little more than the woman's height and build. She was slim, strong-looking, with an upright posture. The grader said something that made Ogino laugh, pat her subordinate playfully on the arm and turn back to the room. Suzuki uttered a quiet gasp. The face she now glimpsed looked quite different to the woman in the file photo.

'Would you like me to call her over?' asked Danno.

'No, no,' Suzuki said quickly, turning away. 'I just wanted to see what she looks like. Your staff photos—are they taken only once?'

'Yes. When the employees first enter the company. Why do you ask?'

'What time do they finish?'

'D Section? At six p.m.'

Suzuki glanced at her watch. She gave Danno a hurried thank-you and left the building. In the taxi, she pulled a rice ball from her handbag and ate quickly, ignoring the curious glances of the driver all the way back to the hotel.

***

Teizo was not among the fisherman casting from the pier later that same day. Even if he had been, she'd not have had time to acknowledge his wave as she hurried around the harbour and back to the Tokai Pearl company gates. She arrived as the first employees were exiting, young women laughing and chatting as if the menial tasks they'd just spent hours performing were now a distant memory. Suzuki positioned herself across the road outside a convenience store, a cup of coffee in one hand, a mobile phone in the other, and, for effect, pretended to play Candy Crush.

The workers streamed through the gates. Gone were the formless blue uniforms that had reduced them to a single entity, a human resource to be watered and fed and paid out monthly. They wore fashionable blouses, colourful accessories, boots and form-fitting skirts with bolero denim jackets, clothes that revealed their individuality and character.

Amidst the outflow, sporting a striped blue and white sweatshirt, black jeans and pink Vans sneakers, Reiko Ogino appeared. She broke from the crowd and crossed the street towards the convenience store. Suzuki looked down in panic: she'd forgotten the sleuth's most valued accessory, sunglasses. As Ogino reached the store entrance she made an evasive sidestep to avoid an outgoing patron. It brought her close enough for Suzuki to smell Ogino's sandalwood fragrance and steal a close-up glimpse of her face, which was radiant, relaxed—and unblemished.

***

The following day Suzuki attended an open day at her daughter's kindergarten, taking the morning off work to meet the teachers and chat with the other time-pressed, work-harried parents. They clustered at the back of the classroom listening to their children sing songs about pulling giant radishes, and a story about a boy who marched off to battle demons in a distant land—just like any single mother, Suzuki thought, except that the demons were disguised as beer, bills and a bad back.

That evening she viewed the CCTV footage again, focusing her attention this time on the happenings inside D Section. Each time Ogino came into view, Suzuki slowed the footage, noting the ease with which the supervisor interacted with her co-workers, in particular her habit of leaning in close when speaking to the younger employees with a laughing and smiling manner, as if work wasn't the only thing they were discussing.

After an hour, with her eyes strained, Suzuki had to admit there was nothing untoward about the supervisor's behaviour. In fact, Ogino's seemingly compassionate and professional manner impressed her. She went to the fridge and pulled out a beer. Then she remembered: the laundry. With a heavy heart she replaced the can and from the bathroom lugged a full basket of damp clothes to the balcony. The city shimmered beneath her; a bullet train passed seamlessly through the constellation of streetlights, heading west to Fukuoka. Out to sea, freighters and night ferries floated like starships across the celestial stream, heading east with the tide. It was a view Suzuki could not savour until three generations of women's socks, stockings and underwear had been strung beneath the moonlight.

***

A breakthrough came two days later. Suzuki, having decided to walk to her dental appointment in Motomachi, spotted Ogino in Chinatown. Sidestepping into a kitchenware store on Nankin-machi Street, Suzuki pretended to examine the woks and noodle sieves, watching as Ogino disappeared inside a store nearby. She re-emerged a short time later and, in her trademark casual way, merged easily back into the crowds of tourists and sightseers.

Suzuki crossed the street and stepped up to the window of the Kanpō Satsuma medicine store. She pushed on the door, which set a small bell jingling, and entered. Aromas of spice and herbs filled her nostrils and, while not unpleasant, again reminded her of a school science lab. It was a small shop, uncluttered, and from behind its counter an elderly man in a batik shirt stood watching her approach through horn-rimmed glasses.

'Do you treat skin problems?' she asked.

'What kind?' he asked.

'Acne.'

He turned to the wall of miniature drawers behind him, ran his finger down the labels of faded characters and pulled on a drawer handle.

'Dokudami,' he said, spooning a tiny sample of dried brown leaves onto some wax paper. 'Add hot water, drink as tonic.'

'I thought dokudami was a weed?' she said, holding the sample to her nose and sniffing.

'It's cheap as weeds.'

'Got anything else?'

He looked thoughtful. From another drawer he pulled a vial of white powder and placed it on the counter.

'Add this to moisturising cream, cleanser or lotion, once daily.'

'What is it?' she said, holding the glass tube up to the light.

'Akoya.'

'Pearl?'

'Pearl powder.'

'How much?'

'Eight thousand yen.'

'Eight thousand!'

'Why do you think I offered dokudami?'

'Why so expensive?'

'Specialty medicine. Won't find a gram under a thousand yen anywhere else. Eight thousand yen gets you twenty percent discount.'

She turned the vial slowly, noting the dull white colour of the contents, its icing sugar consistency. 'Who buys this stuff?' she said.

'Chinese. Off the cruise ships—'

'Yes, yes, I know. Where do you get it from?'

He peered over his horn rims and his smile disappeared.

'If you are thinking of going into business, don't. There are cheaper and more popular medicines out there. Pearl powder is not one of them.'

Suzuki left the store with the vial in her handbag, and a receipt that she hoped she could claim as a business expense. After bathing that evening, she mixed a small amount of the powder into her moisturiser and applied it to her face. On waking the next morning, she inspected her face in the bathroom mirror. Was it the power of expectation or was her skin really smoother?

***

There was no proof that Ogino had ever used pearl powder, and it seemed unlikely that a woman who handled pearls every day for a living would spend eight thousand yen to buy her company's own product. But how could the transformation in her appearance be explained? Quite easily, Teizo might have suggested: modern medicines were effective in treating all kinds of skin conditions, and there was no shortage of cold creams and steroid ointments one could get from a doctor nowadays. But what if a severe acne sufferer had tried them all, and to no effect? What if such medicines caused allergic reactions? What if someone was so desperate to find a cure for a debilitating condition that they were prepared to steal for it? The questions came thick and fast as Suzuki made her way along the esplanade towards the hotel the next morning.

At lunchtime she joined her co-workers in the staffroom for bento box lunches and green tea. But while the other staff chatted about the day's strange house guests, next summer's fashions and the current Korean TV dramas, Suzuki's mind was elsewhere. That was, until the woman beside her gave a sudden cry and clutched at her throat.

'What's happening?' one of the staff cried, giving the choking woman several firm slaps on the back.

'Swallowed a plum stone,' the woman said, coughing.

They rubbed her back and someone said, 'Don't worry, it will come out in your poo.' This caused the others to erupt in guffaws. But Suzuki wasn't laughing; she was deep in thought.

***

Friday night arrived, and with her mother at calligraphy

class and her daughter storied-out and purring quietly in the next room, Suzuki poured herself a long shot of Suntory black label, added ice and soda, and set herself down at the kitchen table. She opened her laptop and inserted Danno's USB. Eight hours of viewing CCTV was out of the question with a bottle of whisky in front of her. But she knew what she was looking for, and intuition told her she would most probably find it in the hours that followed the lunchbreak. She fast-forwarded to 13:30, just as D Section were returning from their break, and watched as each grader took her seat and resumed the mundane job of classifying pearls. Ogino took her own seat at a window-side terminal and set to work typing. This scene continued unchanged for quite some time. Suzuki yawned, thankful her own job allowed her to converse with people of all types, and that no two days behind the reception desk of an international hotel were ever the same.

She poured another whisky, tempering it with soda, and fast-forwarded the MediaPlayer to 15:30. It was then that something curious happened. As D Section's tea-break began and the staff filed out of the room, Ogino lingered. She remained at her own workstation, swivelling her chair away from the ceiling camera. She then made a series of short upward movements with her hand—not once but half a dozen times. Suzuki peered closer at the grainy image on her monitor, not exactly sure what she had just witnessed. She rewound and viewed again, slowing the film and noting that Ogino's movements were both swift and deliberate. She paused the player, froze the frame and zoomed in on her reflection in the window. She clicked 'save' and transferred the image to her desktop. She then resumed the video, watching curiously as Ogino turned back to her desk, lifted a drink bottle and took several sips. Suzuki reached for her own glass, saw that it was empty and splashed in some whisky. She swallowed the shot whole.

***

She awoke early, a hangover threatening, but not enough to bring on grumpiness. She prepared breakfast, a chore she performed on weekends to give her mother a break from feeding them before work and school. Then grandmother, daughter and granddaughter caught the train to the Mosaic shopping mall to hunt for summer clothes. June through to August were the months Suzuki detested most. The crushing humidity, sleepless nights and general irritability of the Kobe populace made the detective business less a test of acuity than one of mental and physical endurance.

After a cheap lunch at a family restaurant they took a stroll along the harbourfront, passing knots of high school lovebirds, wedding-goers dressed in their finest and Chinese-speaking tourists, all of whom made the port esplanade the best place to people watch in the city.

Teizo stood among the weekend fishermen, a bucket beside him, his suntanned head wrapped in a knotted white towel. The three women gathered around to inspect the wriggling rockfish he held up, much to the delight of Suzuki's daughter.

'Any luck?' he asked Suzuki.

'Some,' she replied, then turned to her mother, asking her to buy ice-creams for the four of them at the terminal kiosk. As soon as they'd gone, she said, 'I'm almost certain I know who it is and how they're doing it. I just don't think this person is doing it for the money. I mean, for personal gain.'

'Motives usually make the least sense. Remember that shoplifter? Eighty-five years old. He didn't need a can of corn. All he wanted was someone to notice him, to talk to.'

Mother and daughter returned with the ice-creams, and for a moment the only sound was the lapping of fast-melting softcream. Later, as the three women walked back along the esplanade to the subway station, Suzuki's mother nudged her daughter's shoulder. 'He's my type,' she said.

'Everyone's your type,' Suzuki said, and the two of them burst into laughter.

***

Sunday evening was the one time in the week when the general populace, having slept, shopped and supped, spent the dying hours of their weekend at home watching TV or preparing for Monday's onslaught. It was the perfect time to cold call.

Wearing navy blue business pants and a crisp white shirt, Suzuki stepped from the train at the Suma station and rechecked the address in her notebook. The sun had dipped below the suspension bridge that connected Awaji Island to Honshu and only the highest buildings on the hillsides now caught the last of the golden light. Once a fishing village, Suma had long since been swallowed by Kobe's westward sprawl, and as such, one had to follow the same confounding system of numbered districts and blocks to locate a business or private residence. Here, one gave directions using local landmarks, and when this failed they stepped into the street to meet visitors or delivery persons. Suzuki expected no such courtesy—canniness and gut-feeling were a private detective's best friends.

It was on dusk when she reached a small park near the top of a hillside. A swing, a slide, and a sandbox strewn with forgotten plastic toys marked it as a place of activity by day. But the aromas of curry-rice and okonomiyaki that now carried on the evening breeze said life had moved elsewhere.

Suzuki felt a pang of nervousness. Confronting suspects was not her strong card, and it rarely happened. But when she felt something amiss, something that couldn't be explained, or when clarity could only come from a face-to-face encounter, she would make her move. There was risk in this, to be sure. However, Suzuki picked her battles and always abided by the mantra 'fear the person who has nothing to lose'. Ogino did not seem like such a person.

She descended the lee of the hill, through neighbourhoods that were older and more densely packed than the sea-facing side, crowded with young families, factory workers, university students and the elderly, much like Suzuki's own further east.

Presently, a monument to brown stucco and seventies-era imagination appeared. Whoever had named the apartment building 'Laguna Heights' had high hopes and a low budget. Suzuki stepped into the foyer and scanned its mailboxes. The names ran in vertical rows, typed except for one at the very top—number 411. In black marker pen, someone had written neatly the name 'OGINO'.

She took the elevator, still unsure of what she was about to do or say until she stepped onto the fourth-floor landing. She counted off the numbers, making her way along a shared landing cluttered with pot plants and children's bicycles, until she reached number 411 at the very end. The doormat said 'welcome' in five languages. She inhaled deeply then pushed the buzzer. Moments passed. She pressed again. The door opened and a woman about the same age as her mother peered out.

'Good evening,' Suzuki said. 'May I speak to Reiko Ogino, please?'

The old woman stared back at her for such a while that Suzuki wondered if she might be hard of hearing.

'May I ask who you are?' the woman said at last.

'My name is Mami Suzuki.' Then, knowing that one's company or organisation name carried more weight, added, 'Of Tokai Pearls Corporation.'

The name seemed to register in the old woman's gaze. 'Wait a moment, please,' she said and retreated along a dimly lit hallway. Suzuki peered into the foyer, noted the assortment of keys, goodluck charms and the seaweed-green scent bottle placed on top of the shoe shelf, just like in her own foyer. Murmured voices sounded in a room down the hallway, and presently, into the light stepped Reiko Ogino.

Suzuki sensed her tension; gone was the easy gait and confident smile she had witnessed inside the Tokai Pearls building. A light frown creased Ogino's forehead and her set jaw suggested a defensive mode.

'Yes?' she said.

'Reiko Ogino-san?'

The woman nodded. Her frown deepened.

'My name is Mami Suzuki. I'm under contract by Tokai Pearls to investigate a certain matter regarding their stock inventory.' The formal approach always gave a suspect time to gather their thoughts; it was a technique that afforded both investigator and suspect a little breathing space, a moment to mutually assess the situation.

'I'm sorry, what exactly do you want?'

'I'd like to ask you some questions about the theft of pearls from the company.'

Ogino placed a hand on the shoe shelf. She was about to open her mouth when a soft thumping noise sounded along the hallway. A small child, a boy, appeared beside her wearing Disney pyjamas. He gripped his mother's leg and stared up at Suzuki with unabashed curiosity.

'What a cutie!' said Suzuki quickly, stepping forward and bending down. 'I love your Mickey jim-jams.'

Ogino shifted uncomfortably. She whispered something to the boy and called out to the old woman, who soon appeared and led the boy back off into the dimness.

'He's a nice-looking kid,' said Suzuki. 'How old?'

'Four.'

'Same as my daughter.'

Ogino didn't smile. 'I'm sorry to hear there's been a theft,' she said. 'But I can't help you. All my employees are good women. I trust them. They wouldn't steal from the company.'

'I'm not here to ask about your colleagues.'

Ogino's eyes hardened. Her jaw muscles tightened. Somewhere along the landing a home audio system was playing Queen's 'I Want to Break Free'.

'Would you mind if I came in?' Suzuki said.

'Yes, I would. I'm busy right now—perhaps another time.'

'To tell the truth, there may not be another time.' Suzuki's gaze turned solid, her tone lost its fizz. She was now all business. Ogino sensed the new atmosphere; her eyelids flitted and she wavered a moment. She reached down and drew out a pair of guest slippers, placed them on the carpet in front of Suzuki.

'My house is a mess. I apologise.'

'Don't. It can't be any worse than mine.'

Suzuki stepped into the slippers and followed Ogino into the living room. It was filled with laundered but yet to be folded clothes, toys, a small flat screen TV playing cartoons on low volume, and a beer can on the side table. Ogino led her through to the kitchen where the dishes from the evening's dinner of curry-rice had been stacked and awaited washing.

'Please, take a seat,' Ogino said. 'You want something to drink?'

'I'll have what you're having.'

Ogino reached for a glass and a jug of barley tea from the counter.

'Beer, if you have it,' Suzuki said quickly.

Ogino gave a look of surprise, then shrugged. 'Sure,' she said. She crossed to the fridge and pulled out a can of low-malt beer.

'Sorry, there are no clean glasses.'

'Don't worry, I never use one. Saves washing.'

Ogino gestured to a seat at the table. Suzuki sat down and placed her handbag on the floor beside her. She heard the old lady singing a lullaby in the neighbouring room and the squeal of the youngster being settled.

She took the beer and waited until Ogino had returned from the lounge room with her own half-finished drink, then opened it. They sat at the table and sipped in silence.

'It's like this,' said Suzuki after a while. 'I'm a private eye, a detective, it's what I do. I have a daughter and mother to take care of, just like you. So let's be perfectly clear, this is nothing personal.'

'You're married?'

'Was.'

'Me too.'

Suzuki glanced about the small apartment. There was nothing to suggest a man had ever set foot inside, just like her own apartment.

'Well, now with the pleasantries over, I must ask some tough questions.'

'Go ahead,' said Ogino.

'Are you aware of any theft of pearls from your company?'

'No.'

'You're certain?'

Ogino nodded.

Suzuki pulled from her handbag a copy of a profile photo and pushed it across the table. 'I have reason to believe that this woman is stealing from your company.'

Ogino glanced at the picture and her eyes widened. 'That's not possible!'

'I have evidence to suggest otherwise. I will be presenting it to the company president tomorrow morning.'

'What evidence?'

'I cannot divulge that.'

Ogino looked pained.

'I know Mori-san very well, she's a hard worker, a good worker.' She looked at the photo, then back at Suzuki. There was desperation in her eyes. 'She's not a thief!'

'How do you know?'

'She's my niece!' Her eyes were glistening and Suzuki knew what was about to come. Ogino's lip began to quiver and soon tears streamed down her smooth cheeks. In an unsteady voice, she said, 'She would never steal … It's not her.'

'It's you, isn't it?' said Suzuki.

Ogino shook her head and tears dropped to the tabletop. Strength drained, confidence melted, she grabbed at the tissue box and blew her nose.

Suzuki spoke quietly. 'You aren't greedy. You take only a half-dozen at a time, and I doubt those are what the gemmologists on the sixth floor would call flawless. After tea-time, several days a week, you wait until all the employees have left the room. Then you swallow the pearls. God knows how you manage the next stage of the process—I hope you wash them well because I bought your powder from the Kanpō Satsuma medicine store the other day. Somehow you grind the pearls and put the powder into vials that you deliver to the old man in Chinatown. Correct?'

Ogino sniffled and took another tissue. She said nothing.

Suzuki continued. 'What I would like to know is this: why are you risking your job, your family and your future to steal from a company that pays you a reasonable salary?'

'Because it's not enough,' Ogino said.

'You gamble?'

Ogino shook her head.

'Alcoholic?'

'Not yet.'

'Then why?'

'Because I can't afford to support my child and my mother

on a single salary. My mother is getting senile. I send her to day care five days a week …' She began to cry without restraint, wholehearted weeping that filled the small kitchen with sorrow.

Suzuki leaned back in her chair and breathed out. She felt the weight of the woman's worries, her desperation, her responsibility as a mother and daughter and, above all, her commitment to keeping them schooled, cared for, housed and fed. It was an immense weight. She thought of the Mie sea women searching the cold depths for pearls, for abalone, for food, unable to breathe, unable to see the light until they reached the surface. She picked up her beer and drank it slowly. She felt like crying herself.

Ogino wiped her eyes. Her head now bowed in shame, she said nothing. She did not touch her drink.

'Do you mind if I have another beer?' Suzuki said.

Ogino looked up.

'Sorry to ask.' Suzuki smiled weakly. 'It's just that I find this job rather stressful sometimes.'

'What are you going to do?' Ogino said.

'Honestly? I'd like to get drunk.'

'I mean tomorrow, when you meet the president?'

It was the first time in her five years as a private eye that Suzuki felt the surreality of the moment. Here she sat, a woman divorced, with daughter and aged mother to care for, face to face with a woman of similar age, status and predicament, whose fate now rested in her hands. She reached across the table and took Ogino's quivering hand. She felt its moist warmth and weariness. She gripped it firmly and in a low and tender tone said, 'Let's just have another beer, shall we?'

**

Suzuki sat in the leather chair with her handbag resting on her lap. She wore a smart blue suit with an apricot blouse and camel-brown d'Orsay pumps. Through the window she glimpsed the honeycombed suburbs of Kobe rising up the Rokko mountainside, so near and yet so far.

Her gaze returned, as it had done on her first visit, to the photograph of the solo female diver on the wall before her. A rope was tied around her waist so that should she encounter difficulties she could be pulled quickly to the surface. Sometimes the rope snagged or became entangled and the diver would drown. Her body would be pulled to the surface limp and pale. Slavery it was not, Suzuki had learned: the sea women of Mie were proud of their ability to swim to such great depths and stay under for so long. Theirs was a sisterhood from which one could opt out of at any time, but no one did.

The president cleared his throat.

'Firstly, let me convey to you my gratitude, Ms Suzuki. We are very grateful for the subtle and unobtrusive way in which you have conducted your investigation. Danno here has told me you have some information for us. Is that correct?'

Suzuki cleared her own throat and moved to the edge of the chair. She opened her purse and took out the USB and the CCTV files, which she placed carefully on the glass coffee table in front of her.

'Thank you for requesting my services and for the generous advance payment. I am very grateful. After reviewing the staff files and closed-circuit video footage, inspecting the graders' work environment and undertaking my own fieldwork, I must report that I can find no one who fits the profile of a thief in your company.' She threw a glance towards Danno. 'In fact, I can find no evidence that there has ever been a theft.'

The room fell silent. The president's face was unreadable and Suzuki could not tell if her comments had pleased or displeased him. Without a word, he rose from his chair and walked to the window. He took a moment to consider the harbour before him: the shipyards and submarine docks, the shopping mall and ferry terminal, and finally the city and the mountains beyond. He nodded to his own thoughts.

'Thank you, Ms Suzuki,' he said, turning to face her. 'The pearl industry is filled with insidious and opportunistic characters, and although they make our lives more challenging, they also ensure our wits remain sharp. It is the key to running a successful pearl-trading business. You have brought me peace of mind and I'm only sorry that I couldn't have paid you more. Nevertheless, my sincere thanks to you for your efforts.'

Suzuki gave a short, reverent bow. She thanked him once again and, sensing the meeting had ended, rose slowly from her seat. Danno moved quickly to the door and held it open. 'We have arranged a taxi for you, Ms Suzuki. Would you allow me to escort you to the lobby?'

As the elevator descended, he said in a surprisingly casual tone, 'He does this now and again.'

'Does what?'

'Calls an investigation. It's his way of seeking assurance.'

'Assurance that he is not being stolen from?'

'It wouldn't make much difference if someone was stealing a few pearls—we have the market share in Japan and our profits are rising. No, this is personal. He thinks theft of his pearls is theft of his soul. You see, he is Tokai Pearls and Tokai Pearls is him.'

'Fear blows wind in your sails, they say.'

Danno cast her a quizzical look.

'It's an old proverb,' she said. 'Fear calls us to action, whether that fear is founded or unfounded.'

The elevator doors opened and a black taxi stood gleaming in the sunlight.

'You may be right, Ms Suzuki. Again, thank you.'

As the taxi pulled away from the lobby and passed through the gates, she glanced back to see Danno still standing on the steps. He gave a quick, formal bow and returned inside. From a third-floor window, another face watched her depart. It was one that Suzuki had come to know well, one with whom she had shared her own worries and fears. She realised that she wasn't the only one riding life's ups and downs; sisterhood came in all shapes and forms.

Suzuki gave a short bow towards the window and the face disappeared.

***

The Haru-ichiban was still blowing the next evening as Suzuki entered the alley off Nankin-machi Street. She looked forward to Tuesday nights. With the Monday blues banished, one could face the rest of the week with confidence and resolve, and a bottle of wine to help things along. The mood inside Bar Bon Voyage was thus, where customers engaged in quiet conversation over beer and wine at tables scattered about the low-lit room.

Teizo sat in his usual position at the end of the counter. He told her once it was a habit born of his samurai heritage, that no one, be they assassins or beautiful women, would ever escape his attention from such a vantage point.

'Case solved,' she said, sliding into the chair beside him. Her knee pressed his.

'I'll buy you a drink,' he said.

'No, no. This one's on me. As a thanks.'

'For what?'

'For enlightening me on male fears and mermaid tears.'

She ordered a chilled bottle of Chablis and poured two glasses to their high-tide mark. As they drank she told him the story, ending with how she'd offered Ogino extra work at the hotel if she could manage it.

Teizo listened patiently, sipping his wine, helping the tide run out. 'How did she grind them?' he asked finally.

'Coffee mill.'

Teizo chuckled. 'I'd never have thought of that.'

'That's because you're a man.'

'A man whose only fear is being rejected by a beautiful woman.'

Suzuki smiled. She glanced at her reflection in the mirrored glass of the bar and said, 'You were right about that pearl powder—it does work.'

Oysters to Die For

'Fragrant Harbour', they called it. But Hong Kong was anything but fragrant the night Poh Seng Pang flew in. The air outside the terminal was dank, vegetative, like the smell of the Singapore River in wet season or the streets of the Jurong wholesale market after a deluge. Poh found it strangely comforting.

He checked his Citizen Quartz Titanium: almost dinnertime in Singapore. Betty would be taking first customers at her small chicken-rice stand inside the hawker centre. He tried not to eat on the plane; 'airline food' was an oxymoron and it gave him constipation. But this time he'd missed his wife's lunch in the rush to the airport and had reluctantly accepted the airline offerings, a decision he now regretted as he stood clutching his small overnight bag on the concourse.

Beyond the terminal, rain fell. With no wind to speak of, it drifted down in an almost vertical fashion across the runway, hangars and the harbour beyond. A black Lexus sat idling at the end of the taxi rank, its exhaust steaming the night air. The driver was old-school: silver crew cut, permanent scowl, a real toothpick-chewer. His gaze met with Poh's in the side-view mirror. He lowered his newspaper and the rear passenger door clicked. Poh pulled on the handle and climbed in. They exchanged single-syllable greetings and the car moved away from the curb to join the swirl of courtesy buses, catering trucks, rental cars and limousines leaving Chek Lap Kok island for Kowloon and the night beyond.

Poh was feeling pensive tonight. This would be his last assignment. On his return to Singapore he would formally tender his resignation. At fifty-eight, he was getting too old to be a 'shipping agent'.

He was looking forward to retirement; he'd help Betty at the chicken-rice stand, maybe join a mahjong club, and take more of an interest in his daughter's studies in Australia. Microbiology, wasn't it? What did he know about microbiology? Except that you should always wash your hands after flying because, as his daughter insisted, 'aeroplanes are crawling with bacteria'.

Poh yawned.

The travelling, the hotel rooms, the waiting—the waiting was the real killer. He'd read somewhere that the average human spends a year of their life waiting. The only thing that made the waiting bearable, besides the money, was dining. He loved sampling the specialties of each town and city he visited: dumplings in Taipei, Medan chicken curry in Sumatra, pork noodles in Sabah, suckling pig in Bali. Dining was his real pleasure, but only after a job was done, and even then it had to be a quick meal en route to the airport.

He slumped back in the seat, listening to the timbre of the windshield wipers working away the rain. Why had he chosen this line of business? Actually, *he* hadn't chosen this business—it had chosen him. His talent had been recognised early. The recruitment process had been quick, the training minimal and his first assignment issued within a few weeks.

He had never botched a job. Granted, it was possible. Once, in a Kuching hotel, his gun had jammed. The target had woken with his call girl beside him and he'd had to knuckledust them both. Then he'd smothered the target with a pillow and walked. He never killed women as a rule, and he was glad he'd never been put in a situation where he'd had to choose between a woman's life and his own. It was another reason to retire.

The lights of the Marriott Hotel appeared through the drizzle. The driver eased the car into the circular driveway and drew up to the concourse where a team of red-vested bellhops stepped from the shrubbery. Poh reached beneath the driver's seat, pulled out a slim dark case and slipped it inside his overnight bag.

'Sim cards are inside,' said the driver.

The hotel lobby was crowded, the queue at the reception desk lengthy. Poh didn't mind, he was used to it. Waiting allowed him to survey his surroundings: the vast, open lounge crowded with travellers, the lavish red sofas, a grand piano, and at the centre, an enormous Christmas tree decorated with sparkling, pulsating lights. Though it was only November, he felt slightly cheered.

The receptionist requested his booking card and passport,

glancing briefly at the photo of a man with dark hair neatly parted to the right, a crisp white business collar, blue striped tie and dark-rimmed glasses. On paper he was 'Lee Chee Seng', one of the thousands of shipping agents who came and went across Southeast Asia's big cities every day. He stood out like a grain of sand on a beach.

'I'm sorry, sir,' the receptionist said, 'all of our standard rooms are taken due to a flight cancellation. But since you are a Marriott member, would you accept an upgrade to a deluxe double, with our compliments?'

Poh nodded, thanked him.

'Here is your room key and dinner voucher,' said the receptionist. 'The restaurant buffet is at the end of the lobby. Alcoholic drinks are at your own expense.'

Poh took the elevator, which stopped halfway for a middle-aged Asian man and his two female companions. The man held a large glass of red wine in his hand and smelled of cigar smoke. He smiled at Poh as they exited on his floor and said, 'Have a wonderful evening.'

Once inside his room, Poh turned off the lights, stepped to the window and checked the distance to the harbour. He pulled the curtains, turned the bedlamps to dim and memorised every emergency exit from the diagram on the back of the door. Next he changed over the sim cards for both his phones, then slipped out the slim-lined case, entered a code into the lock and pulled out two QSW 06 pistols from their foam cradles. He checked the firing mechanisms, inserted the magazines and switched both to safety. Finally, he lifted out the two sound suppressors and examined each beneath the bedlamp. Satisfied, he stowed everything beneath the mattress.

Then he turned on the kettle to make a cup of tea.

As he sipped, he looked over the dossier again. The mark was a company president, the owner of Soon Fat Seafood Co. Ltd in Kowloon. Poh noted how similar the two of them looked: the big-boned face, long earlobes, nondescript office worker hairstyle. Poh was just older, slightly more jowled and used hair dye to conceal his creeping greyness.

He put away the dossier and his thoughts turned to old Mister Ng. He had been more of a father than his own father, nurturing, encouraging and rewarding him through his years of service to the company. They'd first met in the garage of his father's logistics company in Jurong Port, where, impressed by the young Poh's mechanical skills, Mister Ng had offered him a job at Ng and Sons Business Solutions Co. Ltd. Not without reservations, his father had assented. Perhaps it was Mister Ng's reputation for getting what he wanted that had persuaded him.

Poh had been ecstatic—someone had at last recognised his patience and precision. At high school he had won trophies and titles for small-bore shooting. He had trialled for the Singaporean Commonwealth Games shooting team, reaching the top three, so that rumours flew thick and fast that he would be offered a coveted place in the team. But when the offer came, his father had refused: his son was too young and his studies should come first. Poh had never forgiven him.

Soon after joining the company, Mister Ng had taken him aside and explained that his 'Business Solutions' were a little different to the usual definition; Poh would be required to travel, usually on weekends for one or two nights, and make good use of his skills. While his new job had required some moral adjustment, his first assignment had been executed smoothly: he had shot dead a man in a hotel hallway in Penang.

Poh had killed many men since, men far richer and more powerful than even Mister Ng himself. Not even the rich and powerful were infallible, and when they messed up, Poh was sent to clean up.

He drained his cup of tea. Sensing a sudden bowel movement, he made hastily for the toilet. After a few minutes of grunting and wheezing, he managed only a dry fart.

Despite his discomfort, he felt suddenly peckish. A good meal might help things along, he reasoned. He had time; the call would come sometime after ten p.m., so until then he could be relatively sure of an uneventful wait. He washed his face, polished his glasses with the pressed handkerchief Betty had given him, turned the phones to vibrate mode and slipped them into his pocket before exiting the room.

Downstairs, at the far end of the lobby lounge, a waitress greeted him and directed him to a window table. Poh picked up a copy of the *South China Morning Post* from a side table. He sat with his back to the window, surveying the restaurant. It was busy and the constant inward flow of clientele kept the white-uniformed staff bustling about behind the buffet counters, replenishing baskets, trays and terrines with sumptuous-looking dishes.

Dining from a buffet required a special strategy. Just like killing a man. That is, to optimise the outcome one had to show restraint and discipline, even caution. A buffet was a visual trap, apt to overload the senses with its colour, presentation and aromas, all of which could foul one's good sense. One had to start small, start light, and not succumb to that trait of many a man's undoing: greed.

He studied the diners around him. He noted how the large, panicky mainland Chinese women built their plates into small pyramids, lips glistening with grease and spittle, and he knew that they would be snoring it off upstairs before he had even given dessert a thought.

He approached the salads first: a small caesar salad with extra croutons and black pepper, a small salad niçoise with extra anchovies, and to accompany this, a glass of dragon fruit juice. He returned to the table and ate.

The buffet itself seemed to have no end: seafood specialties blended into European cuisine, then into Southeast Asian dishes, which became Hong Kongese and Shanghai styles, before finally ending in a faux-British pub servery.

Poh moved on to soup next. Deliberating between the seafood bisque and the clam chowder, he chose the bisque, enraptured by the rich aroma. Then to the seafood corner, presented like a French fish market stall with wooden trays of oysters, mussels and scallops. He lifted the tongs.

'Where are these oysters from?' he asked.

'From New Zealand, sir,' the chef replied.

Poh smiled. He deftly manipulated a dozen oysters onto his plate, took a half dozen prawns, some slices of smoked Tasmanian salmon and two slices of lemon to garnish. Back at the table, he closed his eyes, savouring each juicy morsel, fattened by the nutrient-rich waters of the Southern Ocean, and marvelled at the finest flavours the sea could offer. He ate slowly, forgetting his past, his future, focusing entirely on the present and the wondrous taste coursing through his mouth.

His plate was soon reduced to a small midden of oyster and

prawn shells. Poh drained his soup bowl, took several deep breaths, and made his way to the Hong Kong section. There was roast suckling pig stuffed with rice, which a young trainee busily sliced under the watchful eye of the senior chef, but the queue was too long and Poh moved on. He looked over the Peking duck, which didn't seem much different from the hawker centre in Singapore, and kept moving. He settled on a small eel clay pot with crispy rice and glistening bok choy and, taking a glass of chilled oolong tea, returned to the table.

He ate slowly, again thoughtfully. He was fond of Hong Kong, and though he would not get to visit his favourite haunts on this trip, he looked forward to returning someday with Betty. Then he would take her to Wan Chai and Lang Kwai Fong to enjoy the lively bars, the hustle of the narrow, staircased streets and the fragrances of the flower shops that lined them. Then, after an expansive dinner, he would take her back to Kowloon aboard the night ferry, arm in arm, listening to the great harbour slough and slap about them.

He finished the eel, scooping the last spoonful of rice from the pot and, after dislodging an eel bone from between his teeth, refreshed his mouth with another sip of oolong tea.

Through the shifting throngs, he glimpsed the seafood counter. With sudden excitement, he noticed the staff had replenished the oyster trays. He rose from his table and weaved smoothly between the diners, lifting a fresh plate from the servery and beating two large Chinese-speaking women with exactly the same idea.

The oysters lay fat and glistening in their freshly shucked shells. He picked up the tongs and placed six onto his plate. The smell of the sea excited him. He paused, unable to put down the tongs, oblivious to the mutterings of the women behind him. The chef watched him curiously. Why not, Poh thought—the tray would be refilled again. He took six more oysters.

Back at his table, he lifted the first oyster to his mouth. As the dripping morsel reached his lips, he felt a vibration in his side pocket. He put down the oyster and slipped out his phone, glancing at the time: twenty-five past nine.

The text message read '烏鴉飛行'—crow flying.

'Shit.'

He replaced the phone, picked up the fork and scooped another oyster into his mouth. He chewed quickly, without pleasure. Then a second oyster and a third were dispatched. They squelched between his teeth, and he fought to contain the marvellous juices that exploded from them. He swallowed hard, sipped his oolong tea, and pronged the fourth, fifth and sixth oysters. He chewed and swallowed until only four oysters remained. He paused, took a deep breath, then crammed his mouth full and continued chewing. His jaw began to ache.

Diners at a neighbouring table shot furtive glances at him. The two large Chinese women looked on disapprovingly; one remarked to the other and they shook their heads.

Chewing a piece of oyster rind, Poh hurried from the restaurant. Inside the elevator, he belched. He felt a sharp and sudden pain deep inside, like air being forced through tight spaces. A faint whistle sounded from his bowel as he stepped from the elevator. Entering his room, he lifted the mattress, slipped on the webbing and inserted the handguns, one beneath each armpit, tucking the sound repressors beside them. Then he pulled on a grey windbreaker, zipped it to his neck, picked up his night bag and exited the room.

The reception staff seemed unsurprised by his early checkout—it was, after all, an airport hotel—and wished him a safe journey.

Outside, the black Lexus stood idling at the end of the concourse, the driver chewing a toothpick. Poh climbed inside. He belched. The driver shifted his toothpick and said, 'Good dinner?'

Poh belched a reply, excusing himself. He wondered what the driver had eaten for dinner, besides a bamboo toothpick. His mind now shifted to the job ahead. Taking off his glasses to polish them, he began to empty his mind of petty thoughts and worries, distractions that might cause hesitation and a mistake.

Poh felt the pressure building. A muffled fart sounded. The driver said nothing but lowered the front windows. In rushed the smell of the night, wet, heavy and vegetative as it had been earlier.

Poh farted again.

'Jesus. What was on the menu?' the driver asked.

'Oysters.'

'You're telling me.'

'You like oysters?'

'I like a car that doesn't smell of them.'

'I ate them too fast.'

'That'll do it.'

Poh smiled, but it was more like a grimace. 'Is there a toilet up ahead?'

'Now?'

'I'll make it quick.'

'There's a 7-Eleven after the Kowloon off ramp.'

Poh cringed. He felt a serious pressure building inside of him; it was pushing, prodding, probing his intestine for weakness. He shifted from left buttock to right buttock and back again. Sweat beaded his forehead. The driver glanced in the mirror.

'You alright? You look pale.'

'How much further?' Poh said through clenched teeth.

The driver pressed his foot to the accelerator. 'Soon.'

Rain began to fall again. The lights of Victoria Harbour reflected against the low clouds and now gave the sky a surreal, otherworldly look. The Lexus slowed and veered onto the off ramp. The driver took the first right.

'Stop!' shouted Poh.

'What?' said the driver, alarmed.

'Stop, stop!'

The driver braked, jerked on the steering wheel and pulled into the roadside curb, cursing under his breath. Lorries and container transporters flew off the ramp, sending up sheets of spray as they shuttled past on their way to the port. The convenience store stood on the other side of the road.

Poh pushed open the car door. He stumbled, doubling over for a moment, then regained his composure. He timed his dash between a large Maersk container truck and a city bus and made it across the wet asphalt to the island in the centre. He paused, waiting for a gap in the vehicles passing in the opposite direction. His glasses blurred and shoulders hunched, he leaped out and sprinted towards the light.

***

Inside the cab of a refrigerated lorry, two young men were talking about their girlfriends and making plans for a double date in Wan Chai the following weekend. The passenger passed the driver a lit Lucky Strike. Up ahead, a dark shape moved quickly into their path—an animal? A man? The fleeting figure was hardly discernible in the glare of the headlights and their reflection on the wet road.

'Shit!' gasped the driver.

He rammed his foot on the brake; his passenger grabbed the ceiling handle and braced himself against the dashboard. A dull thud reverberated through the cab, as if a wave of rainwater had hit them only sharper, stronger. The truck skewed, slamming into the curb and sliding to a halt.

The driver hit the hazard lights, leaped from the cab and ran to the rear of the truck. Joined by his passenger, they crouched beside the figure who now lay prone, wet and motionless against the curb. The driver bent down and rolled the body over.

'Mister! Hey, mister!' he shouted. Turning to his passenger, he said, 'Call an ambulance, quick!'

Across the road, a black Lexus pulled away from the curb. At the traffic lights a short distance on it made a U-turn and drove slowly back past the two men attempting to revive the lifeless form lying in the gutter. Then it accelerated onto the ramp and its red tail-lights joined the swarm of others heading towards the airport.

The ambulance arrived and a police car close behind. From their seats, the officers saw a body, two young men standing over it, and behind them a white truck on whose rear cargo doors was written in large blue letters 'Soon Fat Seafood Co. Ltd'.

West Wind

Mori leaned into his old Honda Super Cub, holding it to the mountain road's edges and inside curves. He could make this journey with his eyes closed, trusting his senses to guide him around the contours of the mountainside, past the lake and over the four iron truss bridges that led into the town at the bottom of the valley.

The October morning had dawned cool and still, and it gave him cause to wonder at the strangeness of the previous night's weather. The wind had come from the west, suddenly and violently in the early hours, roaring like a freight train up the valley, felling old trees and fleecing young ones of their leaves. Then, as quickly as it had arrived, it had died.

Mori motored onwards, dodging the debris strewn across

the road, until the lake appeared and the road straightened against its shore. He passed by the shuttered boat rental shop with its colourful dinghies laid upside-down on the pier.

As the road climbed gently back to the mountainside, he revved the Cub, shooting glances at the groves of maple trees where picnic tables afforded the finest views of the lake. In the coming weeks they would be filled with daytrippers from the towns and cities, enjoying the fiery hues of the surrounding hillsides.

Autumn was Mori's favourite season. He looked forward to digging bamboo shoots, harvesting sweet potato and picking the large orange persimmons that hung like light bulbs from the trees his grandfather had planted over a hundred years ago. But this year a great scourge had descended on his farm. It had ravaged his gardens, smashed open his chicken coop, kicked over his beehives and chased off his two goats. Each time he repaired and replanted, it returned by the light of the moon to destroy and demolish again. It was the reason he was making this trip into town —to hire a hunter.

He crossed a bridge and felt the old iron truss shudder beneath him. At the sight of the mountain stream raging far below, he felt a sudden urge to pee. Stopping at the next crest, Mori walked to the roadside barrier and unzipped. Taking in the vast panorama of lake and the mountains beyond, he let go with great satisfaction a golden spout that fell fifty metres to the water below. As the last droplets tumbled, something caught his eye: a plume of smoke. It seemed to be rising from the lake shore further along the road. Odd, he thought; the barbecue crowds had long since gone, and the autumn picnickers were yet to arrive. He mounted the Honda, kicked the starter and set off.

Skirting the bend on the other side of the crest, he saw tyre marks. Where they ended, an iron barrier hung bent and twisted, as if a small elephant had charged through it. He pulled over and peered down. Through the billowing smoke he spotted an upturned vehicle lying at the water's edge. Without removing his helmet, he climbed through the barrier and clambered down the rocky slope.

It had once been a silver Suzuki compact car, but the force of the impact had crumpled it like aluminium foil. The driver's door had been punched in and the windshield glass sparkled like gems strewn across the shore. Mori peered inside but found no one. He scanned the lake shore but found nothing. Squinting into the sun's glare, his gaze settled on a piece of cloth floating just off the shore among the reeds. He ventured into the chill water, careful not to lose his footing, and waded out until he was waist deep. Drawing nearer, it occurred to him that it wasn't cloth but a shirt inflated with air. His eyes widened. Beneath the shirt, the body of a woman floated.

Mori had seen cadavers before, mostly young men he'd helped to pull from bore holes and collapsed shafts of the silver mine on the other side of the lake. But that was years ago, another era, another life. The body now in his arms gave him cause to panic. Her face was as pale as porcelain, her lips thin and blue, and on one side of her head a bruise had spread like a thundercloud.

He shook her gently, then slapped her face and shouted. But she could not be roused. He carried her to the shore, put her on her side and forced his fingers inside her mouth, searching for obstructions. Turning her onto her back, he placed the heels of his hands over the centre of her chest and pumped in quick rhythm. He put his lips to hers, blew, and watched her chest rise and fall. A groan sounded, followed by coughing, and soon came the soft gurgle and wheeze of air flowing.

Certain that she had no broken bones, he hoisted her onto his shoulder fireman-style. At fifty-six years old he was no spring chicken, but a life of manual labour and farming had given him a level of strength unusual for a man of his age. He inched his way back to the road and, leaving the motorbike roadside, set off for home. She was small and waif-like but her deadweight made the journey slow going. Her occasional groans were strangely comforting—it meant she was still alive. By the time he sighted the red roof of his farmstead among the cedar trees, his legs were leaden and his shoulders numb.

The hundred-year-old house had a large main room with a central fireplace. Mori laid the woman on a futon beside it and gently peeled away her damp clothes. He propped her head on a pillow of buckwheat chaff and pulled a winter kakebuton across her to ward off the chill. In his kitchen he heated a pot of water, dissolved in a chicken stock cube and set it aside to cool. But she continued to sleep, and it wasn't until early evening that he decided to let her rest the night.

He sat in the engawa, the long, narrow veranda in which his grandfather used to smoke and look out onto valley. As he watched the sun's rays retreat across the forested mountaintops, he began to fret. Should he have ridden to the town for help? Should he have gone to his neighbour's home to use the telephone? Had it been wise to bring her here? He shut the flyscreens and rolled out his futon across the engawa floorboards. There he lay, shifting restlessly, listening for changes in the woman's condition but hearing only sounds of the outside world: an owl hoot, a deer bark, and a million crickets filling the night with their pulsating symphonies.

In the morning, he left a bowl of rice gruel with some pickled plums and a cup of barley tea beside her futon. He then departed the house on foot. The car was still there beside the lake, blackened and upturned like a chargrilled turtle on its back. He would have to report it to the police sooner or later. The thought weighed on him.

He carried his frown all the way back to the house, but when he slid back the door to the central room, his eyes widened. The futon was empty and the woman's clothes were gone. The rice bowl lay beside the hearth with only the plum stones left inside it. He called out, moving from room to room, but the old house remained silent and still. As he passed along the hallway and back into the large room, he felt a sudden rush of air beside him. Something cold and hard pressed at his jugular.

'Who are you?' said the voice.

The pinprick at his neck forced him to hold his breath. He felt himself pushed into the centre of the room with a force that surprised him. Her eyes were cold and fierce, her hair dark and wild across her face. She was small but capable.

'Who are you?' she said again.

He glanced at the carving knife in her hand. 'Mori,' he said. 'I live here.'

'Where's here?'

'Ochi valley, Kamikawa.'

'My car.'

'You crashed it into the lake. I carried you back here.'

The blade wavered, glimmering, but remained pointed at

him.

'How long have I been here?'

'A day and a half.'

'Who are you?'

'I've told you. My name is Mori. This is my farm.'

Her gaze ranged the room, taking in the rustic furniture, its smoke-stained walls, the old photos of boaters on the lake, and the large wooden fish that hung as a talisman above the fire hearth in the middle of the room.

'Where's my car?'

'You need a doctor.'

'My car!'

'It's down the road, beside the lake,' he said. 'You crashed through the barrier. I pulled you from the water.'

'I must get to the car.'

'It's destroyed.'

'There's something inside.'

Mori watched her closely. He knew accident victims were prone to irrational behaviour. He had seen it in the injured miners he'd wrestled from the shafts. 'Tell me what it is and I'll get it for you. I have a motorbike.'

'It's wrapped in cloth. It was on the seat beside me.'

'What happened?'

For a moment the question seemed to stump her, then she said, 'Something jumped in front of the car ...'

'Probably a deer. They come down from the mountains to forage.'

'I tried to swerve ...'

'It happens.' He glanced at the bowl on the floor, hoping to change the subject. 'Are you still hungry?'

She lowered the knife, stepped back to the hearth and picked up the bowl. 'Thank you,' she said, passing it to him.

***

A heavy dew had settled in the night and the cliff face was wet and slippery as Mori clambered down to the lake. Outside and inside the charred wreck he searched the shattered glass and shards of broken metal, and soon his fingers touched on a bundle of blackened cloth. The object inside was long and stiff and tied with a purple cord.

But when he returned to the house, he found her asleep. The bowl had been washed and placed on the counter, the knife returned to its holder. He placed the cloth bundle beside her futon and retired to the kitchen to prepare lunch. He made a broth with the last drops from a bonito sauce bottle, and to this he added garlic cloves, broken carrots and shreds of Chinese cabbage leaves salvaged from the garden. He ate alone in the engawa, contemplating the slow creep of the autumn hues across the valley, turning now and again to watch her sleep. After lunch he placed a tray of food beside her futon with a flask of barley tea and then set off for the fields above the house.

It was late afternoon when he paused to rest and consider his resurrected vegetable patch. As he gulped from his tea flask, a curious sound reached him. It was a soft, wailing melody, and it seemed to come from the house. Clutching his spade, he stood listening. It was the sound of a wooden flute.

He returned to find her seated in the engawa, facing the valley, with a shakuhachi in her hands. Unsure if she had heard him, he stood in the doorway, captivated by the melody, which plunged and soared like the mountain peaks. It was an ethereal sound, mysterious and fleeting, and for the briefest of moments Mori imagined his grandfather seated at the hearth, his wispy grey beard touching his kimono collar, turning river fish on bamboo skewers over the glowing coals. He too had played the shakuhachi. Could it be that she was summoning his spirit?

The melody stopped.

'Thank you,' she said and turned to him. 'For returning my flute.'

'I must ask you something,' he said.

'Please don't.' Before he could utter a word, she said, 'I will leave in the morning.'

'To where? The only way out is the road to town. Or the trail that runs east across the mountain pass to—'

'Izumo Shrine,' she said.

'In Shimane prefecture?' Mori said incredulously. 'But that's more than fifty kilometres away.'

'There are shrines along this trail.'

'How did you know that?'

'I will be on my way in the morning.'

'In your condition? On foot? You need help.'

'Isn't it you who needs help?'

'What?'

'Your farm.'

'It's nothing,' he said, realising she must have seen him at work.

'Did a typhoon do that?'

'No.'

'What then?'

'A boar.'

'Then why don't you catch it?'

'Because he's too big.'

'Don't you have a gun?'

'I was on my way to hire a hunter in the town when I found you.'

Mori took a seat beside her in the engawa. The sound of crickets had returned and seemed to be coming from directly beneath the floorboards. 'There were many hunters here once,' he said. 'My grandfather was one. But they are almost all gone now and young people aren't interested in such a profession. Deer and boar numbers are rising. They are coming down into the valley to eat our crops.'

'Have you tried poison?'

'Other animals may die.'

'You're afraid of taking life?'

'Everything has a right to live.'

'Even you.'

'I'll manage.'

'Without food? How will you survive? Winter is coming.'

'I'll manage,' he said again with growing irritation.

'Does this boar come often?'

'Now is the season of bamboo shoots. He'll be back soon enough. Look out there—see those over-turned stones? None of them weigh less than a hundred kilograms. Only a huge beast can do that.'

She asked to see the fields. Reluctantly, he led her up the narrow path and through the groves of persimmon and loquat trees. When they arrived at the fields, the rural idyll vanished. Everywhere the soil had been churned and cratered. A line of heavy-duty wire grills lay tossed like a child's playthings along the field's edges.

'That used to be a fence. Just like that was once a cage— over there,' he said, pointing to a stand of wild oak and camphor trees where the mangled wreckage of a large wire contraption lay with its door hanging by one hinge. 'Each time I replant and repair, it returns.'

'When did it come last?'

'Three days ago. With sows and little ones. They ate most of my vegetables and spoiled the rest.'

The sky had turned the colour of copper, and tiny silhouettes now flitted above the treetops gorging on insects in the fading light. Towards the east, the horizon glowed with the promise of a full moon. Mori pondered it for a moment and said grimly, 'It will come again tonight.'

Back at the house he prepared the hearth, placing charcoal in a small pyramid and using a length of bamboo to gently feed in the oxygen. In a few moments, a soft glow had pushed back the dimness of the large room. She took out her flute and played while he set about preparing a dinner of steamed rice and pickled plums in the kitchen. He produced a bottle of shōchū and offered her some, mixing it with hot water and serving it in an earthen cup, which he placed on the hearth beside her.

They ate and drank in silence, watching the pulsing coals.

'Have you lived here all your life?' she asked.

'No. I was born in Tokyo.'

'I don't care for big cities.'

'Neither do I.'

'Is that why you came here?'

'My parents died when I was young. I came to live with my grandfather, then I got a job at the mine.'

'A mine?'

'A silver mine, on the other side of the lake.'

'In this beautiful place?'

'Some would say a vein of silver is more beautiful.' He set down his bowl, picked up the iron tongs and stoked the coals. 'It brought jobs and prosperity to the town. Then the price of silver crashed and it became cheaper to buy from China and Australia. So the mine closed and the miners left. The town is barely a town anymore.'

'But you didn't leave.'

'This was my grandfather's house. He built it himself, with timber from the forest, reeds from the lake, stone from the streams.' He picked up his shōchū and drank deeply. When he returned the cup to the hearth, his face glowed with the intensity of the coals. He wondered what his grandfather would have made of this mysterious woman who sat beside him with a flute in her hands at his fireplace.

***

Despite the chill, Mori chose again to sleep on the veranda. Yet, even after consuming half a bottle of shōchū, he could not sleep; he tossed and turned, sat upright, peered into the large room at the formless shape of her futon, knowing that beneath it lay a living, breathing woman. It had been two summers since a woman had slept there—the mine manager's wife. But all that was a distant memory, just like the mine itself. The moon cast its eerie blue light across the valley until, finally exhausted, he fell asleep.

He dreamed of the lake and a boat painted green; of himself lying stretched out and dozing between the oars, a breeze licking his face and the scent of wild pine washing over him. He heard the laughter of other boaters and felt the breeze strengthen. A cloud passed across the sun, a shadow across his face, and the lake's surface grew ruffled. The boat began to pitch. He grappled the oars and hove to. Now spindrift lashed his face, blinding him, and from somewhere out in the squall came strange wailing cries. The harder he pulled on the oars, the more he stayed still. Great waves towered over him and their steely sides were filled with the faces of miners he had known, dead and gone. They tossed his boat like a cork in a stormwater drain.

He awoke with a start. The house was calm and still. He exhaled, returning his head slowly to the pillow. Then he heard it, a sound so light and fragile that it might have been a valley breeze. He rose from his futon, crossed the floor and pulled back the woman's kakebuton. His eyes widened.

He hurried from the empty futon to the room where his grandfather used to sleep at the rear of the house. Pulling back the old paper doors, he pressed his face to the window and peered up at the fields.

He gasped.

Against a midnight blue sky, her figure sat straight and upright, with the flute to her lips. His first thought was to bring her back to the safety of the house. But a strange paralysis overcame him. He stood transfixed, listening to this new melody that came deeper and more forceful than before. It seemed to reach up through the forest, across the streams, over boulders and into the ravines, as if calling to something.

The realisation struck him like an anvil—he thrust open the window and cried out. But her haunting notes persisted until from high on a forested slope above the field came the whip crack of snapping tree branches.

An enormous form emerged from the edge of the forest and stood silhouetted against the night sky, facing her. Its snout moved back and forth, vacuuming up the scents and odours from the earth, its great curved tusks gleaming in the moonlight.

She did not flinch. She did not stop playing.

Out of the forest others emerged, sows with piglets snuffling and grunting, waiting and watching behind their giant patriarch.

The beast trod nearer until its glistening snout seemed only inches from the woman and her flute. Steam billowed from its huge maw. Mori wondered if he was still dreaming; he had never seen anything so terrifying.

Then, slowly, the woman rose to her feet and with small, nimble steps moved around the huge beast. Playing her flute with one hand, she ran the other along its broad razor back so that it quivered beneath her touch. Beside its left shoulder she stopped. In one smooth action, she twisted the flute so that it became two pieces. Mori glimpsed the flash of steel in the moonlight and a violent spasm rocked the body of the beast. It jerked its head in the air, coughed and fell to its knees.

Mori shoved aside the window and leaped into the garden. As he reached the orchard, the air began to stir around him. Tree leaves rustled. Fruit thudded to the ground. Within seconds, a roaring gale had risen. It forced him to take shelter in the lee of a persimmon tree. Clutching its trunk, he held on for dear life as his farm flew by in an angry swarm.

For how long the wind lasted he couldn't tell, but as quickly as it had come it disappeared. He hauled himself up, gasping. Brushing grit from his face, he waited for the world to right itself. Then he searched the fields and the forest verge, calling out, but hearing only his own breathless voice. There were no footprints in the soil—nothing to say she had ever been there. He realised then that he did not even know her name.

The boar lay at the edge of the field. In the light of the moon, it resembled a small mountain with a dark stream oozing from one side.

He did not report the car accident. In the week that followed, he never heard or saw any report of a missing person; not from the police, nor from his neighbours. The car wreck remained where it was; townsfolk said it must have been joyriders from one of the lowland towns.

As for the boar, Mori cleaned and quartered it himself. He gave some to his neighbours, and some to the police who had visited him enquiring after the abandoned car. The rest he cured in a homemade smoker. The winter would be a long one.

He never told anyone about the woman. Not because it would have brought undue trouble to himself, and to the police who had no report of a missing person, but because of what he found in his grandfather's closet several days later. It was an old Japanese calendar, in which the months of the year were called by different names, and it caused Mori to wonder. He lifted down from his bookshelf a heavy encyclopedia and opened its dusty covers on the tatami floor. Thumbing the brown and brittle pages, he stopped near the middle and his finger came to rest on the following words:

'October is known as Kaminazuki, or Month of the Gods. This is due to the popular belief that Shinto gods from all over the country depart their own shrines to gather at Izumo Shrine in Shimane.'

Night Fishing

'Stringbean' Riggs jiggled his cup and drained the gin to the rocks. He peered out of the window, first at the clouds, then at the earth, wondering if the lush and otherworldly island beneath him was Cebu or just another green jewel in the Visayan Sea.

The plane dropped like an elevator. A woman gasped. The old man in the seat behind uttered a Hail Mary and Riggs thought he heard rosary beads chatter. Presently the cabin attendants appeared, the prayers subsided, and passengers took comfort in the bored faces of the two young women who seated themselves in the bulkhead facing them.

Riggs crushed an ice cube between his teeth as he scratched the nub of pink skin where his left hand used to be, and caught one of the attendants watching. She smiled quickly and said,

'First time to the Philippines?'

'No,' he said.

'On holiday?'

'Sort of.'

'Staying long on Cebu?'

'That depends.'

She smiled again, but it was purely professional. Riggs didn't feel much like small talk. His attention drifted back to the window and the sugarcane fields and mango tree plantations that grew greener and more voluminous as the plane descended. He glimpsed a lorry, a cane truck perhaps, crawling beetle-like along a dusty highway towards a hamlet in the distance. So different to the dishwater-grey sprawl of London, now twenty-two hours behind him.

He felt his armpits leaking. The gin had worn off and the unease had crept back. It was the same deep and ominous feeling he'd had opening the small brown envelope that had dropped through his mail slot five weeks earlier. Five postage stamps of General Douglas MacArthur and 'Mister Allan Riggs' scrawled in a curious hand across the creased, travel-worn paper. He touched his chest pocket, confirming that the letter with the polaroid photograph was still in his possession. In less than forty-eight hours he would be standing face to face with its sender. The stains beneath his armpits grew darker.

The plane banked and in a wide arc the aircraft's nose was brought into the wind. The sea lay below them, whitecaps whipped by the wind and racing to shore. The plane came in low and uneven across the outer reef, skimming the turquoise lagoon until the land reared up in a green blur and flight PI420 kissed the hot tarmac of Cebu island.

Like MacArthur, Riggs had returned. He hadn't planned to. In fact, he had vowed *not* to after what had happened in Angeles City seventeen years earlier. He half-expected the immigration officer to say, 'Mister Allan Riggs? We have been expecting you, would you please step this way.' Or, from the gallery of glistening faces on the other side of the arrival hall doors, 'Welcome back, Stringbean, you crazy sonofabitch!'

For better or for worse, time works its magic on a man, widening his girth, thinning his pate, shrinking his gums, leeching him of testosterone. No one recognised him as he moved through the immigration corrals, the customs gates, and out into the arrivals hall. He was just another tall, balding dayuhan, with one good hand and a duffel bag, moving solemnly and sluggishly through the concourse throngs to the taxi stand.

'Sampaguita Guesthouse? Legaspi Street? Yeah, I know it,' the driver said, casting his cigarette to the ground. 'Seventy pesos. Get in.'

They drove in silence through the cane fields, then the industrial parks, passing the sun-bleached slums on the city limits until they reached a traffic signal and the driver stopped, wound down the window and dispatched a wad of phlegm onto the steaming asphalt.

'Know what sampaguita means?' he said, wiping his mouth.

'Jasmine,' said Riggs.

'Means jasmine. Jasmine Guesthouse.'

'I know,' Riggs said.

'First time to Cebu?'

'No.'

'You want marijuana?'

'No.'

'You want a girl?'

'No. I want to sleep.'

'You want to sleep with a girl?'

'I want to sleep till I'm dead.'

'Dead no good for business. I bring you a girl and marijuana to Jasmine Guesthouse tomorrow, okay?'

Riggs rubbed the stump of his wrist; the heat made it tingle. He watched the crazed choreography of bikes, buses and jeepneys swirl past. He glimpsed the roadside fry-stalls and juice stands, mangy dogs and half-naked kids roaming between them, and everywhere people talking, smoking, drinking and laughing. Were people who lived near the equator happier than those who lived near the poles? Did cheerful poverty trump miserable wealth? Could *he* call a place like this 'home'? Time would tell.

'What happen to your hand?' the driver asked.

Riggs glanced at the rear-view mirror. The driver's greasy face gleamed in the late afternoon sun.

'Lost it in Saudi Arabia,' Riggs said.

The driver shot him a quizzical look but said nothing until they reached the periphery of the old town. There he turned off the main road and into a narrow tree-lined street. Outside an elegant colonial-era building with a purple bougainvillea vine cascading over its iron gate, he pulled up and cut the engine.

'Eighty pesos,' he said.

'You said seventy,' said Riggs.

'I burn rubber to get here.'

Riggs reached beneath his trouser belt and wrestled with

his crotch. The driver's eyes narrowed, watching the dayuhan pull a fistful of damp pesos from between his legs and throw them onto the front seat.

'Cut your hand off,' Riggs said.

'What?'

'For stealing in Saudi Arabia. They cut off your hand.' He took his bag and exited the car, leaving the driver to utter a string of Cebuano curse words and count his money.

The guesthouse lobby was cool and dimly lit. Riggs' nose twitched at a familiar scent. He searched the room for its source, spotted the floral arrangement at the end of the teakwood counter and leaned down to fill his nostrils.

'You like Arabian jasmine, sir?' the elderly receptionist enquired.

'I'm a gardener,' Riggs said, scrawling his name into the guest register and pocketing his key. 'Thank you.'

The upstairs room overlooked the street. A desk, a ceiling fan, a small bed and a painting of a woman combing her hair beside a waterfall were its only comforts. After sluicing himself, he put on a fresh shirt and bought two cans of San Miguel from reception. He must have passed out because when he awoke, sounds of laughter and pop music drifted up from the street. From the window, Riggs peered down onto dozens of mobile kitchens that had sprung up along the tree-lined thoroughfare. Night had wrapped the city in a suffocating stillness and its fragrant fug pressed in on him as he left the guesthouse in search of food. Sodium lamps dangled from the trees, casting a warm glow over the tables where Cebuanos sat laughing, drinking and gorging themselves. Riggs stopped to watch a woman carving a roast suckling piglet. He took a seat and ordered a beer. The lechon arrived soon after, sliced thickly and piled high on a plastic plate. He ate the succulent meat hungrily.

''Scuse me, mate,' came a voice behind him. Riggs turned to find a gaunt foreigner standing over him. His eyes were bloodshot and jaundiced, and his chest bones pushed through his faded batik shirt like an old washboard.

'You American?' the man asked.

'British,' Riggs replied.

'Been here long?'

'Couple of hours.'

'Staying?'

'Maybe.'

The man considered Riggs for a moment, then his gaze fell to the suckling pig. He pulled out a stool and sat down. 'Listen, mate, I'm in a bit of a tight spot …'

Riggs chewed his mouthful, waiting—the best storytellers in the world were Australians.

'Some cunt stole mc wallet while I was in the shower this mornin'. Bastard cleaned me out like a Kolkata curry.'

Riggs swallowed his mouthful and washed the gristle down with beer. 'How much?'

'I'm not begging, mate. I'm not one of those shitty begpackers you see everywhere.'

'How much do you need?'

The man gripped the table and leaned closer, his voice falling to a desperate whisper. 'I gotta get outta here, mate. I gotta get to Manila.'

Riggs looked about at the families and office workers clustered at the makeshift tables, enjoying their dinner beneath a constellation of tiny light bulbs. He looked back at the man's face and saw something he recognised. It was fear—fear of dying, fear of living, fear of never finding peace? He wasn't sure. But he had seen that look in a mirror.

'How much do you need to get to Manila?'

'Can you spare a coupla thousand?'

Riggs put down his fork. He slipped his hand beneath his belt and pulled out two thousand-peso notes and laid them on the table. The man trembled as he raked the money towards him; his fingers reminded Riggs of an old skeleton money box he'd owned as a kid.

''Preciate this, mate. Really do.' He rolled the bills into a tube and, holding them tightly, extended his other hand.

'Barry's the name.'

'Allan,' Riggs said, and their greasy palms locked together.

'Gimme your address, Allan. I'll pay you back.'

'Forget it.'

'Nah, nah, I'm not gunna forget it, mate. Gimme your address and I'll send you the money from Manila.'

'Just do the same for someone else in need and we'll call it even.' Riggs called over the stall owner and paid the bill.

'Here, write it down,' the man said, pulling an old biro from somewhere and taking a tissue from the dispenser. 'C'mon, mate.'

As Riggs scribbled, the man mouthed the words.

'Stringbean Riggs, London Royal Parks ...'

'Best of luck, Barry.'

'Geez, mate, what happened to your hand?'

But Riggs did not reply. He was on the move, weaving between the tables of diners, putting distance between himself and what he might have become seventeen years ago had a sympathetic Australian not helped him.

'Stringbean! Mate, I'm gunna get that money to ya!' the man shouted, loud enough for diners to turn and glance in his direction. Had he looked back, Riggs would have seen the traveller slump down at the table and start hand-sifting his greasy leftovers.

***

Riggs lay half-naked beneath the ceiling fan with the letter fluttering against his hand. He knew the contents by heart. The pure, simple sentences—childlike in construction, earnest in their intention—had shaken him to his core. He picked up the polaroid and held it to the bedside lamp, studying the face of the figure who gazed awkwardly back at him. He'd scoured the recesses of his mind for the name 'Cruz', but could not recall anyone he'd ever met in Angeles City by that name. Yet the familiarity of the face was unmistakable; it had left him sleepless and agitated, night after night, day after day, until he'd been able to stand it no longer. Taking leave of his job, he paid rent two months in advance and bought an air ticket to the other side of the world.

One day a groundsman for the Royal Parks of London, tilling horse manure and talking peonies with lonely old women, next a middle-aged man adrift, holed up in a cheap hotel in the Philippines awaiting a dawn bus to carry him north to a boat that will ferry him across the Visayan Sea to an island where someone who perhaps represents his past, present and possibly his future awaits.

He returned the photo and letter to his money belt, set his alarm, and turned off the light.

***

In the dawn light, a bus terminal vendor sold him a cup of steaming coffee and a banana pancake. Then, as the sun fingered the tops of the office towers, the bus crawled out through the shanties and joined the Grand Nautical Highway heading north. Hidden from view by the riotous foliage, the sea made its presence known on the cool, briny air that rushed in through the open windows. Curled up against each other, older passengers availed themselves of the rhythm of the road and dozed. The younger ones let their gaze wander the lush landscape, perhaps thinking of the family and friends awaiting them at the end of line, or of those left behind.

The bus veered inland, passing ramshackle villages and flooded rice paddies where farmers sat smoking, watching their water buffalo wallow. Seventeen years earlier, on a bus from Manila to Angeles City, Riggs had been too drunk to see anything but the smashed insects on the windowpane. Now the roadside flora beguiled him with its size, colour and variation: the fiery red flowers of the dap-dap tree, the cream-white blossoms of the bani tree, which spread like a huge umbrella over the highway, and the rampaging hibiscus—all so different to the delicate, manicured gardens of England.

When they stopped for breakfast at a roadhouse, Riggs joined the melee at the buffet, piling his plate with pancit noodles and adobo chicken, adding two cans of San Miguel to ease his nerves and drawing knowing smiles from the older men. When he climbed back aboard the bus, the seat beside his had been taken by a young Filipino who introduced himself as Vincent. He wore a white business shirt and pressed trousers, and his white teeth flashed when he spoke.

'You're going to Maya?' he asked.

'Yes,' said Riggs.

'There's nothing in Maya. So I guess you're going to Malapascua Island?'

'Yes.'

'Beautiful place. The water is so clear, you get dizzy just looking down. Your first time?'

'Yes.'

'You're a scuba diver?'

'No.'

The man looked at him curiously. 'But there's nothing else to do there.'

'That's why I'm going.'

The man smiled, but his eyes failed to hide his puzzlement. He changed the subject and for a while Riggs, politely as he could, kept their conversation to home towns, jobs and the weather in England. He learned that the man was an English teacher in a small village school, and that he was fulfilling his Department of Education training to work for one year in a remote rural area of Cebu.

'I miss my family,' the teacher said. 'You're married?'

'No.'

'But you have family in London, don't you?'

'No.'

'No brothers or sisters?'

Riggs shook his head.

'I'm sorry to hear that. Filipino families are big—many brothers and sisters! We say children are a gift from God.' He flashed his teeth.

Riggs smiled back, but his gaze returned to the world of light and colour beyond the window. He thought of his mother and father, worm-eaten and frigid beneath the frosty turf of London Cemetery, and a feeling of melancholy overcame him. He hadn't exactly been their gift from God; his reckless ways had driven his mother to tears and his father to kick him out of home on his eighteenth birthday. By twenty he was squatting in a south London flat, peddling Moroccan hashish to west London rich kids.

The bus descended onto a plain and a vast plantation of sugarcane stretched before them. The asphalt faded to coral dust and soon the passengers and their possessions were covered in a fine grey powder. When a small farming town appeared and the bus drew into its clapboard roadhouse, the teacher rose from his seat and said, 'This is my stop.' He took his Boston bag from the rack and shook Riggs' hand. 'Sorry to be rude, but I've been wanting to ask: how did you lose your hand?'

'Scuba-diving accident,' Riggs said.

'That's what I thought!' The teacher nodded vigorously. 'I tell my students, humans are land creatures. We don't belong in the water. Me, I can't even swim.' He flashed a smile, the doors closed after him and the bus lurched away.

Ruffled by the dry breeze, the sugarcane fields rolled on in endless design. Riggs extended his legs, glad for the extra space and the absence of an inquiring gaze. He pulled the letter from his chest pocket and re-read the sender's instructions, worried that he may have missed some small detail that could delay his arrival. With his head against the rattling window, the words seemed to dance before his eyes and soon their meaning was lost to the rhythm of the road.

He awoke to a furnace blast scouring his face. He gasped, then coughed, and felt the letter whipped from fingers by the

hot gust. He turned to glimpse it fly out the window and flutter up into the dust clouds. His first impulse was to dash to the driver and ask him to stop. But the request would have sounded absurd and he slumped back gloomily in his seat.

They sailed on through the sea of green, the bus tossing its passengers this way and that, until the growl of the engine abruptly ceased and Riggs sensed the vehicle drifting to a stop on a long stretch of highway. The driver announced that the engine had lost power. There would be a delay. Outside, Riggs kicked at the grey dust. He looked about at the old men with tired eyes, the drowsy teenagers sipping warm Coke, and the giggling women who disappeared into the sugarcane to relieve themselves. He felt out of his depth—a one-handed, middle-aged English gardener treading water in the deep, slow-moving torrent of humanity that was not his own. Gazing out onto the fields of sugarcane and the long white ribbon of coral dust that shimmered behind him, he felt a crushing solitude. He had no idea what to do.

At the rear of the bus he found the driver wrestling with the bus's innards. A snapped drive belt lay like a dead snake in the dust at his feet. Riggs recalled what a workshop mechanic had once told him and said, 'Pantyhose.'

The driver looked up, first at Riggs' face, then at his

missing hand.

'What did you say?'

'Ladies' pantyhose. You can use them as a drive belt until you get to a garage.'

The driver chuckled. 'You want to ask around?' He gestured to the middle-aged and elderly women squatting in the shade of the bus then returned to his tinkering, leaving Riggs to search the cloudless sky for an answer. It was now late afternoon. With Maya several hours away, he worried that he might not make the ferry.

A plume of dust rose in the distance. In a short while, a convoy of cane lorries emerged from the heat mirage. When the lead truck drew alongside the bus, its sun-blackened driver thrust out his head and exchanged words with the bus driver; phone calls were made and then came an announcement. An excited chatter rose from the gathered passengers and Riggs soon found himself hoisted up by a burly cane cutter and into the walled tray of an ancient Fuso. There he squatted with a dozen others as the lorry lurched forward and resumed its northward journey. The roar of the engine and the swirling cane chaff rendered all communication pointless, so passengers took refuge in their own thoughts and prayers, hopeful like Riggs that they would reach Maya by nightfall.

The hours passed and the air grew gradually humid. The sugarcane faded into fields of mango trees, and soon clusters of ramshackle homes with fishing nets slung between their eaves appeared. Passengers shook off the dust and rose to their feet to push their faces into the warm, salty breeze. Maya emerged in the distance, a scruffy port town clutching the shores of the Visayan Sea, which stretched like a plain of brushed silver beyond it.

Inside the ferry office, Riggs bought a one-way ticket to Malapascua and a bottle of Coke. Pressing the frosted glass against his wrist to sooth its itchiness, he fretted, sipped, and fretted some more, until an ancient tannoy speaker crackled to life and a sleepy female voice announced that the ferry was ready for boarding.

The outrigger 'pumpboat' had wide, ungainly stabilisers that reminded Riggs of an albatross with its wings extended. Passengers boarded by way of a gangplank extending from the rocky shore to the boat's prow and then to the shelter of a blue canvas awning that stretched beneath the wheelhouse. The engine belched and grunted, and the propeller churned the brine to a green froth as the captain eased the boat out of the lagoon and through the reef channel. Riggs sat near the prow, happy to leave behind him the hot breath of the land and feel the cool, briny breeze against his face. He scanned the horizon but saw nothing more than the melding of sea with sky. Now and again, flying fish broached the surface and winged ahead of them.

He felt a hand touch his arm and turned to find an elderly woman pointing out to sea. 'Turtle,' she said, indicating a huge creature whose head bobbed for a few moments then quickly dived.

While the thrum of the propeller and rocking motion of the boat as it slipped through the velveteen swell held the passengers in a strange hypnosis, Riggs could not shake free of his apprehension; he felt like a meteorite hurtling towards the Earth's atmosphere, unable to change course or turn back, but strangely resigned to his fate—the moment he would fully realise that actions have consequences.

Darkness crept across the Visayan Sea, the lights of fishing boats scuttling back and forth along the horizon resembling comets or satellites sailing across an inky space. Again, he felt the woman touch his arm. 'Malapascua,' she said, pointing to a tiny cluster of lights peeping above the skyline. 'You come for the festival?' she asked.

'What festival?' he said.

'Lawihan, the thresher shark festival. It's tomorrow, you know. Everywhere boats coming from other islands, music, a parade and roast pig—lots of lechon! You like lechon?'

He nodded, but his gaze remained unshifting.

The lights of the island grew brighter. Soon the propeller's rhythm slowed and the bow wash flattened as the boat veered towards the island's leeward side. Riggs strained to see the lay of the land ahead. The moon had risen, silhouetting a small hillock at one end, and below this a white sand beach rimmed a crescent-shaped cove. Coconut palms studded its shore and a single building stood with a light shining above it. The scent of the land drifted out to greet them, causing Riggs' nostrils to twitch; he smelled jasmine.

As the captain throttled down, manoeuvring the ferry between vessels already moored in the cove, the deckhands rushed forward to ready the gangway. Passengers in jeans rolled them to their knees; those in skirts hitched them into their underwear. The ferry's keel pushed into the sand, and after the plank had been lowered, passengers splashed ashore with their boxes and cartons held high. Riggs watched the whole procession move past the boathouse and up a sandy path, disappearing into a grove of coconut palms. He stood alone on the damp sand, shoes in one hand, duffel bag in the crook of his other arm. His stump itched terribly. Save for the crew, who now busied themselves securing the ferry, the beach was completely deserted. A terrifying thought flashed through his mind: had he landed on the wrong island? But no, the old woman had been right—a sign above the boatshed announced 'Malapascua Island Ferry Co.'.

He followed the sandy path that the others had taken until he reached the top of the knoll and stood looking down on a sprawling village with tin rooftops glinting in the moonlight. Somewhere a rooster crowed and a child cried. He descended onto a sandy street lined with shop houses, each one festooned with paper flowers and flags advertising Tanduay rum fluttering in the light breeze. He stopped outside a bar of sorts. Seated at tables scattered across its sandy forecourt were a few old-timers drinking beer and playing fan-tan. When they glanced up from their card game there was a curious recognition in their faces. It seemed to Riggs that they were expecting him.

'Anna!' one of them called out to the bar. Through the open door a middle-aged woman appeared. She had a large, gleaming face and wore a pink t-shirt with a Rolling Stones tongue stretched across her breasts. When she saw Riggs, her eyes widened. She rushed forward.

'Mister Riggs?'

'Hello,' he said.

'We thought you weren't coming,' she said breathlessly. '*Thank you* for coming.'

'My bus broke down.'

'Ronnie's been waiting. He thought you'd changed your mind.'

'Where is he?'

She turned and shouted something through the door. Two young boys appeared, barefoot and wearing football jerseys. She spoke quickly in Tagalog and the youths stared wide-eyed, first at Riggs' missing hand, then at his face. 'My sons will take you to him. He's out on the reef, fishing for octopus.' She stepped closer and held out her hand. 'I'm Anna Cruz, Ronnie's aunt. Gracie was my older sister. We worked together in Angeles City.'

It was the moment Riggs had been dreading, when his past would fly up into his face and slap him publicly. *Actions have consequences.* 'I'm so sorry for your loss. I'm sure she was a good mother to Ronnie,' was all he could muster.

'He was all she had. She didn't tell him about you until just before she passed away. She was proud and stubborn and we all loved her,' she said, her eyes glistening in the lamplight.

'Ronnie found me on the internet?'

'You must have given Gracie your address. My eldest son found a photo of you online. You won a gardening contest in London—'

'A long time ago.'

She smiled with delight. 'Go on, Carlos and Joshua will take you to him. He'll be so happy.' She wiped her cheeks. 'Leave your bag. Go!'

The moon now hung large and full and set the coral sand beach at the end of the street aglow. A king tide had emptied the lagoon like a kitchen sink; far out across the shallows, all the way to the reef's foaming edge, lanterns drifted back and forth like glowing sentinels. These, the boys said, were the octopus hunters.

'Wait, please,' the oldest boy told Riggs. He scampered across the sand and waded into the lagoon until only his silhouette was visible against the moonlight reflected in the water. A short while later, one of the lanterns ceased moving. Riggs' heartbeat quickened. His nerves tightened. He sucked on the salty air in short rapid breaths.

Actions have consequences. One night a man walks into a bar in Angeles City. Blind on drink, he is beguiled by a beautiful Filipina. One night in her company turns into a week and he blows all of his money on uppers and downers and everything in between to keep the fantasy alive—and almost dies trying. He wakes up in a police cell, bloodied and half-naked, with charges of public indecency and assaulting another dayuhan to his name. Then from somewhere steps an Australian, an older, wiser man whose face he's never seen before, or can't recall, who posts bail and puts the foolish young man on a bus to Manila and a flight home.

'Did a shark do that?' Riggs turned to find the youngest boy staring at his pink stump, and the earnestness in his face recalled his own childhood, when life's mysteries were many and answers from adults few.

'You climb the coconut trees?' he asked the boy.

'Uh-huh.'

'Are you careful?'

'Why?'

'Because one day I climbed a tree with a chainsaw in my hands, and I wasn't.'

Riggs could not know what he was thinking or whether he had even understood. A sudden cry rang out from across the water and the lantern began to move towards them. Riggs stepped down to the water's edge. He felt the cool water wash over his feet, but his body felt on fire. The lantern grew nearer until a tall, slim youth emerged in its glow.

'Hello, Ronnie,' said Riggs.

The teenager's eyelids flickered. A shy smile fought its way to his lips as he stepped forward. Then from his mouth came a sound that was neither Tagalog nor English but another language that Riggs had heard from time to time in the parks and streets of London.

'Ronnie don't speak,' said the younger boy.

The teenager passed the lantern to the oldest boy, then gestured with his hands. The boy said, 'He says, hello.' But it was Riggs who was lost for words; he could not pull his gaze from the long legs, the finely muscled shoulders, the strong cheekbones and soft gaze of the person standing before him. The teenager from the polaroid in the flesh. *His own flesh.*

A look of anxiousness flashed across the young man's face. He hand-signed quickly and the boy translated: 'Ronnie says he's sorry.'

'For what?' said Riggs.

'For not telling you.'

'Not telling me what?'

'That he doesn't speak. He was worried you wouldn't come. He's very happy.'

Riggs sensed a huge weight lifting from his shoulders. He felt his head growing light, as if into the void were rushing seventeen years of lost time. No matter that they spoke different languages; no matter that they were both missing things that others took for granted. Neither of them seemed to notice the other's physical loss. 'Tell him I'm happy too,' he said, out stretching his hand. The young man stepped forward to grasp it, but as their palms touched, Riggs pulled the teenager to his chest and held him tightly. The reek of salt, sweat and octopus did not register. He felt only the warmth of a familial embrace and it was the most electrifying sensation he had ever known.

'Ronnie wants to know if you like octopus,' said the eldest boy, stepping forward and holding the bucket beneath the lantern light. 'The festival's tomorrow but we gonna have a barbecue tonight.'

Riggs peered down at the tangle of writhing grey tentacles and said, 'You'll need more than five.'

The young man smiled broadly. He had somehow understood. He jerked his head towards the reef, hand-signed a message to them all, then stooped down and picked up the lantern.

'Ronnie says, octopus don't jump into buckets by themselves. Let's go fishing!'

Zero Plus Two

From her flight bag Chiharu Kobayashi drew out a Chanel cosmetic purse and popped its clasp. In front of the mirror she touched up her lashes, eyebrows, then her lips. She examined her teeth and made a mental note to pick up a bottle of Hibiki seventeen-year in Dubai before the onward leg to Tokyo. Was it only her mother or did all dentists love malt whisky?

Giggling sounded. Two cabin attendants, immaculate in their midnight blue uniforms and crisp epaulettes, rounded the restroom corner and appeared in the mirror's reflection. On sighting Kobayashi, their giggles ceased. They bowed respectfully and greeted the woman before them with, 'Good morning, flight captain.'

At the coffee kiosk outside, the first, second and third flight officers afforded her similar reverence, then, together as a single unit, they made their way briskly along the quiet hall towards the boarding gate.

Through the gangway's porthole windows, Kobayashi glimpsed the A350-900, sleek and gleaming in the Heathrow mist. The sight of the *Spirit of Kyoto* always sent a pang of homesickness through her. And yet, for sentimental reasons, it also set her at ease; Kyoto prefecture was her grandfather's home.

Outside the aircraft, the first officer finished his inspection and gave Kobayashi the thumbs up. She stowed her logbook, took a few moments to program the autopilot and made a final call to air traffic control to confirm weather conditions. Last but not at all least, she assembled the crew in the galley to wish them well for the flight. It was her ritual; her grandfather had done the same during the Pacific War.

Back in the cockpit, she called the control tower for start-up and pushback clearance. She initiated the first of her two Rolls Royce engines, then the second and, after a short taxi to the apron, waited, watching the golden dawn sweeping the fog from the English countryside. The tower gave the all clear. Kobayashi moved the thrust levers and felt the big engines respond. With nothing but blue sky ahead and three hundred and seventy kilonewtons of thrust behind, her manicured fingers gripped the throttle, shifted it smoothly forward, and there it was—more than the elation of mastery over machine—that freedom to soar.

The English Channel slid beneath her, the French coastline next, and soon the patchworked farmlands of Normandy were lost to the clouds. She brought the aircraft to thirty thousand feet, levelled out and handed over control to the computer. Hot coffee arrived. She cupped its warmth in her hands, marvelling at the sea of altocumulus ahead of her. It recalled the valley-lands of Kyoto in winter, when, many years ago, she'd gone to visit her grandfather for the last time.

***

A green Toyota made its way along an icy road. Snow-covered fields of rice stalk ran to the base of mountains on each side. At a railway crossing, the car halted and from a tunnel a red two-carriage diesel train burst with plumes of white powder into the bright morning light. Wrapped in a pink bomber jacket and wearing a knit cap, the young girl seated in the back of the car looked sullen; neither the landscape nor the funny-looking train held for her any mystery or intrigue.

The car turned into a driveway and a few moments later stopped outside a large wooden and tiled-roof homestead. Craggy rocks jutted from an ornamental garden. There were stone lanterns, plum and cherry trees, and a pine whose trunk had been coaxed into an archway. To a youthful mind it might have harboured dragons, fairies and goblins. But to the young girl peering out of the car window it was simply a garden, cold, still and lifeless.

A kitchen curtain ruffled; a face appeared then was gone. The entranceway door slid back and framed in the doorway was a small woman wearing a faded blue smock and apron, all red cheeks and smiles. The young girl's mother got out of the car and ran to embrace the old woman. They exchanged greetings then turned around.

'Chiharu! Come and say hello to your grandmother!'

The car door swung open, the girl got out and walked towards the women. She swung a backpack beside her, dragging its small Totoro figurine in the snow.

'Who's this young lady?' said the old woman. 'Look how she's grown! I hardly recognise you from the photos.' She stepped forward, hugged her, and the small body softened within her embrace.

'Let me see. You must be nine by now?' the old woman asked.

The girl nodded, smiling shyly.

'Well, come in, come in! Let's meet your grandfather. He's been waiting.'

The homestead was warm and dim inside. Kerosene fumes, steaming rice and incense fought for air superiority as they moved deeper into the house. Chiharu looked about at the earthen walls, the crooked ceiling beams and the paper sliding doors—so different to her two-bedroom apartment in Tokyo, so quiet and still.

The three of them reached the centre of the house and the grandmother slid back a door. Sunlight flooded through the windows and onto the tatami mats of a large living room. The snowbound garden outside seemed otherworldly. In one corner of the room, a sacred alcove held a hanging scroll of a tiger crouching in bamboo; beneath this a set of deer antlers stood with a samurai sword cradled in the horns.

Chiharu's attention moved to the opposite corner and a purring kerosene heater, a flask of sake bubbling on its mantle. Her gaze was suddenly arrested by a stirring movement at the low table in front of her. She hadn't noticed the body tucked beneath the futon of the kotatsu. Slowly, it rose and turned.

'O-tosan,' her grandmother said, 'they're here! It's Megumi and Chiharu.'

The old man wore a strange leather hat, the kind that Chinese or Russian people wear in winter. Lined with wool, the side flaps curled up like dog ears. The old man's eyes were watery, his skin ivory. Though he smiled, he seemed at first not to see them.

The girl's mother rushed forward to embrace him. They talked in whispers for a short while, her mother tearfully holding his hand, until the grandmother said, 'And look at Chiharu! The last time you saw her was three years ago, remember?'

The old man turned and studied the girl; his expression changed, as if something from long ago had been suddenly recalled.'

'Chiharu,' he said in a raspy croak.

'Hello, Grandpa.'

He motioned her closer, holding out his dry, creased hand until he felt hers and gripped it.

'You're a young woman.'

Chiharu giggled.

'Would you bring my sake over?'

'Don't be silly!' said the grandmother. 'She'll burn herself.' The old woman took a cloth from the table, lifted the flask from the heater and carried it to the table.

'Did you take your medicine?' Chiharu's mother asked.

'This is my medicine,' he said, fingering the hot flask.

'How's your heart?'

'Still ticking.'

'Well, just don't drink too much, alright?'

He nodded, grunting, but winked slyly at Chiharu.

The two women moved to the kitchen, chattering as they went. The old man patted the futon beside him.

'Sit down here,' he said.

Chiharu obeyed, tucking her feet into the table's warm depths beside him.

'How was your trip?' he asked.

'Good.'

'You like Tokyo?'

'Yes.'

'You must be an elementary school student now.'

She nodded.

'You like school?'

'Yes.'

'Got a favourite subject?'

'Science.'

'I liked science too. When I was young, I wanted to be a scientist and build things.'

She said nothing and he leaned closer to her, so that she could smell the land on his body, the sake on his breath.

'What do you want to be when you get older?'

She smiled shyly.

'An engineer? A nurse? A dentist, like your mother?'

She shook her head.

He reached for his sake cup, an odd-shaped vessel fashioned from brown clay.

'Would you pour my sake? My hands, they're a little shaky.'

She lifted the flask, hot beneath her fingers, and poured with precision—not a drop spilled.

'Well done,' he smiled, then raised his cup and slurped noisily.

They sat in silence for a while, then she asked,

'Why do you wear that funny hat?'

'This?' He patted his headgear. 'This is the only thing that keeps my head warm in winter.' He lifted it from his blotchy pink head and placed it on hers.

'This is a pilot's hat,' he said.

'I don't think so,' she replied.

'It is, you know. It's an Imperial Japanese Navy flier's hat.'

'Where did you get it?'

'It's mine.'

'It smells funny.'

He chuckled, watching her small fingers explore the creases, the furrows and mysterious lines in the leather, as if tracing routes on an old map. He lifted the sake cup to his lips, drained it, and rose unsteadily to his feet.

'Toilet,' he said.

He was gone a long time. From the kitchen, Chiharu heard snatches of conversation, words like 'divorce' and 'separately', words she'd heard shouted with ferocity between warring parties late at night in their Tokyo apartment. She got up and crossed to a low bookshelf that ran along the wall. Her fingers danced across the volumes of old books, stopped and plucked one out. She mouthed its title: *Taiheiyo Senso*. She thumbed the soft, worn pages of black and white images and stopped at a double-page spread. For a while she studied the photo carefully: a line of high school girls waving branches of cherry blossoms at a young pilot readying his plane for take-off on a grass airstrip.

'Nakajima Ki-43 Hayabusa.'

His voice startled her. She turned quickly to find him staring down.

'You know what that means?' he asked.

'*Hayabusa?* It's a bird,' she said.

'Good, good! Most kids these days think it's a motorbike or a bullet train.'

'It's the fastest bird in the world.'

'So it is, so it is. You're very clever.'

'You really were a pilot?'

The old man seated himself, pulled the kotatsu futon over his legs and again reached for his sake flask. He poured a cup, spilling droplets on the table, and took a sip. He looked outside at the frozen fields.

'Yes, I was.'

'You flew the Hayabusa?'

'No.'

'What then?'

'The best plane Japan ever made: a Zero.'

Chiharu turned back to the book and thumbed the pages, but there were no more images of planes, only photographs of dead men on beaches, dirty-faced children and ruined cities.

'The book with gold letters, see it?' He pointed to the top shelf.

Chiharu replaced the book and reached up. It was heavy, but with some effort she laid it on the table in front of him.

'The Mitsubishi Zero A6M5c.' He lifted the cover and turned the pages. 'Fast, light, powerful.'

Chiharu moved closer, peering at the images of a plane so simple in shape and design that it might have been an outline in a child's sketchbook.

At that moment, the two women returned carrying a tray of cups with a teapot on it, and a wooden bowl filled with rice crackers.

'What's that, Chiharu?' asked her mother.

'O-tosan …' the grandmother said gravely.

'She's interested in planes,' he said.

'She's more interested in birds, aren't you, Chiharu?' said her mother, setting down the tray and pouring the steaming hoji tea into small cups. 'Problem is, in Tokyo there aren't many.'

'Yes, there are! There are bulbuls and sparrows and crows,' said Chiharu.

The grandmother passed her the snacks. 'Help yourself, Chiharu,' she said. They took their tea and slurped it noisily.

'Look!' said the grandfather. The three women turned to the garden, where a small bird with metallic green plumage and a white ring around its eye flitted among the branches of the plum tree. 'Know what kind of bird that is?'

'Mejiro,' Chiharu said.

'That's right!' The old man clapped his hands.

'Funny, I've never seen one in Tokyo,' said her mother.

'How did you know that?' said the grandmother.

'From the library.'

'Ah yes, of course. That's where you spend all your time,' said her mother.

'What about sports?' asked the grandmother. 'Don't you play table tennis or badminton with your friends?'

'I don't have any.'

'No friends?' The grandfather looked incredulous.

Her mother sighed. 'The neighbourhood kids are all too

busy with cram schools, ballet, violin lessons—'

'Hooaka!' Chiharu cried. The adults turned back to the garden. Sure enough, a second bird, larger with light brown plumage and a black and white striped head, had joined the first. For a moment they danced madly, loosening plumes of powdered snow from the tree branches, and then they were gone.

'They come down from the mountains looking for insects and farm seeds,' said the grandfather, slipping a rice cracker into his pocket. 'Chiharu, let's take a walk, shall we?'

The two women stood at the window watching the old man and the young girl set out across the snow-covered field. A small Shinto shrine stood at the base of a forested, snow-dusted mountain in the distance.

'How is she doing at school?' asked the grandmother.

'She's having a hard time.'

'Poor thing. Why not move back here? Open a practice downtown. Chiharu can visit us.'

'Kyoto?'

'It's cheaper than Tokyo—and there are lots of birds.'

The girl's mother sighed, her gaze returning to the two distant figures who now seemed to float on a glistening white plane.

'Sometimes I wish *I* was a bird.'

***

The snow sparkled in the sunlight, mesmerising the young girl with each crunching step. She squeezed the old man's hand and shouted, 'Wagtail!', pointing to the shrine up ahead.

A persimmon tree grew in its courtyard and about the branches a flittering movement made by a small, bulb-shaped bird with black and white plumage was visible.

'You've got a sharp eye,' he said. 'Just like a pilot.'

They reached the shrine and entered beneath the torii gate. He pulled the rice cracker from his coat pocket and crushed it in his hand. He cast the golden crumbs into the air, scattering them over the snow beneath the tree. 'They're watching us. You wait, when we've gone ...' He looked skyward. 'Look! A kestrel, see?'

Her gaze followed his to a point high over the mountainside where a raptor whirled on the updrafts in slow, graceful arcs.

'How does it feel to fly, Grandpa?'

'Free, that's how it feels.'

'You weren't scared?'

'Oh, many times.'

'Because you might crash?'

'No.'

'What then?'

'Because there were other men up there trying to kill me.'

She looked thoughtful.

'Come on, let's go home,' he said quickly.

'Aren't you going to pray at the shrine?'

'No.'

'Why not?'

'I don't believe in gods.' He looked back to the sky but the kestrel had gone. 'We've fed the birds. Now I'm hungry.'

'Me too,' she said.

They made a game out of tracing their footsteps back across the snowy field to the house doorstep where they stomped their boots free of snow.

'Grandpa?'

'Yes?'

'Could we build a Zero?'

'What?'

'A model plane, like the one you used to fly. We can buy one—I'll use my new year's gift money.'

'A Zero? Well, I don't know …'

'You can help me build it.'

He stood on the threshold, gazing into her face, so filled with innocence and earnestness that it might have been begging for food.

'No one's ever asked me that before,' he said quietly.

'I like birds and planes.'

'So you do,' he said. 'So you do.' He patted her on the head and together they entered the house.

***

They stood at the bus shelter the next morning, staring out at a world rendered smooth and formless by the night's fresh flurries. Mountains, like great big sugar loaves, rose on each side, stark white against the January sky. Icicles dripped from the bus shelter eaves and the trickling of snow melt sounded everywhere. They waited in silence, Chiharu in her pink feather down jacket, the old man in a brown woollen coat and scarf knotted beneath his chin. The bus arrived with its snow chains rattling and clanking, and soon they too, like the other solemn-looking passengers, peered out at the winter wonderland, each lost in his or her own private thoughts.

'I don't think your grandmother was too happy,' he said.

'About what?' she replied.

'About us going all the way to the city just to buy a plane.'

'Neither was Mum.' They looked at each other and giggled.

The valley grew wider and wider until a large river appeared and townships and factories sprouted along its banks, and then finally the city reared up, all hustle, lights and noise. They got off at Nishi-nikaimachi Street in the heart of downtown and the old man took Chiharu's hand, leading her away from the bustling boutiques and department stores and into a covered arcade where 'old Japan' still lived and breathed, where elderly customers shopped for fish from the Japan Sea and chatted while their tea leaves from northern Kyoto were roasted and packaged.

At a chestnut roaster's stand he stopped to ask directions. A little further on, said the man in the white bandanna and flashing a gold tooth. They arrived outside a corner shop whose sign announced in faded English 'Takata Toys and Stationery'. The grandfather set the doorbell jingling. The interior was dim and stuffy, and the aisles narrow and cluttered with toys from another era. To Chiharu, it seemed like a museum.

From behind the counter, an elderly woman greeted them, listened to the grandfather's question, then directed them to an aisle filled with kit models of battleships, tanks and army men. At the very end, they found the aircraft section.

'Chiharu, we're looking for the Mitsubishi Zero A6M5c. Can you see it?'

She pulled out boxes at random, examining each before sliding them back and pulling out another. She turned it into a quest, a game of matching memory—the picture in her grandfather's book—with the artist's painted image on each box.

'Nakajima Ki-84—' she started, holding a box up to the light.

'Hayate,' the grandfather finished. He took it from her and studied the artist's impression of an aircraft rising from a seaborne carrier, as young men waved their white caps from its deck against a red dawn sky.

'Know what Hayate means?'

'It's a manga story.'

He laughed. 'Not in my day it wasn't. It was a plane. Hayate means "strong breeze". I flew one at pilot school in Korea. Not as fast as a Zero, mind you, but it handled well enough.'

'What about this?' she asked, sliding a second box onto the one he was holding.

'It's a Zero alright. But this one's an A6M3. I flew the A6M5.'

'This one!' she said triumphantly, shoving a third box onto the second so that he now had to hold them away from his eyes to focus. Then something changed in his gaze. A tremor passed through his body, causing his hands to rattle the boxes and almost drop them. His eyes remained fixed on the artist's impression of two Zero fighters soaring sideways over a mountainous tropical island, as an American Liberator bomber tumbled, flaming, into the sea far below.

'It's yours, isn't it?'

'Yes, yes, it is.'

'The pilots have the same hat as you.'

'Yes, they do …'

'Grandpa, are you okay?'

'I am. I just remembered something. Something from a long time ago.'

'We don't have to buy it, Grandpa.'

'No. I promised.' He passed it to her. 'Let's get it.'

After they had picked out a tube of glue, brushes and a half-dozen small pots of paint, they handed everything to the old woman who set to work on her abacus.

The air in the shopping street outside was frigid. 'Hungry?' he asked her.

'Yes,' she said, and so they stopped at a dumpling stall and bought six balls of hot battered octopus, hoisting them into their mouths and sipping Coke to cool their burning tongues.

Snow began to fall as the bus headed back to the valleylands. Through the intermittent blizzards, Chiharu dozed against her grandfather, his arm around her as his own eyelids grew heavier with the locomotion of the bus. Then, as the mountains reared up and they rejoined the river, he too was asleep. At some point, his eyelids flickered and he uttered a murmur. 'Hellcat on your tail, Ando. Pull up, pull up, you're too low ...' His face contorted, he lurched awake and screamed, 'Andoooo!'

He looked about the bus, then at Chiharu, wide-eyed and staring up at him. The bus driver had pulled over and all of the passengers watched him curiously.

'Sir, are you alright?' the driver asked over the speaker system.

The old man took a deep breath and exhaled slowly; he nodded, bowing his head. 'I'm sorry.'

At the bus stop, the mother and grandmother were waiting for them. Inside the car their voices were comforting, their inquiries soft and quietly spoken. Chiharu looked at her grandfather, who quickly put a finger to his lips.

After dinner, as they sat at the kotatsu watching TV, Chiharu took out the box containing the Zero.

'What's this?' her mother said, frowning. 'I thought you were going to buy an All Nippon Airways jet.'

'That mightn't be such a good idea,' the grandmother chimed in. 'For a small girl.'

'The Zero A6M5c's maximum speed was five hundred and sixty-five kilometres per hour. It could fly to eight thousand metres in nine minutes and fifty-seven seconds,' said Chiharu. 'The Americans called it Zeke ...'

The two older women exchanged glances; they turned to the grandfather, who quickly picked up his sake cup and drank it dry.

Later, as Chiharu lay on her futon in the guestroom, she heard her mother speaking in hushed tones to her grandfather next door. Snatches of conversation that, even if she could not understand, were plainly clear by their tone and words like 'psychological trauma', 'dark memories' and 'unsuitable for a young girl'. Then the quiet rebuke of her grandfather that the child showed a passion for 'flight and flying machines', and that he was once a pilot and he understood this better than anyone. But it was her mother who had the last word. 'I do not want her hearing old war stories—or building machines of war. She's a nine-year-old girl, for goodness sake!'

Chiharu rose the next morning to a house becalmed. Snow fell in steady veils across the fields outside. She found her grandfather seated at the kotatsu, the flaps of his flier's hat pulled down over his ears and a flask of sake steaming on the kerosene heater. Spread haphazardly over the table in front of him was a thousand-and-one-piece jigsaw puzzle.

'Where is everyone?' she asked.

'Farmers' market. Shopping for dinner,' he said.

'What are you doing?'

'Building Kinkakuji—the Golden Pavilion. Want to help me?'

'Why don't we build the plane?'

'I don't think it's a good idea. Your mother—'

'We don't have to tell them.'

Her gaze held his, and there it was again: that intense look of earnestness and determination. It was too much for him to bear. A conspiratorial smile worked to his lips. He pulled the box from its hiding place under the kotatsu and placed it on the table.

'Trouble is, my eyesight is bad and my fingers shake. You're going to have to help me.'

She joined him on a cushion at the table.

'The A6M5 Zero was the Imperial Navy's best fighter plane in the Pacific War,' he said, producing a small pair of scissors. 'I painted the pieces last night, after everyone had gone to bed.'

'What about the instructions?' she asked.

'Don't need instructions—I know this plane by heart.' He passed her the scissors. 'You can cut out the pieces.'

In a short time the tabletop was covered with them, and Chiharu looked with uncertainty at her grandfather. 'I think we need the instructions, Grandpa.'

'I used to fly this, remember? Just follow my directions.'

The snow fell silently, surely, across the mountains, fields and valleylands as they started assembling the aircraft, piece by piece.

'This is a Nakajima Sakae engine. Eleven-hundred horsepower,' he said, passing her three round silver discs. 'Thread these onto the propeller shaft,' he instructed. Next, he handed her a set of curled silver-painted pipes. 'This is the exhaust propulsion system. Gave a top speed of five hundred and sixty-five kilometres per hour. But you know something? I clocked five-eighty-five once over Rabaul in … let's see now, that was May 1942.'

'Where's Rabaul?'

'In Papua New Guinea. Right above Australia.'

'You shot someone?'

'No, no—I was escaping! One of my guns had jammed, the other was out of ammunition.'

He picked up two long black-painted gun barrels. 'The Zero A6M5 had two seven-point-seven-millimetre machine guns and two twenty-millimetre belt-fed cannons on each wing,' he said, holding them away from his eyes. He passed them to her, his hands shaking. 'Now glue the holes in the middle of each wing section and insert these.'

'Did you travel the world, Grandpa?'

'During the war?' He chuckled. 'Oh, no, no. But I saw more than enough of it, let me tell you. When I was seventeen, I went to the Imperial Navy college in Mie prefecture, and after that to Korea for pilot training. Then I joined the Tainan Air Group and we flew in China, New Guinea and the Solomon Islands. After that, I was sent to Yap. You know it?'

She shook her head.

'It's a tiny island in Micronesia.'

'In the Pacific Ocean?'

'It was beautiful.' A spasm reached his throat. He coughed, hacked, took a tissue from the holder and wiped his mouth. 'But war doesn't care for beautiful things. The Americans were getting closer and I was eventually sent home to defend our country.' He passed her the left and right wheel units. 'You know where these go, don't you?'

She nodded, applied glue to the wing cavities and inserted each wheel strut.

He continued. 'Our name was changed to the 251 Air Group and many of us experienced fliers were ordered to train the younger pilots. I went to Kure.'

'Near Hiroshima?'

'Yes. Don't forget the antenna, it goes in that tiny hole near the wing tip.'

'Did you shoot down many planes?' she asked matter-of-factly, while skilfully pushing the black needle into its hole.

'Yes.'

'Why?'

'Because that was my job. I did it because I had to.' He rose slowly from his cushion and took the steaming flask of sake from the heater's mantle. Returning to the table, the grandfather poured his cup full. He raised it to his lips, drops sprinkling the table, until it was empty, wiping his mouth with the back of his hand. 'You've done well. Now attach the wings to the body and we're almost done.'

'Is that why you had a bad dream on the bus yesterday?'

He poured another cup of sake and, as if to fortify himself, took a sip.

'We were fighting for our lives by the war's end. I was an instructor, but I flew with our group because we had only eleven pilots left. Just teenagers, they were. The Americans were close and our losses were terrible. One day, four of us took off and headed south for Kyushu, but I got engine trouble. I turned back, had the engine fixed and joined the second four Zeros on the runway. But as we prepared to take off, we were attacked. Corsair fighter planes from an American carrier swooped in over the hills and hit us while we were still on the ground. Ando, my master sergeant, was shot down on take-off. I survived only because I was last in line. I jumped from my cockpit and ran. My plane was hit right after that.'

'What about the other pilots?'

'The first three? They never came back. Everyone else was killed. Except me.' He rose from his cushion.

'Grandpa, where are you going?'

'I forgot to give you the most important part of the plane—the pilot.'

He returned carrying an old paulownia wood box, which he placed on the table. Then he opened it and drew out a folded piece of red and white cloth. Chiharu watched curiously as he spread it across the table.

'Hinomaru,' she said quietly, eyeing the old flag. It was covered with the names of men.

'Those are all the pilots in my group. Fifty-five men. They're all gone now.'

'What do you mean?'

'I'm the only one still alive.'

He took from the box another item—a wristwatch.

'This is my flier's watch. It's a Seikosha. I think it still works. Let's see …' He twisted the crown several times and the second hand leaped forward. 'It does!' He passed it to her.

'This is for you. For helping me build the plane.'

'But you were helping me,' she said with wide eyes.

'Oh no!' he said, looking beyond her out the window. 'Here they come!' She followed his gaze and in the distance spied the small Toyota making its way up the long driveway towards the house. 'Hurry, put everything in the box. We'll hide it under the kotatsu.'

'But where's the pilot?' she said quickly.

'Oh, I almost forgot. Here,' he said, pulling from his pocket a small figurine and placing it in the palm of her hand.

She stared at it. 'But why did you paint him with a pink jacket?'

'Because it's not a "him", it's you.' He smiled. 'Now hurry up, put it in the box before they see.'

She obeyed, and together they quickly cleared the table.

When her mother and grandmother appeared they were still huffing and puffing from the weight of the fresh produce boxes they had brought into the kitchen. Sliding back the door to the living room, their expressions turned to surprise.

'What's this? All this time and you haven't even started the jigsaw puzzle?' said her mother. 'What have you two been doing?'

'Just talking,' Chiharu said.

'About what?'

'Flying.'

The grandfather turned back to the window and gazed out at the sunlight now casting through the snow clouds, directly onto the roof of the Shinto shrine. It looked almost heavenly.

***

A shrill scream split the dawn.

Chiharu listened to the sound of hurried steps moving between rooms, and then the grandmother's voice into the kitchen telephone, requesting an ambulance.

He had died during the night. Of heart failure, said the doctor, but peacefully. There was nothing that could have been done. What had seemed strange to them all was the paulownia wood box, which had been placed at the foot of Chiharu's futon. Inside was a note written in his hand:

> *To Chiharu,*
> *May your spirit soar—always.*
> *Your Grandpa.*

Only after the ambulance had pulled away and begun its descent of the valley road did the mother and grandmother notice her missing. They hurried inside, calling her name, but there was no answer. Then, through the lounge window, they glimpsed a small figure wearing a flier's hat and scurrying across the white field. Tied about her neck like a cape, a piece of red and white cloth billowed. The hand, raised high into the freezing air, held in it what looked like a small aeroplane.

***

'Captain, are you alright?' The voice was quiet beside her. Chiharu Kobayashi jerked upright, still clutching her coffee, and looked up at the third officer.

'Yes, yes, I'm quite alright,' she said, wiping the tears away with her hand.

'May I take your cup?' he asked.

She thanked him, then turned back to the console to confirm that all was well with the *Spirit of Kyoto*. With the altocumulus far below, the morning sky stretched blue and unfathomable ahead. She drew back the cuff of her shirt and examined the old Zero flier's watch.

It was still ticking.

Never Say Goodbye

Whenever I visit Rouen I call ahead to Walter, the maître d' at Brasserie Paul. I ask him to reserve the corner table that overlooks the square and the great gothic facade of the cathedral. Though it may seem unremarkable with its paper tablecloth and cluster of old bentwood chairs, this table holds special memories for me. If you crane your neck low enough, you can see all the way to the spire. It's the tallest in France, you know. When you have grown up in Rouen, all other spires seem ordinary.

I live in Paris now. Retired from the public service, I spend my days capturing the city's beauty, and ugliness, through the lens of an old Leica. I've had exhibitions, printed postcards, sold photos to famous people …

But I digress.

Every year on the twenty-ninth of April, if I can manage it, I take the train from Gare d'Austerlitz and return to Rouen. I don't come to look up old acquaintances in the cobblestoned laneways, or to wallow in the nostalgia of the smoky cafes and bars where I spent my youth. I come to honour the memory of my two dear friends who shared with me the greatest feeling on earth: to stand atop the highest peaks in France and to know what it means to be close to God.

Walter is Austrian and in his eighties now. He still recognises me and calls me 'Madame Juliette de Rouen'. The restaurant is cheerful and busy; the paper tablecloths, the polished cutlery and the ambience are all exactly how I remember them forty years ago. If it's on the menu, I order calf kidneys and mashed potatoes, with a small glass of Fitou red. Then, after my lunch, I cross the square to the cathedral and enter through the Saint Etienne door. Inside, beneath those magnificent high stone arches, I light two candles and take a seat beside the stained-glass window of Jeanne d'Arc at the Siege of Compiègne. I think of this magnificent young woman who died at the stake, not more than a few streets from me. I think of my own life, its ups and downs and round and rounds. But mostly I think of my two dear friends, Pascale and Rodolphe, who, on a grey March day many years ago, turned my darkest hour into a memory that would burn brightly forever.

***

Brasserie Paul was crowded for a Monday night. I suppose it was the Atlantic cold front that had driven the homebound

workers indoors, seeking a hot meal and like-minded bonho-
mie. There was not a vacant table in the whole place. Outside,
the bells of the cathedral clanged seven times. I glanced at my
watch, half-listening to a tourist couple at the next table de-
bate the backwards flow of the Seine River that afternoon. The
man said it was because the wind was strong that the water
only appeared to flow backwards. His partner disagreed; she
said it was the tide pushing in from the English Channel. They
referred the matter to Walter, who shrugged his shoulders and
said it might be a combination of both, which ended the
conversation.

I sipped my wine. It was my elixir, and despite the doctor's
advice to take it easy, I felt the need for more of it than usual
tonight. A sudden commotion pulled my attention back to the
door. A party of office workers entered, jovial and boisterous,
and proceeded to fill the reserved seats at the table along the
wall.

Behind them stepped a tall, slim man in his mid-twenties.
He wore the blue and white uniform of the Club Nautique et
Athlétique de Rouen, and his curly brown hair and goatee were
glistening with rain. His eyes were quick and alert, and as soon
as they found me, he grinned. In three strides he was kissing
my cheek and embracing me.

'You look blue,' he said, falling into the chair opposite.

'It's this weather,' I lied. 'Where's Rodolphe?'

'He's got to close the shop. Be here any minute.'

Walter brought over the chalkboard and greeted Pascale.
We said we'd wait for our friend. In the meantime, Pascale
ordered a glass of vin de Pays d'Oc, and myself, a second.

'What's the occasion?' he asked.

'No occasion.'

'Monday blues?'

'I told you, it's this weather.'

As the wine arrived, so did another man, bursting through the door with a frigid Atlantic blast at his back. He was compact and muscular, and beneath his crew cut a frown creased his tanned forehead. His jacket pocket bulged with a packet of Gitanes cigarettes. On sighting us, his solemness turned to sunshine.

'What? Dining on Mondays? Don't you still have a hangover from Saturday, Pascale?' He embraced me and slapped his friend hard on the shoulder.

Pascale sniffed the air. 'Hmmm, oysters,' he said.

'You wouldn't be smiling if you had to shuck ten dozen of the bastards,' Rodolphe said, slumping into the chair beside him. He fished out a cigarette and readied his Zippo lighter. Suddenly, Walter appeared.

'I'm sorry, monsieur, we are non-smoking.'

'Since when?'

'Since March the first. New regulations.'

'You're telling me a Frenchman can't smoke in a French restaurant?'

'I'm telling you what the law is telling me. To drink?'

Rodolphe returned the Gitanes to his pocket with great theatrics. To compensate, he ordered a bottle of wine for the table. Walter returned again with the chalkboard of the day's specials. I ordered the calf kidneys and mashed potato, Pascale the quail in wine sauce, and Rodolphe the roasted lamb medallions. I pulled a camera from my bag—a small point-and-shoot that I used for recording our escapades—and asked

Walter to take our photo.

There was no small talk about sports or politics. Climbing was our passion and all we ever talked about when we got together. It was what had brought us together. We had grown up in the same neighbourhood climbing everything that sprouted from the earth. Our parents called us mountain goats. We had started on apple and horse chestnut trees, and later, with borrowed ropes and clips, secretly scaled the elms and oaks of the parks and squares all over Rouen, mostly at night. We had broken four arms and one wrist between us and still we climbed. In high school we had been members of a rock-climbing club and spent the weekends clambering over the buttes that loomed high above the Seine. On summer days, when we could see all the way to the Atlantic coast, we had felt like kings of Normandy. Rodolphe, still seventeen, used to slip out his cigarettes and we would sit with our legs dangling over the abyss, smoking, contemplating the patchwork of emerald farmland through which the Seine cut a long, lazy swathe.

I was more at ease with Pascale and Rodolphe than I was among the other schoolgirls, who would tease me for being a tomboy and a dangerous 'wild card'. You see, Pascal and Rodolphe were like me—poor, spirited and crazy—and as we grew older, we sought bigger thrills. We joined a climbing club run by middle-class snobs, and because we couldn't afford the expensive boots, harnesses and carabiners, we had to beg, borrow and rent. Whenever one of us got into trouble, the other two would come to the rescue. Once, climbing La Roque in Haute-Normandie, Rodolphe punched a guy on the jaw after he publicly observed that I had a nice arse.

Pascale and Rodolphe were the brothers I never had. Later,

when our part-time jobs put money in our pockets, we took trips to the Massif Central and Switzerland. We hiked, we climbed, we drank and we danced. Climbing was our passion but we weren't out to prove anything to anyone. We did it to free ourselves. And while we loved Rouen, we all knew that the real excitement lay at higher altitudes.

Rodolphe raised his glass. 'To Pic du Balaïtous!' he said, loud enough to attract the attention of the tourists and office party. We raised our glasses, knowing full well he would get louder if we didn't. The meals arrived and we ate hungrily, ordering another bottle of wine to last till the cheese arrived.

After graduating from high school, our classmates moved away to take up studies at universities in Paris, Lyon or elsewhere in Europe. For most of them, Rouen was a shithole where nothing happened. To us, it was home, familiar and safe. Which is why, upon reflection, I find it strange that we pursued such a dangerous pastime. Perhaps it was the great equaliser, that from high risk came high return, and it was this equation that made the humdrum of daily life bearable. I often wonder if the same mindset had driven Flaubert to write *Madame Bovary*, or Monet to paint the cathedral's facades, or Jeanne d'Arc to lead her army into battle.

Drizzle fell across the square. I now felt sufficiently drunk to tell them why I had called them to Brasserie Paul that night. I would not be going with them to the French Pyrenees. Pic du Balaïtous, in all its 3144-metre glory, would have to wait for me.

At first Pascale and Rodolphe said nothing. Their expressions said I was joking and that it wasn't funny.

'I have brain cancer,' I said.

The restaurant suddenly sounded very loud. The office party laughed and swayed, a kitchen hand dropped a wineglass, while patrons went about their cheese and fruit, clinking their cutlery against the bone china.

I told them my headaches had been not from hangovers but from the growing tumour. What a CT scan had picked up, an MRI had confirmed. The operation was scheduled for the coming Friday.

'How serious is it?' asked Pascale.

The question might have sounded stupid to anyone else, but to me, it was all my friend could say at that very moment.

'They'll know when they take a sample,' I said, recalling the doctor's exact words: 'Let's wait and see.'

'We're not going without you,' said Rodolphe.

'Don't be stupid,' I shot back. 'I'll be in hospital for a week, with a month of rehab after that. Besides, everything's been booked. We've been planning this trip for so long.'

'We'll cancel,' said Pascale.

'You're not going to cancel. Go!' I felt like crying because I knew how much it meant to them, and how much my friendship meant to them. I couldn't tell which was gloomier: the cold, wet night on the other side of the window or the faces of the two men before me.

'You shouldn't be drinking,' said Rodolphe.

'You shouldn't be talking shit,' I said. He shook his head and smiled the saddest smile I have ever seen, and for a moment I thought I saw a tear rise in his eye. I slid a hand over each of theirs, gave them the bravest smile a bottle of Brasserie Paul's cheapest wine could muster, and said, 'I'll be fine. I've got Jeanne D'Arc sitting on my shoulder.'

And that was that. We left the wine and cheese unfinished, paid up, and thanked Walter. Outside, the rain had eased and the run-off between the cobbles of Rue Saint-Romain glistened under the street lamps. A seagull's mournful cry carried over the rooftops of the medieval timber houses. There wasn't much to say; none of us felt like talking, so we walked three abreast with arms linked until we reached Rue Armand Carrel. There, beneath the glow of a lamp, we embraced and kissed. They made me promise to tell them my hospital room number; they would visit. I told them I'd like that. Then, in different directions, we walked off into the night.

I admitted myself late in the afternoon, my anxious mother and father accompanying me. The Seine-Maritime Hospital was a modern building painted the colour of vanilla ice-cream. It stood beside the Seine on the opposite bank to the old town. There were four beds in my room on the sixth floor, but since I was the only inpatient, the head nurse let me choose a bed near the window. From there I could see the traffic flowing across Pont Boieldieu and glimpse the ant-like figures of old men and young couples who lived aboard the péniche barges, and who rode their bicycles along the quay with dinner baguettes peeping from their baskets each afternoon. High above the rooftops, the cathedral's spire stood sentinel over all.

At five p.m., after returning from a series of tests followed by bed visits from the oncologist, anesthetist and surgeon, I was exhausted and quickly fell asleep. I was awoken by the duty nurse who said I'd had visitors while sleeping. 'They left a message for you,' she said, passing me a crumpled white envelope. She changed my IV drip and after she had left the room I opened it and read the wildly scrawled words:

'Cathedral spire tomorrow at seven a.m.' It was unsigned but I recognised the handwriting.

I awoke several times during the night to peer across the river at the old town, which now seemed so far away. Here and there I glimpsed the apartments of insomniacs, night owls and those who had gone to sleep with their lights on, or could not sleep without their lights on.

Would I die? Probably not. But the great unknown we call life is exactly that, and although I had faith in the doctors, modern medicine and technology, I began to ponder the very thing that young people spare the least amount of thought for: their own mortality.

Dawn arrived with a bluish glow. Had the cloud been lower it would have forced the seagulls to land. The duty nurse entered at six-thirty and took my readings, said everything was fine, and wished me well for the operation. I asked her to draw back the blinds, and as soon as she had left the room I swung my legs to the floor and rolled my IV drip with me to the window.

Dawn crept down the Seine, pushing back the fine mist that lingered on the rooftops of the old town. The cathedral's spire seemed to hold up the sky as the sunlight tried desperately to pierce the clouds. I glanced at my table clock: six-fifty. I turned back to the window. Something moved against the spire. Then a tiny silhouette appeared, and soon there were two of them. They moved insect-like towards the tip of the spire.

At seven sunlight burst through the clouds. It was a blinding shaft of gold, like the ones you see in the baroque paintings of angels descending, or saints rising. It struck the spire just as the two tiny figures reached the pinnacle. Something like a long white ribbon unfurled beneath them, and in that instant the sunlight streamed through a fissure in the clouds. It was a banner, hand-painted in black. I felt my heart stumble and my jaw unhinge, the word 'INVINCIBLE' broadcast to the whole of Rouen.

I doubt many would have noticed at that early hour. It hung only for a few minutes before the two tiny stick men furled it and began their descent. Soon they were gone and the wail of a police siren reached me from across the Seine.

Pascale and Rodolphe visited me two days later. My operation had gone smoothly. A tiny hole had been drilled through my skull and a sample of tumour had been extracted. It had been sent for testing and the results would return soon. The surgeon and the oncologist were positive. It was after five when Pascale, still in his sports club uniform, and Rodolphe, smelling vaguely of shellfish, entered bearing flowers and fruit. I waited until the nurse had left the room, then said, 'Why did you do it?'

'Do what?' said Pascale with mock surprise.

'You know what I'm talking about. What if you'd fallen? What if you'd died?'

'God was on our side,' said Rodolphe.

'Don't bullshit me. What about the police?'

Rodolphe and Pascale looked at each other, and Pascale said, 'Ever see a pig catch a monkey?'

I shook my head but it hurt. 'Come here, you baboons,' I said, holding out both hands for them to clasp. 'Thank you, but don't ever do that again.'

They squeezed my hands and grinned.

'You're still going, right?' I said, although I already knew the answer.

'You'll be with us in spirit,' said Pascale.

'No monkey business,' I said, knowing full well that it was me who balanced their crazy souls, who ensured that none of us pushed beyond our limits and that we never took unnecessary risks.

I felt the mood sink. My head ached. They sensed it too, and they leaned down and kissed my cheeks. Then they were gone. I wanted so badly to go to the window and watch them cross the Pont Boieldieu to the old town, but I had begun to feel dizzy and pressed the nurse call button.

Mount Balaïtous is what happened when Iberia collided with Eurasia a hundred million years ago. Climbers from all over Europe flock to its base in summer in order to test themselves against the granite peak that sits squarely on the border of France and Spain in the Pyrenees. The Spanish called it Pic de los Moros—Moors' Peak.

The three of us had spent six months planning our route, saving our money and training our bodies, so as to be ready for the climb by the end of April. We planned to take the train to Paris, fly to Lourdes, and from there catch a bus to the small village of Arrens-Marsous. Then we would hike up the valley to the foot of Balaïtous and make our ascent, weather permitting, as quickly as possible. We wished to beat the summer rush that would see the valley turn into a tent city from June onwards.

The test results arrived the following day and the oncologist presented them to me with a warm smile. Later the surgeon arrived to inform me that, although the tumour was benign, non-cancerous tumours were sometimes known to turn malignant. He recommended full removal in a week's time.

My heart sank.

The river traffic came and went, the cathedral bell tolled the hours and the seagulls wheeled and cried over the rooftops of the old town, just as they had always done. At times I felt as if the workaday rhythms of Rouen passed unnoticed to all but myself, confined to my hospital room like Rapunzel in her tower, longing to be free. It was now mid-April and the days dawned earlier; blossoms began to appear in the hospital garden and the pale blue sky revealed itself more frequently.

Rodolphe and Pascale visited each day to cheer me with their joking and fooling around until either the head nurse would tell them to leave or Rodolphe's urge to light up one of his Gitanes would drive them out. The day before my operation they came to say good luck and, with less enthusiasm, goodbye. They would be leaving on the next morning train for Paris.

'I have something for you monkeys,' I said, opening my bedside drawer. I passed them three copies of the photo Walter had taken of us that Monday night at the corner table in Brasserie Paul. I'd had my mother make prints. 'When you reach the peak, leave one there for me,' I said. Then I burst into tears. Like Jeanne d'Arc, I wasn't afraid of dying—I was afraid of never seeing them again.

To my surprise, Rodolphe took my hand in his and Pascale's in his other and said in a voice loud enough to wake the entire ward, '*Unus pro omnibus, omnes pro uno*—one for all and all for one!' It was the laughter we badly needed to keep our tears at bay. They kissed and hugged me, and then they were gone.

***

Now, whenever I take my seat at the corner table in Brasserie Paul, awaiting Walter with my glass of Fitou red, I wonder if my photo is still there, high on the windswept granite of Pic du Balaïtous. I wonder if the dry, frozen air has preserved it, or whether it has been turned into dust and cast like confetti across the Pyrenees. I reach the same conclusion every time: that it no longer matters, because I can proudly say that two years after I learned of the avalanche that swept Rodolphe and Pascale to their deaths, I myself reached the summit of Balaïtous to place our photo in their honour.

The Convenience Store Ballerina

Car headlights swept Tanaka's face, rousing him from his doze. He peered out at the car park, still glistening with rain, wondering for a moment where he was. The truck's passenger seat was empty. Then he remembered: Watanabe had gotten off downtown. All that remained was for him to return garbage compactor #28 to the northside depot.

A convenience store stood on the other side of the car park and Tanaka watched a car that had entered now make an exaggerated arc over the wet asphalt towards it. He lowered the window, letting in the night air, cool and dank as a harbour tide. He inhaled deeply. Was he the only garbage collector in all of Japan who looked forward to the rainy season? He was certainly the only albino garbage collector.

Across the car park, two teenage boys and a girl climbed out of their small Honda. The driver remained inside, bathed in the glow of a dash-mounted TV. Tanaka watched the youths enter, hover over the cup noodle section and make their choices. They approached the counter where a clerk stood watching them. She was young; probably a university student filling in for the old coot who usually worked the graveyard shift, Tanaka thought.

The youths paid, tore off the seals and filled the cups from the hot-water dispenser on the end of the counter. Outside, the driver joined them—a thin girl, older, with braided hair, low-slung jeans and a white baseball cap—and together they squatted on their haunches, council-like, dealing the noodles into their mouths wordlessly. When they had finished, they rose and walked back to the car.

Tanaka stiffened, the furrows on his brow deepening. He flicked his headlights. The youths glanced in his direction but did not stop. Tanaka punched the ignition button, dropped his boot and let the roar of seven thousand cubic centimetres of combusting diesel fill the night. Startled shadows leaped onto the convenience store wall as the five-tonne Hino leaped forward with its headlights blazing. It skidded to a halt metres from the youths and Tanaka thrust his head out of the window.

'Kurrraah!' he yelled. 'Chanto hokase-ya!'

The youths froze, gaping at the enormous pink head with its silver crew cut and gold earring. The boys traded glances, but the girls were already scooping up their dinner mess and stuffing it into the garbage containers outside the store. Tanaka watched their red tail-lights fade to black. Night-time was playtime for the city's neglected youth. He didn't care what these kids did with their time, money or imagination so long as they cleaned up after themselves. He revved his engine and turned out of the car park.

A few blocks from the depot, his chest pocket vibrated. He pulled over and glanced at the text missive: 'Green tea ice cream please.' Why did insomniacs love sweets so much, he wondered. Was it because they loved sweets that they *were* insomniacs? All that sugar turning their bloodstream into an Indy 500. Or was it simply that his mother worried about him?

At the next green light he made a U-turn and was soon back at the convenience store. This time he left the truck idling roadside and made his way across the car park on foot. Nearing the store, a sudden movement inside caught his eye; it might have been the clerk running through the shop. Young people did that, ran when they should be walking.

Drawing closer, he heard music. The sensor activated, the doors parted, and a great orchestral wave washed over him. A woman's cry sounded above it. Then came loud tumbling, crashing noises. Tanaka stepped inside and peered around the corner into the aisle. His eyes widened. Sprawled on the floor, engulfed in tea and coffee packets, lay the clerk. She glanced up and gasped. Tanaka was used to such reactions; his mother said he stood out like a tarantula on a cheesecake. But this young woman's face wasn't fearful, it was glowing with embarrassment. She leaped to her feet, rushed to the counter and punched a button on the sound system. There was an awkward silence.

'You okay?' he asked.

'I'm sorry,' she said.

'For what?'

She bowed her head, said nothing.

'That was quite a tumble.' Tanaka looked back at the mess on the floor. 'Need a hand?'

'I can manage,' she said, slipping past him.

He didn't doubt her; she was small, lithe, almost catlike as she crouched and gathered up the tins of coffee and packets of sugar and returned them to the shelves. He noted her dark hair, twisted and tamed behind her head so that it exposed the nape of her slim neck. She glanced up and caught him staring. He made for the freezer section at the back of the store.

At the counter she avoided eye contact, swiping the barcode and dispensing the monologue of all convenience store workers throughout Japan, ending with 'thank you very much' and 'please come back soon'. He considered berating her for offering a bag—the town didn't need more plastic bags blowing like tumbleweeds through the night-time streets—but thought better of it. It would only have embarrassed her. He walked to the door, but at the threshold he hesitated.

'I've seen you before somewhere ... You work at the orphanage of the Western Light Temple?' he said. She looked suddenly guarded, so he added quickly, 'I collect the temple's garbage on Tuesdays.'

Her gaze fell to his uniform, the Department of Sanitation insignia and the green 'Safety First' symbol. She nodded. And that was that.

Halfway across the car park he threw a glance back at the store. She was at the window, arranging the comics in the magazine rack. Watching him, but not watching.

He climbed into the truck cab and thumbed a text message to his mother: 'Mission successful.'

Seven days of rain fell on the city. Down at the port, the old fishermen blamed the Black Current for sending a low-pressure system up from the Philippines. Privately, they were happy to drink beer, play Japanese chess, and let the rainwater gush and gurgle its way through the neighbourhood sluiceways. Gardens grew unchecked, hydrangeas of powder blue and pastel pink nodding in the deluges. As the humidity climbed, ripples like tidal marks appeared on the paper sliding doors. Tanaka's mother found her first slug on the bathroom wall. The wet season was upon them.

Inside the Department of Sanitation depot lunchroom, the banter was not of the weather but of the five million yen in cash that a worker had discovered inside an old Seikosha wall clock at the city recycling plant. Tanaka and his colleagues spoke begrudgingly of this because it was they who delivered the trash, and treasure, to the plant.

There was a standing vow among all the depot's garbage collectors that, should any one of them be so lucky, the 'treasure' would be divided equally among themselves. Tanaka knew there would be other chances. So long as people regarded the banks as thieves then money would always find its way between walls, inside futons and wall clocks. But there would always be those unlucky few who took the secret of their hiding places to the grave.

Was his a thankless job? It all came down to perspective. The way Tanaka saw it, garbage collecting wasn't about cleaning up after others: it was a civil duty, a responsibility to keep the town clean, *his* town, and get paid for it. Besides, he enjoyed the solitude and the restfulness of the city after dark.

But there were nights when the city wouldn't sleep. When

he and Watanabe would happen on strange things, like husbands beating their wives, kitchens on fire, high-schoolers petting in parks, passed-out drunks—both men and women—and sometimes altercations. Once they watched a foreigner—an Englishman, someone said—stand on a roof in his underwear and scream down at the police, who were forced to dodge roof tiles pitched at them by the crazed gaijin. Night-time was for those who couldn't handle the daytime.

Saturday was the other garbage collection day for the city's northern neighbourhoods, and because most people dined out on Sundays, generating little household refuse, Tanaka and Watanabe would almost always finish early on Tuesday nights. So it was that, after having dropped Watanabe off downtown, Tanaka found himself back at the convenience store, once again being woken by headlights, this time a newspaper delivery man on a motorcycle. With his arrival a cat appeared from the shadows, and this was followed by a second and third animal. The rider dismounted, entered the store and returned with a packet of cigarettes. He stood smoking, watching the felines, watching the night sky—rain was the bane of every newspaper delivery person—and when he'd finished, he stepped back inside the store. He returned with a tin of cat food which he opened and scattered about the car park.

Tanaka growled.

After crows, the city's feral cats were the worst culprits of torn-open garbage bags. But he checked himself because he saw the paradox—that those with little gave to those with even less. Wasn't that a time-honoured trait of the working class? Wasn't it their greatest weakness? Or could it be that a simple act of giving brought the greatest pleasure?

The rider straddled his motorbike and kicked the starter pedal. The machine gave a muffled fart, lurched forward and carried the man and his news sheets off into the night.

Tanaka lowered his window and held out an arm, feeling for rain. But instead of droplets he felt a tickling sensation, like the ripples on a pond or the undulations of a spring breeze reaching him through the humid night air. He pushed out his head and listened.

It was classical music.

All at once, the clerk appeared inside the store. She launched herself down the aisle in a spinning motion, arms rising and falling, her face to the garish light so that Tanaka could see for certain it was the same young woman from a week before. When she reached the end of the aisle, she pivoted then she whirled back towards the counter. Her poise and precision reminded him of an expertly cast spinning top.

He left the truck and, moving closer, felt the vibrations strengthen, the music growing strangely familiar—a tune stored in the recesses of his memory, too far away to recall, too weak to decipher. He was halfway across the car park now. It sounded like—Tchaikovsky.

It *was* Tchaikovsky. His grandmother, God rest her soul, used to play it up loud on summer nights. The music of Europe's great opera theatres would fill the narrow alleys all the way to the port so that house lights would turn on and the neighbourhood boss would have to pay them a visit.

Headlights swept Tanaka's face. He wheeled about, pretending he'd forgotten something, and walked briskly back to his truck. Meanwhile, the clerk had hurried back to the counter, fiddled with the sound system and now stood waiting, watching, as a taxi pulled into a parking bay and the driver stepped out. The signal was lost.

***

He awoke the following morning to the drumming of rain on the roof tiles and murmured voices in the lounge room. He remembered his mother's appointment to discuss his grandmother's upcoming Buddhist memorial ceremony with the family priest.

Tanaka rose from his futon and trod quietly down the hallway to the room his grandmother had kept. It was a small salon, sparsely furnished and still vague with the smell of sandalwood incense. He slid back a cupboard door, reached inside and pulled out a wooden box filled with records. His fingers worked through the faded jackets until he pulled out the *The Nutcracker*, placed it on an old Onkyo turntable he'd rescued from a trash heap, and let the needle rise and fall on the dusty grooves. The first notes of the mysterious melody he'd heard the night before now filled the small room. 'Dance of the Sugar Plum Fairy' had been his grandmother's favourite.

He lay down on the tatami mats and closed his eyes. He must have dozed off because when he came to, the record was rotating soundlessly and whomever was peering through the gap in the paper door was suddenly gone. He listened to footsteps fade along the hallway and heard his mother say, 'He loved his grandmother very much.'

***

Tanaka phoned in sick the next day. The doctor said it was a summer flu and rest was prescribed. So he stayed in bed, flipping through manga comics and slurping bowls of warm rice porridge that his mother delivered. To fend off restlessness, he moved the record player into his room. Brahms, Bach and Beethoven drifted from the house all afternoon, causing the neighbourhood boss, who lived at the end of the alley, to cock an ear and look thoughtful.

The following Tuesday, after dropping Watanabe off downtown, Tanaka returned to the convenience store. He waited and watched, eyeing the night creatures that came and went—the cats, bats, drunks and insomniacs—occasionally catching a glimpse of the clerk as she went about her mundane chores.

Then all fell quiet. The store stood lifeless and empty. Tanaka waited. He glanced at his watch: 12:45 a.m. The depot would be closing soon. All at once the doors opened and the clerk appeared wearing gloves and carrying fresh garbage bags. Tanaka watched her sort through the trash, tie the bags and carry them to a garbage disposal pen on the other side of the shop.

He felt his chest pocket vibrate. 'Vanilla ice-cream, please', read the message. A flicker of movement inside the store caught his eye. Not a flicker, more like a floating movement—a floating woman. With her hair pulled tightly behind her head, she drifted through the aisles of snacks, coffee and noodles, her hands moving in short graceful motions as if she were swimming. On reaching the magazine racks, she sprang from one foot to the other, lifting each one high over the manga comics and fashion weeklies, until she reached the end of the aisle. Then she stopped, wheeled about and in ever-quickening revolutions danced back alongside the front window, so fast that Tanaka worried she might spin out of control and crash through the glass.

The squeal of vehicle tyres startled him. A small Mazda with hubcaps missing swerved in from the street and attempted a tight U-turn across the car park. A black Jeep followed, its driver clawing the wheel, skidded to a halt and blocked the smaller car's path. The Jeep driver leaped out and ran towards the Mazda. Perhaps panicked, the driver of the smaller car reversed but, miscalculating his speed, sent the car leaping across a concrete buffer and crashing into the storefront. Tanaka watched in amazement as the entire front window of the convenience store imploded and rained down with a roar.

Now shouting, the Jeep driver hammered his fists on the Mazda window. Managing to pry open the door, he reached inside and grabbed the driver.

The clerk had retreated behind the counter. Tanaka glimpsed her holding a phone to her ear and speaking quickly. He jumped from his cab.

'Yamero! Yamero!' he bellowed, bounding across the car park. The Jeep driver turned. At the sight of the huge albino in a mint-green Department of Sanitation uniform rushing towards him, he froze. It gave Tanaka enough time to reach inside the Mazda, grab the ignition key, and keep the two angry men apart until the distant wail of a siren materialised into a patrol car. Strobing red and blue lights were joined by three more police vehicles, two motorbikes, and a gaggle of sleepy-eyed tenants from the surrounding apartment buildings.

The police eyed Tanaka curiously but quickly moved

on to the drivers, whom they escorted to separate cars for questioning. A young officer returned to Tanaka a short time later to take down his version of the events. As the clerk made her own statement to a female officer inside the store, Tanaka noticed that her gaze kept shifting towards him.

A tow truck soon arrived and the onlookers drifted back to their homes with news for their friends and co-workers. Tanaka finished with the officer and entered the store. He picked out a tub of vanilla ice-cream and laid some coins on the counter.

'Thanks,' she said, taking his money.

'For what?'

'For breaking it up.'

'Thanks for calling the cops.'

'What were they fighting about?'

'A woman.'

'How do you know?'

'Didn't you hear them shouting?'

'I was scared.'

He laughed. 'So was I.'

'Why are you watching me?'

Tanaka flinched. He felt his face burn and his mouth turn to wood. 'I ... like classical music,' he said. Then quickly, 'The N-N-Nutcracker's my favourite.'

Her eyes narrowed.

'My grandmother was a music teacher,' he said, then regretted it.

'Is that right? So you're a Mozart fan?'

'Tchaikovsky.'

A smile worked its way to her lips.

'Yes, of course,' she said. 'Tchaikovsky.'

'Why do you dance at night?'

'I need to practise.'

'You're a student?'

She nodded.

'You must be busy. Two jobs …'

'Tuition is expensive.'

The automated doors rattled open and in strode the store manager, breathless, crunching glass underfoot. His gaze met with Tanaka's and his anguish turned to surprise. He looked questioningly at the clerk.

'Thanks,' said Tanaka. He slipped the ice-cream into his pocket and left.

***

Rain drifted in long veils across the city. The meteorologists said the wet season had only days to run. Tanaka still savoured the cool, moist nights, but it was his newfound love of classical music that contented him as he passed through the night-time neighbourhoods with the audio system on high volume. *Swan Lake* and *A Midsummer Night's Dream* drowned out the compactor's roar, and even Watanabe sighed and gave up competing for airtime with *Cinderella* and *The Sleeping Beauty*.

There were times when Tanaka suspected she knew he was watching, brief moments when she'd glance at the window and probe the darkness with her wistful gaze. What did that mean, that a ballerina might be thinking about a garbage collector? That was truly the material of an opera yet the thought pleased him.

One night, on a circuit of the northern neighbourhoods, Watanabe climbed into the truck cab with a roll of copper wire. 'This for a turn behind the wheel,' he said dryly, tossing it into Tanaka's lap. It became a new way of killing time while awaiting the Tuesday night performances in front of the convenience store. He would sculpt sections of the wire into tiny figurines of ballerinas and set them along the truck's dashboard. Watanabe began to look at him strangely.

Then one day it happened. Saito and Sugimoto, who drove the #26 compactor, were clearing junk piles on the city's east side, near the river, when they happened on a set of stereo speakers that were unusually heavy. The two men pried off the timber backing and struck gold—literally. They reported their find, first at the depot, and then at the police station. The bullion, cast into twelve-ounce ingots, was taken into custody and there it stayed until one month later when, still unclaimed, it became the rightful property of the two garbage collectors.

They kept their word, honouring the vow, and the bullion was evenly divided between themselves and their co-workers. Tanaka went straight to the bank, exchanging his share for a tight brick of cash. He bought his mother a new bathtub and deposited the remainder into his savings account.

While his co-workers regaled each other with tales of dining on Kobe beef and buying new football boots for their kids, Tanaka remained silent, his mind elsewhere. He could think only of the young woman who danced at night, who had ignited his love of classical music and given him something to look forward to at the end of his shifts. For several more weeks he marvelled at her impromptu performances, turning his audio system down low, wrapped in the warmth of the night, appreciative.

Then one Tuesday afternoon he paid a visit to the bank and made a large withdrawal. That night he left the truck and crossed the car park to the row of garbage bins that stood next to the convenience store. From his jacket he took out a small cardboard box and stuffed it quickly into the container farthest from the door.

A half hour passed. Tanaka checked his watch: 12:35 a.m. From inside his truck he could see her stocking the fridges, filling shelves and mopping the floor. At 12:42 a.m. a vagrant limped out of the darkness. He was wild-haired with stained shorts and legs covered in bandages. Tanaka leaned forward in his seat, watching him approach the garbage bins, reach into the one nearest the door and fossick. Tanaka's pulse quickened. The vagrant came up empty-handed and moved on to the second bin. He fished out a half-eaten bento, sniffed it over and tossed it back. His attention then turned to the last bin.

Tanaka opened the truck door and placed one foot on the ground. As he readied himself to dash across the carpark, the convenience store's doors parted. Out stepped the clerk wearing gloves and carrying garbage bags. The vagrant gave a start, retrieved his hand from the container and limped off, back into the night.

Tanaka slipped back inside his cab. He watched the clerk pull out the bins and sort plastic and cans into separate bags. She paused a moment, lifted out the small box and held it to the light. She pried open the lid. For a moment she stood very still, staring inside, then looked up quickly. She spotted the garbage compactor and began walking slowly towards it. Cloaked in the shadows of his cab, Tanaka watched in terror.

His heart began to race. Sweat beaded his brow. She was midway across the car park when three youths carrying skateboards approached the convenience store doors and entered. She hesitated, staring at Tanaka's truck, then ran back to the store.

***

Tanaka did not return to the convenience store for many days. Foolishness and regret swept through him, clouding his mind and causing him to make mistakes; he grazed the truck against a power pole and once left Watanabe standing with bags in his hands while he drove off down the street. Coworkers asked how he'd spent his loot, but he just said he was saving it for a 'rainy day'.

Then one hot night in August he resolved to explain himself, to step up to the mark and tell her it had been him watching her from the shadows all this time, to thank her for the performances, to apologise for being a creep.

He parked in front of the convenience store. Stepping from the truck, he sensed something amiss. The store doors parted and the sugary beat of a girl-band J-pop tune smacked him in the face. Women's laughter sounded. At the sight of the huge albino, the two middle-aged clerks chanted stiffly, 'Irasshaimase!'

'Where's the woman who works here Tuesdays?' said Tanaka.

The clerks traded glances. 'You mean Murakami-san?' the plump one said.

'Murakami-san?' he said.

'Murakami Junko.'

'Junko …'

'She quit.'

'When?'

'A few weeks ago,' the slim clerk chimed in, her tone suspicious. 'Are you an acquaintance of hers?'

'I'm ... I *was* a regular customer.'

'Well, she quit,' the other said with finality.

'Know where she went?'

'Russia.'

Tanaka searched their faces for some hint of a joke but there was none. The women returned his stare.

'She said she was going to a place called ... St Petersburg. To study,' the plump one said.

'She's a dancer, you know,' the slim one added.

'I know,' he said, and the sound of his own voice made him want to cry. He pulled out of his pocket a copper wire figurine and placed it on the counter. 'If she comes back, please give her this?' He left the store with women's eyes on him and this time he didn't look back.

***

Tanaka got a new partner the following summer. His name was Kenji Takahashi, a young kid straight out of technical high school, strong and hardworking. They got along well. Takahashi suggested Tanaka buy a dash-mounted TV. All the other drivers had one. If they finished early, they could drink hot canned coffee and watch TV before returning the truck to the depot.

Tanaka suspected the kid just wanted to keep up with the baseball and football scores. He bought one for the both of them that winter, as a Christmas present.

It was three days after New Year when they sat in the car park of a convenience store watching a variety show, clutching their hot coffee, as snow fell thick and heavy across the city. Tanaka, fed up with cheesy jokes and fake laughter, flicked through the channels, searching for a show with more substance. He stopped at an arts program and there it was, *The Nutcracker*, being performed on stage somewhere in the world by ballerinas with painted faces and bodies that seemed as light as feathers. Takahashi laughed, said he had seen fat middle-aged men do that on a variety show once. Tanaka shushed him curtly. The performance cut to a male reporter interviewing a young Japanese woman dressed in a thick winter coat and fur hat. Snow swirled about her. Tanaka leaned closer to the TV screen. On the woman's coat lapel, a small figurine gleamed beneath the lights of the camera. Tanaka's eyes widened. The reporter laughed, concluding the interview, and asked the young woman how to say 'thank you' in Russian.

She turned to face the camera and, smiling broadly, said, 'Bol'shoy spasibo!'

Atomic

Carpathian Solutions head office, Budapest, Hungary

'Thank you for coming at this early hour, Ms Burskayal. My name is János Szabó. I'm the head of strategic solutions here. Would you please take a seat? Some coffee?'

'May I smoke?'

'I'm afraid that is against our policy.'

'Then I'll have coffee—black, thank you.'

'Here you are. Now, let's begin, shall we? Please relax, this is not an inquest.'

'Is this being recorded?'

'Yes, I was about to mention that, for our records. It is just a chance for us to hear your side of what happened in Vienna last week. Would you kindly state your full name and begin please?'

'May I ask who he is?'

'This gentleman here is Mr Tóth, representing our Russian client, Atomoprom. He will be observing.'

'Will this affect my position within the firm?'

'This is not an interrogation. It is merely an opportunity for you to tell us what happened. Please go ahead.'

'Alright. My name is Masha Burskayal. I belong to the research solutions department at Carpathian's Prague office. I've been working at this firm for—'

'Yes, I know. Please proceed with Vienna.'

'On September fourth I departed Prague. I arrived by train at Vienna Hauptbahnhof on a Slovakian passport, travelling under the name Tatiana Yevchenko. As per my brief, I waited at the Schwendergasse apartment near the station for further instructions. On September fifth I received a message from operations saying the Japanese nuclear scientist had arrived and that he was checking into Hotel Sacher behind the State Opera Theatre. His name was Dr Masanobu Mochizuki, but we codenamed him 'Atom Boy'. He had also just made a ticket reservation for the opera the next evening.'

'September sixth?'

'Yes. I was told a seat had been reserved for me, and that if I didn't have suitable clothes I was to go shopping immediately.'

'The International Atomic Energy Agency conference was the next day?'

'At nine a.m.'

'And the meeting with the Galliatome Corporation representative?'

'The day after, at one p.m. Atom Boy would fly out the same evening.'

'Giving you forty-eight hours to get the dossier.'

'It sounds easy, doesn't it?'

'I'm not judging you, Ms Burskayal. Only confirming what—'

'So the next day I bought an orange one-piece with matching heels, but on the subway train to the opera, a drunken gypsy passed out on me and I had to clean off his filth at the subway station. That's when I realised my phone had been stolen.'

'Don't you carry two phones?'

'The one that operations supplied me with froze. I didn't have time to get a replacement. I was in a hurry to pick up my ticket for the opera.'

'Which opera?'

'The State Opera Theatre. I've already told you.'

'No, I mean, what was the name of the opera you were attending?'

'*Carmen*. Is that important?'

'No—it's just that it's a story with a gypsy and a tragic ending.'

***

Taiga Corporation, head office, Tokyo, Japan

'Doctor Mochizuki?'

'Yes?

'My name is Sato. Would you step through here, please?'

'Thank you.'

'Take a seat, please. As you know, this is an immense embarrassment to the company and to the president, Mr Aoki. He is very disappointed. He is *deeply* disappointed. If what transpired in Vienna last week is made known to our competitors, or to the media, there will be grave consequences. I'm sure you understand.'

'Yes. Once again, I sincerely apologise for—'

'You have already apologised. What we need from you now is the full story of how this huge mess came to pass.'

'But I've already been debriefed by Mr Hara from overseas operations.'

'I am Mr Hara's boss. Above me there is only the president. Today, man to man, face to face, I would like to hear your version of the events.'

'Can I smoke?'

'There's an ashtray over there.'

'Sorry, do you have a light? Thank you. So, I arrived in Vienna on September fifth. I went directly to the hotel—'

'Which hotel?'

'The Hotel Sacher. I checked in, had dinner, then went to bed.'

'Did you notice anyone suspicious, or anything unusual, between the airport and the hotel?'

'Everything was unusual. It was my first time to Vienna. There was no one following me, at least I don't think so, if that's what you mean.'

'Go on, go on.'

'I spent the next morning in my room preparing for the conference at the International Atomic Energy Agency, and checking my dossier and notes for the Galliatome meeting the following day.'

'Where?'

'The Vienna International Centre.'

'The Galliatome Corporation meeting?'

'No, the IAEA conference. Galliatome was to be held in a private room at the Hotel Sacher.'

'So you didn't leave the room all day?'

'Only to walk in the park next to the hotel.'

'And you didn't notice anything strange, or anyone following you then?'

'No.'

'Did you leave the hotel that night—the night of September sixth?'

'No.'

'Not at all?

'I ate in and watched an opera on TV.'

'Which one?'

'Why?'

'I'm an opera fan myself.'

'*Carmen*.'

***

'Ms Burskayal, could you tell us what happened at the opera on the night of the sixth?'

'As I said, I was in a hurry and I was late to the ticket box. The opera had begun by the time I got inside. It was very dark and because the audience was large I could not locate Atom Boy. So I waited until the end of the first act, then I went to the second-floor bar. There were many Asians—'

'Did Operations send you a photo?'

'It was grainy, so I went on feeling. I tried the outside balconies looking for a single middle-aged Asian man of that description, and I found him. Sorry, do you mind if I have more coffee?'

'Go ahead, and please continue.'

'I pretended to admire the night view, the Stephansplatz cathedral, the Museum of the Arts, the street trams running down Kärntner Straße … He noticed me, but seemed shy, in that way men try to look at a woman without being seen. So I lingered. Then the buzzer sounded and I waited for him to return to his seat—left wing, upper balcony. I could see him from my seat. At the end of the second act, he went to the bar. That's when I made my move. I was behind him and he let me go ahead to the counter. On the balcony I thanked him for being a gentleman. He told me he'd smelled my perfume— Zara Sandalwood—and that it reminded him of Japan. We talked about the performance. He asked me if I was a classical musician.'

'What did you tell him?'

'I told him I was a doctoral student studying religious history at the University of Vienna.'

'And he believed you?'

'Do I look like a cello player to you?'

***

'So, Doctor, to confirm, you stayed in the hotel on the night of September sixth?'

'Yes.'

'Alone?'

'Of course alone. Why wouldn't I be?'

'Because it just so happens that my acquaintance at Nelio Systems was also attending the IAEA conference. He was staying at Hotel Sacher that night too. He said he saw another Japanese man, of similar appearance to yourself, with a woman in the lobby early next morning. Medium height, young, blonde—care to explain?'

'I met her in the elevator on the way from my room to the restaurant. We had breakfast together.'

'Who was she?'

'She said her name was Tatiana something. A student at the University of Vienna.'

'A bit luxurious, don't you think?'

'What?'

'Hotel Sacher, for a uni student.'

'Maybe she has a rich father, I don't know. Russian oil businessman …'

'She was Russian?'

'I didn't ask. Why are you asking me all of this?'

'Well, it just seems strange that you checked into the hotel alone and that you should have a woman with you in the morning.'

'She wasn't *with* me. We met in the elevator. Are you insinuating that I got it on with a callgirl studying for her PhD in religious history?'

'Alright, go on. What happened on the seventh?'

'I attended the IAEA morning sessions at the International Centre, then I ate lunch at the venue restaurant and later returned for the afternoon sessions. At three-thirty I delivered my presentation, took questions, and finished around five-thirty.'

'Refresh my mind—the title of your presentation?'

'Dismantling and Disposal Procedures for Damaged Nuclear Reactors.'

'Yes, of course. Did you meet with anyone after the conference?'

'Who would I meet?'

'A simple yes or no will do.'

'No.'

***

'Ms Burskayal, you met with the Japanese scientist after the conference on the seventh?'

'Yes. I arranged to have dinner with him in the Innere Stadt once he had finished his business.'

'How did you contact him without a phone?'

'Operations had replaced the broken one. Could I have some more coffee?'

'You like coffee, don't you?'

'It's a habit you pick up in Vienna. Thank you. At six p.m. we met at Cafe Central near Saint Stephen's Cathedral. Then he surprised me. He had two tickets to the opera.'

'Again?'

'He likes opera.'

'*Carmen* twice?'

'*Salome.*'

'*Salome*?'

'You know it?'

'The story of a beautiful young woman who seduces a king to get what she desires. Yes. What happened after the performance?'

'He invited me for a drink at his hotel, in the Blaue Bar. That was around eleven. We drank a bottle of wine then we went up to his room.'

'You stayed the night?'

'No. I slipped a flunitrazepam in his wine. When he passed out, I searched his briefcase and found the dossier. I couldn't photograph it because my phone had frozen again. I couldn't go to the front desk. So I left the hotel and went to a convenience store to make copies.'

'You were seen?'

'Yes, but not noticed—the hotel bar and cafe were crowded. The lobby was crawling with high-end callgirls.'

'But you had some trouble, I understand.'

'On the way back to the hotel, a taxi pulled up beside me. The driver spoke German with a Russian accent. He asked if I needed a ride. I kept walking, but he persisted. So I told him to go fuck himself in German and that made him more excited. I slipped into the subway and lost him under the State Opera.'

'Could you describe him for us?'

'Middle-aged, dark features, heavy-set, glasses. A real pig.'

'Thank you. Please continue.'

'When I got back to the room, Atom Boy was still snoring it off. I replaced the dossier but realised I'd left the original documents on the copy machine in the store.'

'A little amateur, don't you think?'

'It's a little amateur giving me a phone that breaks twice, don't you think? Try using Nokia instead of Samsung next time.'

'Noted.'

'If I'd been able to photograph the dossier, none of this would have happened.'

'I've noted it down, now please continue.'

'Atom Boy had prepared the client's dossier in a blue plastic folder. Behind the title page were the documents. I needed to make the folder look somehow full, so I went back down to the bar.'

***

'Where did you dine on the night of the conference?'

'Why is that important?'

'It's just that there was a dinner for delegates and my acquaintance from Nelio Systems did not see you there.'

'I ate at a cafe. Vienna's famous for them, you know. Then I took a walk to the cathedral to buy some souvenirs for my wife.'

'And all of this time, you never felt that you were being watched or followed?'

'No.'

'How did you spend the rest of the evening?'

'I returned to the hotel, freshened up, and after that I went down to the hotel bar for a drink.'

'I know.'

'You know?'

'My acquaintance said he saw the same Japanese man with a woman later that evening in the bar. His description of her matches the one of the young woman you said you met in the elevator earlier that morning. Care to explain?'

'Alright, it *was* the same woman. At breakfast she'd asked if I'd like to meet for a drink after the conference and I said yes.'

'Doctor Mochizuki, do you know what they call Vienna?'

'Opera Capital of the World?'

'They call it the Spy Capital of the World. Every industrialised nation has an embassy there. There are over four thousand diplomats and six thousand government officials stationed there. It's the headquarters for OPEC, the European Space Agency, the Comprehensive Nuclear-Test-Ban Treaty Organization …'

'What are you saying?'

'I'm saying that not every callgirl is a university student trying to make ends meet.'

'Are you again suggesting I was with a callgirl?'

'I'm suggesting that the woman you were with was not who she said she was. Look, I know this could be difficult for you, you have a wife ... But all we wish to do is ascertain how this mess occurred. Did you check your dossier before the meeting with Galliatome?'

'I checked it on the sixth.'

'And you didn't check it again?'

'Why should I? I wrote the contents myself. The dossier was in my hotel room the entire time.'

'Which brings me back to the young woman. Did you, at any time, allow her entry to your room?'

'Can I have another cigarette?'

'Go ahead.'

'May I … your lighter again? Thanks.'

'Let me say that what you do in your private time is none of my business, but on this occasion I must insist that you answer the question directly. Did she enter your room?'

'I don't recall she did.'

'Then how is it that the Galliatome Corporation representative received a copy of the Hotel Sacher dessert menu instead of our reactor dismantling bid?'

'What can I say? The apple strudel was wonderful.'

'You see humour in this? We lost a multibillion-yen contract to Rastrom!'

'No, no, I'm sorry. I didn't mean anything by it … I'm just a little tense right now. Humour relaxes me. I apologise.'

'Well, perhaps you would like to sample the apple strudel in Phnom Penh.'

'Excuse me?'

'Mr Aoki has asked that, following this interview, you be reassigned.'

'Reassigned where?'

'To Taiga Corporation's new community-based project in Cambodia.'

'Cambodia? Doing what?'

'Clearing landmines.'

***

'Ms Burskayal, let's discuss the morning of the seventh. You copied the documents and replaced the originals. Kudos to you, but what happened next?'

'I left the hotel and caught the last subway train back to the Schwendergasse apartment. That was around two a.m. Just before the Volkstheater station, an elderly woman next to me began to behave erratically. She seemed to be having a seizure, or a panic attack, or something like that. She was gasping and grappling to get off the train. So I assisted her when we arrived at Volkstheater. Only after the doors had closed did I realise my purse had been opened. No money was missing, but the dossier copies were gone.'

'Please describe the woman.'

'She was elderly, heavy-set with dark features. She smelled of mothballs.'

'Did you return to the convenience store to search for the originals?'

'No, not right away.'

'Why not?'

'Because the creep in the taxi might have been parked outside. I returned later that morning at seven but the staff said the garbage had been collected two hours earlier. So I contacted operations for instructions.'

'Which were?'

'Return to Prague immediately.'

'Ms Burskayal, I'd like to give Mr Tóth a moment to say a few words. What he has to add is very interesting. Mr Tóth?'

'Thank you, Mr Szabó. Ms Burskayal, please take a look at these. Do you recognise any of the people in these three photos?'

'The man in the first photo looks like the gypsy on the train. But the woman, and this man in the pilot's uniform—no, I've never seen them before.'

'They are all the same man, just as the gypsy, the driver, and the old lady were all the same man. His name is Radovan Mikić, a Serbian national and a master of disguise. He was most likely hired by Rastrom to intercept you. Galliatome accepted their bid ahead of ours and Taiga Corporation's a few days ago in Paris. So, you see, you were good, but this time the competition was better. That's all I have to say. Mr Szabó?'

'Thank you, Mr Tóth. Do you have any further comments, Ms Burskayal?'

'Are you sure this won't affect my position at the company?'

'Not at all. However, due to the huge disappointment of our client and the enormous embarrassment to us, we are reassigning you.'

'Pardon me?'

'We are opening a new office in Southeast Asia. There are many European businesses currently operating in the region and your skills will be put to good use there.'

'Southeast Asia?'

'Phnom Penh, to be exact. Cambodian coffee is very good, I hear.'

Spirited Away

Yuzuru Ono rolled from his futon and crawled across the tatami mats to the low table at the centre of the room. He gulped three cups of barley tea from a flask, relieved himself in the basin and, still wearing the clothes he had slept in, descended the stairway to the guesthouse lobby. At the genkan he slipped on his scuffed leather shoes and placed a hand on the sliding door.

'Going out, Mister Ono?'

Ono flinched. Turning, his gaze met with the manager's.

'Oh, good morning,' he said, a little too quickly.

'It's good afternoon,' the manager said, rising from his seat behind the counter.

Ono glanced at the wall clock behind the man's head. 'Yes, of course.' He offered a feeble smile that was more like a grimace; speaking caused his skull to shudder, as if someone were pitching cannonballs against its insides.

The manager eyed him coolly. 'Big night?'

'A work dinner,' said Ono cautiously, hand still on the door.

'Nice food and drink?'

'Yes, as a matter of fact.'

'As a matter of fact, you left your nice food and drink all down the hallway to the bathroom. The maid spent the entire morning cleaning it up. I had to pay her an hour overtime.'

Ono licked his lips, ran a swollen tongue over the fur of his teeth and exhaled a foul wind. 'I'm terribly sorry,' he said. 'I will pay any extra expense.'

'I've already added it to your bill. You are checking out today?'

'Yes, yes, I am,' said Ono. Then in a pleading tone, 'Is there … a bathhouse near here?'

The manager studied the middle-aged salesman—his rheumy eyes, uncombed hair, crumpled clothes and pall of death-by-shōchū hanging over him—and smiled. 'Certainly, Mister Ono. There happens to be one at the end of this street. Just turn left when you reach the Takase River.'

Ono felt his stomach rising. His cheeks puffed in and out. Giving muffled thanks, he jerked on the door and exited at a frantic trot. Ignoring the stares of two elderly women who stood chatting in the street, he vomited into a stormwater drain.

'Arrrgh, 'scuse me,' he said, dropping his Kyoto airs for the rough Banshū dialect of his home town. The women frowned with disdain as Ono wiped his mouth on his sleeve and staggered off—another barbarian from the western provinces, they probably thought.

Half-trying to recall the previous night's outing, half-trying not to, Ono limped towards the end of the street. How had he gotten back to the guesthouse the night before? A searing white pain stabbed at his brain. Then he remembered: he'd gone to Pontocho district to celebrate winning a contract! Single-handedly, he'd won the right to supply the Kyoto Holiday Inn with futons for their Japanese-style rooms. Although 'won' wasn't quite the best word. He'd have to phone his boss and explain that the margin was a little slimmer than he'd hoped for. Come to think of it, there wasn't any margin. But what did it matter—he'd come to Kyoto to win confidence in his company's product, and if an order of fifty futons at break-even price wasn't a measure of confidence then what was?

The street widened and a small bridge appeared. Ono soon found himself on the bank of a narrow river. What had the manager said—turn left at the corner? Or was it right? The river's clear, shallow water ran beneath weeping willows and ducks puttered between purpose-built huts anchored to its banks. The scene was a Kyoto idyll, but Ono's appreciation for the idyllic extended no further than a steaming hot tub at that moment. He glanced downstream at the old houses nudging each other in eel-nest fashion. He looked upstream. Through the shifting willow branches he glimpsed a tall, slim chimney. In a few minutes he stood outside a nondescript building painted in French vanilla with a faded blue entrance curtain that bore the symbol ゆ for 'hot water'. Over this hung a sign announcing 'Ume-yu'—Plum Bath. He lurched forward and entered.

The air inside was warm and vague with the scent of bath salts. He slipped off his shoes, placed them in a locker and, pocketing the wooden key, passed through a sliding door.

A high wooden counter straddled both male and female changing quarters inside, and seated behind it on an impossibly high stool, an elderly woman watched Ono enter. Her surprise gave over to curiosity as he stepped up, mumbled a greeting and asked her the price.

'How much would you like to pay?' she said.

An odd question, Ono thought. Then again, Kyoto people *were* rather odd. They had their own set of rules, manners and mindset, just as the western provinces folk had.

'It's a hundred yen in Himeji city,' he lied, reaching up and placing a single coin on the counter.

'I remember those days,' she said, raking the coin into a drawer. 'Have you been drinking?'

Ono glanced up at her. He wanted to ask what business it was of hers but didn't. This was Kyoto, after all.

'No, I have not,' he said flatly.

She pointed a gnarled finger at a wall poster beside the door that read 'The imbibing of alcohol before taking a hot bath is not recommended by the Kyoto Association of Medical Practitioners'.

Ono shrugged. He turned and ducked his head beneath the entrance curtains. The male changing room was empty. Looking about, he noticed that every basket was taken, each filled with a set of clothes, dark in colour and immaculately folded. He peered about, searching for signs of life. Mist clung to the other side of the bathroom door and he saw no one.

After slipping out of his clothes and piling them onto a stool in the corner, it suddenly occurred to him that he'd forgotten to bring a towel. He stood naked at the centre of the room, wondering what to do. On a drying rack he spied an old piece of frayed cloth no bigger than a handkerchief. He snatched it up and, covering his jewels, slid back the bathroom door and stepped inside.

The mist was warm and comforting. Gurgling and gushing noises sounded, and there was the quiet hiss of a steam maker. The sounds put him at ease; public bathing was about sharing a common desire for cleanliness, relaxation and hadaka no tsukiai, or getting along on equal terms with your fellow men. Not that Ono felt in any mood to be social as he ventured into the billowing steam. He hoped to meet no one.

Unable to see more than a few feet ahead, he edged cautiously along the wall. His foot nudged something hard. He bent down and grappled at a wooden stool and a plastic bowl on the tiled floor. Lowering himself to the seat, he felt about for the tap. The water was scalding, so he filled his bowl to let it stand for a few moments. What luck! Someone had left behind a small bar of soap. He dampened his cloth and proceeded to soap himself, scrubbing first his torso, then his legs, feet and, finally, his nooks and crannies. He brought the soap to a thick lather and ran his hands through his hair, purging it of the night's izakaya grease and tobacco odours.

Ono ceased scrubbing. He cocked his ear and listened. Did he just hear words uttered? Blinded by dripping soap suds and unable to rinse off for fear of scalding his face, he rose from the stool and moved towards the sound of gurgling water. Warm drafts wafted about him. He felt a strange presence but heard nothing, saw nothing. Reaching the bath's edge, he sluiced the suds from his face and opened his eyes. The voices had ceased.

Ono lowered himself into the hot water, allowing a deep

sigh to escape his lips. His eyelids grew heavy, and for a while he dozed off.

Loud, booming laughter startled him awake. Wavelets slapped at his chin. The water around him suddenly bubbled. Then from it something emerged that pulled Ono's eyeballs taut in their sockets: a horse-like creature with a mane of golden flames and fiery hooves and tail. Ono gaped, watching it pass through the mist and disappear.

He cried out, 'Who's there?' but there was no reply.

He spun about, searching for the bath's ledge, but in his disorientation he must have moved further out into the water. Only mist surrounded him.

Splashing sounded nearby. He turned to find a creature covered in emerald scales, with flaming nostrils and a pair of glistening eyes that ogled him. Ono opened his mouth but no scream was forthcoming. He backed away frantically, searching for the ledge. But instead, his hand fell to something warm and slippery. He swivelled and this time he did scream. Two giant carp—one red, one blue—bore down on him, whirling in unison and with eyes as big as dinner plates.

Ono leaped up and stumbled through the water. He fell down, then crawled and swam, coughing up mouthfuls of water as he groped desperately for the hard edge of the bath.

When he reached its cool tiles, he collapsed onto his back. His heart hammered against his chest, his lungs clenched and unclenched like a fist. He rolled over onto his soggy cloth, snatched it up and clawed through the mist to the door. He tugged on the handle—and froze. An immense weight rested on his shoulder. Whimpering, Ono turned and looked up into the eyes of Raijin, the god of thunder.

'You forgot this,' his voice boomed from the mist. The hand unfolded and in its palm Ono glimpsed the squished remains of his soap.

He gave a shrill scream, leaped through the door and into the changing room. Charging through the curtains past the bemused matron, he bounded barefoot into the street. Clutching the cloth to his crotch, he sprinted along the riverbank, causing cyclists, tourists and dog walkers to stop and stare at the pink-skinned, wild-eyed streaker.

The guesthouse manager jumped up from his seat, scattering his sudoku puzzles onto the floor.

'Good God, Mister Ono, what happened? You look like you've seen a ghost,' he said at the sight of the steaming, naked man before him.

'I have! That bathhouse, it's full of them!' Ono cried.

'What on earth are you talking about?'

'Ume-yu! Ume-yu!'

The manager gazed blankly back at him. Then a grin worked its way to his lips. 'I said turn left, not right, Mister Ono.' The manager struggled to contain his mirth. 'That bathhouse belongs to the Aizukotetsu-kai.'

'Aizu … what?'

The manager glanced through the open door behind Ono. The garden was lifeless, the street empty. He leaned across the desk and whispered.

'The yakuza, Mister Ono, the yakuza.'

Crossing the Ditch

You struggle with your hand luggage, trying to keep up with your parents as they close in on the boarding gate and its flashing final call sign. Your younger brother and sister trail you like salmon up a mountain stream, panting with Weet-Bix breaths because they didn't have time to brush their teeth before the airport taxi arrived.

The Continental Airlines' staff have run out of smiles. 'You're the lucky last, kid,' one of them says. But you don't hear their requests to present boarding passes, don't notice the Chanel No. 5 vapour trail of the stewardess or her Wild West accent; you just follow her outstretched hand down the aisle, and though you've never flown in a Boeing 747, or any aircraft for that matter, you instinctively know that seat 44E is located behind the huge, chuckling Samoan who has already jettisoned his footwear in preparation for take-off.

Across the aisle, your mother checks your brother and sister's seatbelt. She glances furtively at your father, who is beside you, then slumps back into her seat. Relief floods her face. You know what she's thinking: *Farewell to laundering sheep shit from rugby jerseys every weekend. Sayonara to butter-fried sheep's brains. Adios to town hall dinner parties with all the intrigue of watching Dulux dry.* Sixteen years of New Zealand rural life served—gone in a cloud of exhaust fumes, disappeared through the grimy rear window of a blue Toyota Corolla with three suitcases strapped to its roof. A teary-eyed goodbye to Grandpa, a road trip to Auckland, a last supper of pizza with relatives, then a few hours of sleep before the dawn taxi to the airport. She closes her eyes, exhausted.

But your adrenaline is pumping, beating like a war drum against your temples. Your primary senses creep back: you feel the *whumph* of the cargo hold doors closing, hear the engines whine and smell the aviation gasoline fumes permeating the cabin. You avail yourself of the 1184 kilonewtons of thrust, let it ease you back in the seat and allow this great force to separate you from the land in which you were born.

The engines roar, the overhead compartments rattle and lurch; your fingers tighten around grey vinyl armrests as the big bird rises and Aotearoa slips away.

Craning your neck, you glimpse the mudflats and mangroves of Manukau Harbour, then, as the plane climbs ungainly, the greater suburbs of Auckland, rough-edging the chartreuse-coloured farmland of Northland.

You wonder if you'll ever see your homeland again. A

pang of fear strikes at your gut. In a few hours you will land in Melbourne, a teenage immigrant. There is freedom in that, your mother says. But you aren't so sure. To arrive in a foreign land with no home to speak of, no friends or relatives, only the clothes on your back and a suitcase in your hand, seems problematic. Your brother and sister don't seem to comprehend the enormity of what is happening, but for you, there is an elephant sitting on your chest.

Your family isn't chasing freedom—it's fleeing crushing boredom, the kind that gets small-town teenagers pregnant, tempts young men to smoke pot and drive fast, goads older ones to rustle cattle and other men's wives.

You are high now. High enough to glimpse Manukau Heads and through them the turquoise water of the harbour rushing to marry the cobalt blue swells of the Tasman Sea over which you are poised to cross. You read somewhere that the Aussies call this stretch of water the 'Ditch'. Your father laughs when you tell him this and says, 'Well, something's gotta separate honest cricketers from dodgy ones.'

Your gaze holds onto your motherland as the last slither of coastline slips beneath the clouds and is gone. Your favourite band, Split Enz, once sang about the pioneer who acknowledges no frontier, but you find no solace in their words as you ponder the frontier that lies ahead of you.

Australia.

Where will you fit in this vast, red and desiccated land peopled by tall, sunburned men with zinc-creamed noses and twangy accents, and blonde-haired women called 'shielas' who drive trucks as long as trains across night-time deserts, and lightning storms that set the land on fire, and deadly snakes with names like 'taipan' and 'tiger', and sharks as big as buses, and …

The seatbelt lamp switches off and the cabin fills with the click-clack of metal clasps releasing. Soon a tall, black American steward approaches in a beige waistcoat. 'Larry' announces his gold name badge. Larry passes out impenetrable plastic bags filled with headphones. Later he returns pushing a drinks service trolley. The university students in row 45 request miniature bottles of vodka and gin, three apiece. This causes Larry's eyebrows to rise like duelling caterpillars and in a rich baritone he enquires, 'Y'all can drink that much?'

Your father asks for a Budweiser, your mother a gin and tonic and 'Cokes for the kids'. Larry serves the drinks and salted peanuts, but you give up trying to liberate your nuts from their bag and turn to liberating your mind. You gaze through the window at the altocumulus clouds scattering like a million sailboats across the Tasman Sea and you wonder what your mates are doing right now. You imagine them slumped behind pockmarked desks, bored, restless, awaiting the lunch hour when their pent-up energies can be spent on a pigskin rugby ball and a muddy paddock.

You miss your best mates B. and S., those two happy-go-lucky twits who got you into and out of trouble in equal measure. Remember when the three of you slipped inside your neighbour's son's abandoned sleep-out? The one wallpapered in *Penthouse* magazine centrefolds of Asian women with big hairdos, and you held a contest to see who could come the furthest but quickly abandoned it when a car pulled into the driveway, and then risked your manhood on a rusty tin fence in the mad rush to escape.

They say Australia is dangerous, but you survived sixteen years of small-town New Zealand: got chased by billy goats, dive-bombed by magpies, knocked over wasp nests and fell out of trees. You survived winter floods, earthquakes and spring storms that machine-gunned hailstones as big as golf balls across the land, killing ducks, geese and newborn lambs, and the wonder of it was that those hailstones melted in your hand.

You survived the Mongrel Mob, that bunch of social dropouts who swaggered about town in leather jackets and German war helmets, flicking cigarette butts at motorists and swigging from bottles of DB Draught while they peed on parked cars. They gave you no trouble because trouble could never pedal as fast as you.

Someone said it was the Mob who blew up the TAB betting office one year. You watched detectives in beige suits from the Hastings Criminal Investigation Branch sift for clues among the splintered wood and glass that covered High Street, pocketing a piece of the debris when they weren't looking, which won you 'best show and tell' at school later that morning.

Larry appears through the curtain pushing hot lunches and the quiz show question: 'Chicken or fish?' You guess 'fish' and win a fillet of rubber cod in cheese sauce with a rock-hard bread roll.

You have been reminiscing about the river you left behind, the one whose Māori name means 'muddy water' but whose waters, fed by snowmelt from the Ruahine Range, were crystal clear and filled with rainbow trout that you caught, gutted and stuffed with butter and bay leaves and, under your mother's eye, oven-baked for family dinners. Funny how trout always tasted of the river itself, water-weedy with a hint of silt.

Summers were for fishing, but when the trout weren't interested you'd toss your rod on the riverbank, climb an overhanging tree and, with your mates, plunge like madmen into the cool, tea-coloured water. After you'd dry yourselves on warm riverbed rocks, watch the fish leap at nymphs in the sunlight, and when the potatoes you'd tossed into a small fire a half-hour earlier were done, you'd tear off their blackened skins with your teeth and scoop out the fluffy core, knowing nothing could taste better.

Remember that bull carcass you found downriver one summer, drowned and bloated like a Zeppelin? Your mate wanted to stab it with his sheath knife 'for the hell of it', but you stopped him for fear the beast might explode hot maggots all over you.

You feel your stomach rise. The plane bucks on the Tasman's thermals, sliding up and down invisible slopes and causing the seatbelt sign to illuminate with an electronic ping that sets off more metallic clicking sounds. You close your eyes and wait for these small moments of terror to pass.

Time has taken on new meaning. Once it measured the number of 'sleeps' between birthdays and Christmases. Now it marks your progress across the Earth's surface: a five-hour road trip from a small country town to a big city, a forty-minute taxi ride from a motel to an airport, a three-and-a-half-hour flight across the ocean to an even bigger city in a country twenty-nine times larger than your own.

You open your eyes and your tray is gone. Through the window you sight land, a vast plane of brown and gold, mottled by cloud shadows and veined with waterways, which stretches to the horizon. It is endlessly flat save for formless humps that rise here and there and that remind you of your backyard where Ricky is buried. When your dog died, your father planted a lemon tree on the grave. It produced so many lemons you couldn't give them away. Years later, over a lemon meringue your mother had baked for dessert, your brother asked the question everyone had thought of but had never ventured: 'Are we eating Ricky?'

The pilot banks the aircraft and for a brief moment you glimpse a small kingdom rising in the distance.

Melbourne.

Your pulse quickens.

The gap between you and your new home closes and the cabin grows strangely quiet. Soft music plays from the speakers but fails to conceal the occasional gasp from an elderly passenger as the plane dips sharply and continues its descent.

Then a mighty surge grips you. Your sphincter tightens and you feel yourself thrown forward as Australia leaps up to greet you.

Touchdown.

Applause fills the cabin. The huge Samoan chuckles with glee and thrusts his enormous feet back into their shoes. While the aircraft taxis to the terminal, Larry appears and, joined by other cabin attendants, passes along the aisle spraying us with insecticide, 'By regulation of Australian Customs and Quarantine.'

You thank Larry and the Wild West stewardess, step from the plane and into beige carpeted halls along which you are joined by other passengers, all of you surging like a river towards corrals and gates with glowing immigration signs.

The officer in the blue shirt and shiny badges is a big man with a gallery of faded tattoos on each arm. He winks at you, stamps your passport as if killing insects and waves you through. At the baggage carousels, with your brother and sister fidgeting, you watch with nervous excitement as your bags mysteriously appear through a hole and rotate towards you.

You help your father load the trolley and then guide its squeaking wheels through the sliding doors and out into a sea of expectant faces. For an instant, they all recognise you. Then their gaze leaps to the person behind and you push on, anonymous, through the throngs of hugging families and kissing loved ones, towards the money change booths where your father exchanges green-tinged pictures of Queen Elizabeth II for pink ones.

Outside on the concourse the air is dry and pepper-scented. 'Eucalyptus,' your father says. He finds a taxi and asks something of the driver, who shoots a glance at you and your family and the mountain of bags and shakes his head. But soon another driver appears and your belongings are brusquely loaded. Your father and sister ride in the first car, your brother, mother and yourself in the second. But as you watch the string of crystal rosary beads dance from the rear-view mirror and hear the radio news broadcasting in a language that isn't English, you wonder if the Continental Airlines pilot has mistaken Austria for Australia.

'On holiday?' the driver asks.

'We're emigrating,' my mother says.

'Here?' The driver laughs and shakes his stubbled head. 'But no jobs, no jobs, and everything so expensif!'

Your brother clutches your mother's arm and you hear him whisper, 'I want to go home.' But your gaze fixes on the road and the small kingdom rising ahead of you.

You no longer feel sad, lonely or worried. No—you feel that life is just about to get interesting.

Holiday

As the nine-fifteen p.m. shinkaisoku express pulled into Kobe Station, Shugo Kugo felt his pulse quicken. Beads of sweat surfaced on his brow and his hands grew clammy. He snatched up his satchel and shuffled forward, watching the blur of commuters inside the carriages slow to a halt and their pale, fathomless faces stare blankly back at him. The doors hissed open and the crowd surged forward, carrying Kugo with it.

Pressed against the damp suits, he glanced about and recognised others like himself: young men and women fresh out of university, stiff in their Suit Company business attire and clutching satchels still new and shiny. What was going through their minds, Kugo wondered. Were they thinking how lucky they were to have an inbox of trivial queries to answer each morning? Or how lucky they were to attend afternoon meetings that never concluded without a consensus? Or to have to apologise to senior colleagues for delays caused by impossible deadlines, then be coerced to drink until drunk by these same colleagues, only to ride home, bathe, sleep and wake up so they could do it all over again?

'Welcome to company life,' Kugo's elder brother Hyugo had said dryly after congratulating him on getting his first job.

Ever since his induction into the Setouchi Shipping Company, Kugo had grimly accepted that his position in the corporate food chain amounted to something only slightly smaller than krill. His senior co-workers, the mullet heads, took advantage of this, heaping on the new recruits the most menial of tasks, smirking at the way they performed their morning calisthenics as if training for the Olympics, and when out of earshot calling them not freshmen but 'fresh meat'.

So why had he spent three years studying English and Spanish at a prestigious university (which his parents had paid for) and worked three part-time jobs to fund a graduation trip to Europe, only to wind up as fish bait in a seaboard shipbuilding company? The answer was as sad as it was simple: to please his parents.

More passengers forced their way aboard at the next station, thrusting Kugo deeper inside the carriage until his face met with a businessman's armpit and his crotch with the sharp edge of a woman's briefcase. With no handle to grasp, nothing to stop him from being swallowed by the morass, a sense of doom filled him. He wanted to cry out; he wanted to kick and beat his way to safety; but mostly, he just wanted to breathe the cool night air ...

A gap appeared, a fissure in the wall of passengers revealing the platform outside. He saw his chance and leaped. The doors clamped shut as he landed, catching his briefcase between them. He tugged violently, tearing the handle but managing to wrench it free. The pale faces inside stared back as if he, not they, were a ghost. And soon they were gone, slipping away with the red tail-lights of the train into the night.

Kugo slumped down on a platform bench, closed his eyes and inhaled deeply. Once again he would have to take the slower, less crowded local train home. When he opened his eyes, the airbrushed faces of two young women smiled back at him. Swathed in colourful summer kimonos, their sprite figures filled a floodlit billboard on the opposite side of the tracks. 'Visit Hot Spring Heaven. Visit Beppu!' their voice bubbles shouted as they strolled hand in hand along a quaint street lined with the glowing lamps of traditional bathhouses. In the hoarding's top corner, a gleaming white ferry eased through blue swells; the accompanying words read, 'Berth, Bath and Breakfast Included.' He stared at the billboard and his expression changed. The lights of the local train soon appeared, and by the time it had drawn into the station, Kugo had the free-call number scrawled on the back of his hand.

***

Next morning, he joined the rank and file as they marched wordlessly from the train station to the company gates. It was only Tuesday and a pile of specifications for the soon-to-be-launched LNG supertanker lay waiting on his desk, to be sifted and sorted and written up as PR prattle for the in-house magazine by Friday. The morning drifted until the electronic clock above the section chief's desk tolled lunch hour, and the rank and file rose from their workstations and marched wordlessly to the cafeteria.

Following a bowl of greasy ramen and a sad green salad, Kugo left the smokers to their post-lunch ritual and stepped into the bathroom. He entered the cubicle at the far end and locked the door. From his wallet he took out a folded piece of tissue and unwrapped it, inspecting the grains of red chilli powder. Then he held the tissue to his nose and snorted. The effect was immediate: his eyeballs swelled, his tear ducts gushed, and mucus flooded into his nasal tracts, causing him to cough and sneeze all the way back to his workstation. Once there, he guzzled a half bottle of water, which only made him splutter more.

A senior colleague frowned. 'What's the matter, Kugo?' he asked.

Wiping his nose and eyes, he said, 'Think I'm coming down with something.'

The colleague said nothing but slipped on a white face mask and hunched lower behind his monitor. The section chief, who had been talking on the phone, hung up and walked over.

'Kugo, you sick?'

'Don't feel so good, chief.'

'You don't look so good.'

'It's probably nothing,' said Kugo, grabbing a fistful of tissues and blasting them full of mucus.

'It's probably something. Best you get over to the clinic and get it looked at.'

'There's a virus going around,' said the colleague, without

looking up.

The chief took an indiscreet step backwards. 'Get it looked at, Kugo. Then take the rest of the day off. You can finish the ship-launch story at home.'

Coughing and wheezing, Kugo gathered his things and left. On the way to the clinic he bought a can of heated coffee at a vending machine and tucked it inside his armpit. When he handed the thermometer back to the physician a few minutes later, the old man nodded sagely. 'Common flu,' he said, and prescribed sachets of orange powder and pink pills.

Outside the train station, Kugo tossed the medicine into a garbage container and headed for the coin lockers. He glanced about, then inserted his key and removed the Boston bag he had deposited earlier that morning. Next he boarded an eastbound train for Sannomiya, and once there transferred to the monorail service bound for Port Island. As the train glided quietly over the harbour, he spied the cranes and gantries of the Setouchi Company's shipyards. He could just make out the black hulk of the new LNG tanker lying like a beached whale on slipway number two. A grin worked its way to his lips and he chuckled. Did he feel guilty for what he was about to do? He laughed loudly.

At the Port Island terminus there was a waiting shuttle bus, and in a few minutes he stood dockside, gazing up at the magnificent white lady of the Seto Inland Sea, the *Sunflower Ferry*. A column of smoke drifted lazily from her stack, while below container trucks rumbled up her stern ramp, stewarded inside by shouting stevedores.

At the ticket counter Kugo gave his phone booking number and paid in cash. And what luck! A double berth on the top deck with single occupancy all the way to Kyushu. A celebration was in order. He stowed his baggage, bought a can of beer at the kiosk and set out to explore the ship.

Stepping onto the observation deck, he sucked in the cool, briny air of the late afternoon and looked back towards Kobe city. The waning sun had cast the Rokko mountains in deep copper hues. Jet vapour trails blazed like a meteor shower across the azure sky above them. Kugo popped the tab on his beer, slurping off the bitter foam. He wondered where those planes were headed; he wondered if their passengers were feeling the same elation he was at that very moment.

Save for a solitary figure who stood on the lower deck looking back at the city, there were no other passengers outside. Kugo guzzled his beer and crossed to the ship's port side. A fleet of mackerel boats motored towards port, returning from the Pacific Ocean with a whirling cloud of hopeful seagulls in pursuit. Out to sea, tankers, barges and bulk carriers were making their way westward. The sight reminded him of what an 'old salt' from the shipyard had once said, that the inland sea traffic was timed to the tides—there was money to be saved in sending a ship with the tide rather than against it—and for this reason one could almost always judge the movement of the current by the direction of the shipping. Kugo glanced at the lower deck; the solo traveller had gone. A fresh breeze had risen and it caused him to shiver. He drained his beer and went below in search of dinner.

The cafeteria had filled like a rock pool at high tide. Kugo joined the queue of long-distance truck drivers, university students, retired couples and backpackers that flowed along the buffet counter. With his tray piled high, he took a window table overlooking the bow and watched the stevedores wave them off as the ship pulled away from the pier. At the far end of the cafeteria sat the solo traveller from the deck, a man of similar age wearing a dark business suit like himself, eating his dinner, pondering their departure, just as Kugo himself was doing.

Soon they had entered the shipping lanes and joined the westward run of maritime traffic towards Kyushu island and their destination, the hot spring towns of Oita and Beppu. Kugo finished eating and returned to his berth to collect a sweater. He bought several cans of whisky highball and returned to the observation deck, eager to toast his escape from Kobe.

In a short while the Akashi Kaikyō Bridge loomed before them. Toy-sized traffic drifted back and forth between Awaji island and Honshu, which caused Kugo to marvel at this feat of engineering that had produced the longest suspension bridge in the world. As the ferry slipped beneath the vast iron trusses, he glanced down at the currents surging around the massive concrete pillars. Where they came together again, swirling vortexes of phosphorescence appeared. He wondered what would happen to anyone who got caught in one; the thought made him shiver. He checked his watch and decided it was bath time.

Outside his room, as he inserted the key card into its slot, he had a sudden sense of being watched. He glanced sideways in time to catch sight of someone entering the room at the far end of the hallway but could discern nothing more.

There was only one other bather in the ship's communal bathroom, an elderly man whose deep sighs of satisfaction started to grate on Kugo's nerves as he sat soaking in the deep bathtub. Nevertheless, the motion of the bathwater as it shifted with the ferry's passage through the swells lulled him into a deep sense of wellbeing. Later, after he had towelled off and made to exit the changing room, he almost collided with an incoming bather. Their eyes met, and in that split instant Kugo recognised him as the solo traveller whom he'd seen in the cafeteria. There was an awkward moment as both men moved left, then right, and apologised before finally passing.

Kugo fell asleep quickly. Occasionally, the distant moan of a ship's horn or the raking beam of a passing lighthouse would pull him from his slumber and he would sit up and look around, wondering where he was. But the steady, reassuring thrum of the propellers far below him quickly summoned back the sandman every time.

***

Rubbing the sleep from his eyes, Kugo peered through the porthole at a chain of ragged mountains emerging from the dawn mist. A sprawling coastal town came into view. Like Kobe, Oita also wrapped itself around the base of steep hillsides—a captivating scene to anyone arriving by sea— and Kugo mused that, in another time, the giant hand of a Shinto god might have shaken Oita like a blanket and sent its buildings tumbling into a heap at the seashore, because that is exactly how it appeared.

Dressed in blue chinos, a hooded sweatshirt, and a red LA Dodgers cap to clamp down his bed hairdo, he gathered his bags and joined the passengers disembarking at the gangway. The air outside the terminal smelled strongly of sulphur. As he made his way through the empty streets of the port, he noted the iron chimneys that sprouted from homes, hotels and bath-houses, tails of thermal steam escaping like fleeing spirits. At Oita train station, Kugo bought a ticket for the short ride to Beppu, the famed 'hot spring capital' of Kyushu island and his final destination. There he knew he would find the bathhouses of his billboard dreams, the young women with wistful smiles who strolled the lamplit streets in their colourful yukata, and maybe, just maybe, one who might go for a drink with him.

The train hugged the rocky coastline, passing in and out of tunnels and mist-filled fishing ports and villages that came and went like the turning pages of a history book. Far from his family, far from his office, Kugo felt as light as a feather. He looked about the carriage, noting the sleepy high-schoolers and early-bird office workers who dozed with their heads on each other's shoulders. The train took a sharp bend and through the opened door he caught a glimpse into the next carriage. Seated at the far end and looking back at him was the solo traveller from the ferry. The train entered a tunnel, plunging the carriage into darkness. When it emerged, Kugo strained his neck but the man was nowhere to be seen. Odd, he thought. Then again, Beppu was the logical destination for tourists arriving by ferry in Oita. Any further thought on the matter was pushed from his mind by the appearance of the tiled rooftops of a steam-shrouded seaside town. 'Welcome to Beppu,' announced the conductor.

On disembarking, Kugo placed his bags in a train station locker, and after a light breakfast of toast and coffee at a railway cafe, he visited the restroom. Inside the cubicle he took out his phone and placed a call to work. Pressing a handkerchief to his mouth, he uttered some muffled words about a virus and 'superspreader' but promised to be back at work by Friday. The section chief sounded cautious. 'Make it Monday,' he said.

Pleased with his growing skill in the art of deception, Kugo took a walk around the station. He inspected the placards offering morning and afternoon trips to the thermal attractions and hot spring bathhouses about town. He settled on the shortest and cheapest tour, the curiously named Jigoku Meguri, or Burning Hell tour. The return ferry to Kobe would depart Oita at nine p.m., and until then, Beppu's local delights were his to sample.

After purchasing his ticket and boarding the waiting bus, a classic diesel-powered Isuzu, he was happily surprised to find the tour only half-full. A middle-aged woman in a 1960s-era powder blue air stewardess uniform, complete with a pillbox hat, greeted him at the door. Then, as the tour got underway, a strange thing happened. Rather than speak, the guide began to sing. It was a haunting melody, not terrible, and somewhat beguiling, like a mezzo-soprano's last song before her execution in a French opera. It occurred to him that she was singing the tour commentary. As they passed along the narrow streets, she sang about the old town market, the paved-stone highway once used by the palanquins of the samurai era, the tea houses filled with geisha and, as the street climbed higher up the slopes, the hot spring resorts where the wealthy and famous once stayed. Kugo took a moment to savour this atmosphere, so far away from the sombre stillness of his family home, so far from the beige-walled bell jar of his shipping office. Her songs weren't the only thing of interest: each time she turned sideways she presented the most curvaceous profile he had ever laid eyes on.

He felt strangely aroused.

The bus continued higher up the winding road until a large parking lot appeared and the guide brought her opera back to earth by announcing they had all finally arrived at the Garden of the Hells.

The tour group entered through the ticket office and set out to explore the immaculate gardens over which the thermal attractions were scattered. Everywhere, the earth belched and burped, filling the air with an odour like egg broth. Steam billowed from fissures, and streams hissed and gurgled. Eager to explore, Kugo separated from the main group and trod carefully along the stone trails, noting the signs that warned of death by boiling should he try to venture off them. He stopped first at Umi-Jigoku, Sea Hell, to marvel at its milky blue water and champagne fizz, then later at Oniishibozu-Jigoku, the Monk's Head Hell, where boiling mud burst in bubbles the size of a man's bald head. He carried on to Yama-Jigoku, Mountain Hell, and Kamado-Jigoku, Boiling Hell, until he reached Shiraike-Jigoku, the White Pond Hell. There he stopped to rest, contemplating the wisps of steam that danced like sprites across the water's surface. All at once, a gust of wind swept the lake clear of steam and Kugo's eyes widened. Standing opposite, watching him from across the water, was the solo traveller from the ferry.

Unease crept through him. The steam clouds closed in again but Kugo didn't wait. He made his way briskly across the miniature bridges and back through the ticket office and shop, without stopping to buy rice crackers or onsen puddings, until he reached the car park. There he found the tour guide smoking a cigarette behind the bus. She had removed her jacket and Kugo found himself momentarily distracted by the tautness of her blouse.

'You're early,' she said, butting her cigarette. She smiled. 'Hell too hot for you?'

'No,' he said, stealing a glance over his shoulder. 'Are we departing soon?'

'Are you in a hurry?'

'It's just that I want to see everything before my ship leaves …'

'You came on the *Sunflower Ferry*?'

'Yes.'

'Oh! I've always wanted to ride the *Sunflower*. I've heard it's wonderful.'

'Can I get back on the bus?'

'Actually, Chinoike-Jigoku is just down the road. We can walk.' She looked suddenly enthusiastic. 'And there's a crocodile farm ...'

'Crocodile farm?'

'Didn't you read the pamphlet?'

'I just looked at the pictures.'

'They left the photo out. Too gory.' Her gaze swept him lightly. 'Are you travelling alone?'

He almost said, 'I hope so,' but then, 'Yes, I'm travelling on business ... with some time off for pleasure.'

'We all need time off for pleasure,' she said. Looking about, she plucked a business card from her chest pocket. 'I give these to all the solo travellers.' She sang shrilly, 'Yooookaku!', then tittered.

He took the glossy pink card, reading the words aloud. 'The Candy-Candy Bar?'

'It's my sister's place. Downtown.' Her smile faded.

'Are you okay? You look a little pale.'

Before he could answer, the other tour members returned and, after deciphering the guide's sing-song explanation, together they all set out on foot for the next attraction. Kugo fell in behind them, glancing back occasionally, frowning as he descended the road. Was he being followed? Had the section chief put a tail on him? He'd be fired for sure …

Shit!

What would he tell his parents? He felt a sudden wave of anxiety wash over him. Would the chief really go to the trouble of having someone follow him all the way from Kobe? Then Kugo remembered: the files. In his satchel were the specifications for the new LNG tanker, due to be launched in two weeks' time. Could the man following him be an industrial spy? It was definitely possible—competition was fierce among the shipbuilders of the Osaka seaboard. Contract bidding was cutthroat, bribes were not out of the question, and the yakuza sometimes got involved.

Kugo cringed.

How foolish of him to bring the files to Kyushu! He wanted to pound his head with his own fist. Why had he not left his satchel in the Kobe train station locker?

Up ahead, billows of reddish steam rose sinisterly against the rocky outcrops of the mountainside. As the tour group grew nearer, the guide sang the praises of Blood Pond Hell, then launched into a tragic love story about a beautiful local girl whose love interest is thrown into the boiling pond by a jealous samurai lord.

Kugo cringed again.

Outside the park another tour bus had arrived and Kugo found himself quickly swept up by the disembarking passengers and carried through the ticket gates. Preoccupied by his situation, he climbed the hillside to a pergola and looked out over the steaming red lake. But rather than appreciate this mysterious, otherworldly scene, his gaze jumped between the faces of the sightseers who came and went from the viewing platform below. Suddenly, he heard footsteps approaching. He swivelled to find the guide smiling coyly at him.

'What's this? All on your little old lonesome?' In three strides she was beside him, bending across the pergola rail and peering down at the steaming lake. 'I can see why you chose this spot,' she said. 'Just look at that view! You wouldn't want to fall, would you?' She gave a shrill laugh and patted his arm. 'Just joking. Come on, let me show you the best place to try a hot spring boiled egg. It's divine.'

Reluctant to leave the safety of higher ground, Kugo nevertheless allowed her to lead him down through the lush gardens to a small lakeside pavilion. Inside, behind a rough-hewn wood counter, a retinue of elderly women in white aprons and headscarves busied themselves lifting wire nets of corn on the cob and hard-boiled eggs in and out of the steaming hot spring water.

Kugo had to admit that the eggs were delicious; they reminded him of how hungry he was. Halfway through his third egg, he glanced up and his jaw locked. Silhouetted in the doorway stood the solo traveller. Their eyes met momentarily, then the man looked away and stepped to the counter to place his order. Kugo crammed the remainder of the egg into his mouth and took his chance to slip unseen through the pavilion's side exit.

'Is something the matter?' the guide asked outside the front gate. 'You didn't like the boiled egg?'

'No, I did.'

'You did?'

'I did!'

'Well ...' She looked at him curiously. 'You're a little early, but you can wander down to the crocodile farm if you like. I'll direct the others as they come out.' She handed him a ticket.

'Couldn't I just sit in the bus?'

'All by yourself?'

Kugo returned a weak smile.

'Oh, come on,' she goaded. 'The crocodile show is great. You'll love it. They feed those monsters whole chickens!'

As Kugo descended the road, he tried to rein in his runaway mind. Life was filled with coincidences, he reasoned, and all visitors to Beppu took tours of the hot springs and bathhouses. On the other hand, wasn't it strange that of all the passengers who had boarded the ferry in Kobe, only this one man kept reappearing? And each time he did, he seemed acutely aware of Kugo's presence. Again he wondered if the section chief had sent someone to keep an eye on him, to make sure he wasn't selling secrets to rival companies. Could this mysterious man be an employee of his own company? He did look vaguely familiar. Then again, almost all of the Setouchi Shipping Company were of average appearance and had black hair.

Kugo glanced at his watch: ten-fifty a.m. He decided that the crocodile park just might provide the much-needed diversion for his overactive mind. He gave a sulphurous burp, flashed his ticket to the gate attendant and entered. The smell hit him immediately: a vile cocktail of turgid water and rotting meat. It set his nostrils flaring.

It was now almost eleven o'clock and a sizeable crowd of tourists had swelled around a large brothy pool that, according to the sign, housed crocodiles from Malaysian Borneo. Kugo watched as the keeper climbed his ladder with a bucket of plucked, pink chickens and dangled one over the iron grille barrier by its legs. This gesture set the water churning and foaming as the huge lizards slid across one another to get within striking distance. The first chicken landed in the jaws of the largest beast, and the sound of its cracking bones raised a murmur of excitement around the enclosure. Faces pressed against the grille, the audience was neither thrilled nor appalled but instead seemed transfixed by the limp flying chickens, the rip-tearing of flesh and the ensuing fight for morsels. Kugo felt his stomach turn. He yearned for fresh air, to escape this vile place of filthy water and rotting meat. He turned and pushed through the crowd, hurrying to a side gate and exited onto the road.

Ahead of him, a man in a dark suit stepped from a public convenience and started briskly in the same direction uphill. Kugo slowed his pace, halted, his eyes on the back of the solo traveller. Breathing fast, he dived quickly into the conveniences, stepped to the window and pretended to urinate. Peering out, he watched the road until his tour group began to trickle out of the crocodile farm and make its way uphill towards the car park. When Kugo spied the tour guide behind them, he gave her a short, harsh hiss. She stopped, looked about, searching for the source of the noise. Spotting Kugo's face in the toilet window, she tottered over.

'What are you doing?' she said.

'I've decided to walk back to town.'

'What?'

'I want the scenic route.'

'But we take the scenic route.'

'I want to experience the local culture.'

'Are you feeling alright?'

He nodded vigorously.

She looked left, then right, and said, 'Are you sure?'

'Yes.'

'Well, I'll have to inform the bus driver.' She looked flustered. 'Happy travels, and don't forget to visit Candy-Candy.' Then she too was gone.

Kugo exhaled. Wasn't this supposed to be a holiday? Wasn't he meant to be stepping out of hell, not into it? He washed his hands and checked the mirror. His pale face with its furtive gaze and tight jaw shocked him. For God's sake! He smacked his cheek with his wet hand. Was he losing his nerve?

He descended the mountainside into a neighbourhood of ancient tiled-roof and wooden homes. Staircases linked the winding narrow streets; here and there, elderly residents sat chatting with their baskets of fish and freshly pulled radishes beside them. Kugo had little to offer except a greeting as he passed, heading into the town centre.

Shopping streets soon appeared, lined with the small stores of fruiterers, fishmongers, rice millers, used kimono dealers and bookstores. Red lanterns swung on hooks and their kanji characters advertised the local delicacies to be had within. Kugo felt a pang of hunger strike at his gut. He stepped to the entrance of a small restaurant, slid back the door and entered. A cockroach scuttled behind a soy sauce bottle on one of the tables. He opted for a seat at the counter, surprised but not put off by the greasy cobwebs hanging from the light and the Maneki-neko figurine wearing a furry crown of grey dust. Presently, a toilet flushed and a rotund matron stepped through the small door behind him, wiping her hands on her apron. She gave a one-toothed smile and said heartily, 'Irasshaimase! Welcome to Tori-ten Tengoku.'

Kugo glanced at the shop's name printed on the grimy menu. 'Tori-ten Heaven?'

The matron cackled. 'Beppu's one and only!'

He ordered beer and the signature dish, described in the menu as 'pieces of tender chicken encased in a light tempura coating and served with bamboo salt'. The beer arrived and Kugo wasted no time in draining it. He ordered a second. Halfway through the bottle, a small movement caught his eye. Then something ran along the steel shelf above the deep-frying vat. He looked about but the matron had stepped out again. All of a sudden, a small object fell with a sizzling splash into the hot oil. Kugo leaped up. His jaw unhinged and his eyes filled with horror. A mouse bobbed upside down in the vat, its tail as crispy as a beer snack. Kugo felt his stomach racing to meet the daylight. He fumbled a thousand-yen note from his wallet to cover the beer and left as fast as he could.

It was now mid-afternoon. That the night ferry to Kobe would return at nine-thirty gave him a sense of urgency. It was time to seek out the bathhouse street and the local beauties in yukata who strolled it.

He made his way along the labyrinthine streets of the old

market quarter as they grew progressively darker and more rundown; he soon realised that he was utterly lost. He veered south, assuming that the downward gradient of the street would eventually bring him to the sea. And yet, it seemed to have no end. After a while, neon signboards began to appear above the old storefronts, some of them sputtering, others with letters missing, but everywhere the curious smell of floral deodoriser and disinfectant.

A man in a baggy suit tossed a cigarette to the ground and stepped from one of the darkened doorways. Through yellowed teeth, he whispered at Kugo a 'starting price'. Kugo hurried on. He threw a glance over his shoulder as he rounded the corner and collided with a woman coming the other way. She let out a yelp, and cans of beer and whisky highball tumbled over the paving stones.

'Oh, I'm so sorry,' Kugo said, scrambling about, grabbing the drinks rolling this way and that. It was then he realised that she was wearing a yukata. Only instead of the demure beauty with her hem to her heels, this woman's garment ended high above her knees. Her hair was a Medusa-like arrangement of bronze curls, and as she crouched on haunches, gathering up the drinks, he caught sight of her nipples behind her loosely tied yukata. She caught him staring and stood up, glaring. She was an inch higher on account of her metallic pink heels, and her mascara gave her eyes a fearsome look. Before she could berate him he said quickly, 'You wouldn't happen to know the way to Miyuki Street, would you?'

She jerked her chin in the direction from which she had just come. 'Asoko,' she said. Then she strode off, leaving a strawberry-scented vapour trail.

He carried on down the street, past a convenience store, and at the next intersection he turned left. He found himself on a paved street that extended all the way to the seashore. Lined with turn-of-the-century storefronts and classic bathhouse pavilions, it might have been an elegant thoroughfare down which rickshaws carried bathhouse patrons in another era. Kugo recognised it as the street from the railway station billboard. Sadly, there were no women. In fact, the only other person on the street was an old man who had parked his bicycle and stood urinating into a side drain. Kugo wondered if he had arrived too early as the lanterns had not yet been hung beneath the eaves. But passing by each bathhouse, he peered at their business hours signs and his spirits plunged. They all bore the same message: 'Closed Wednesdays.'

The old man finished draining himself, zipped up and walked over. 'Looking for a bathhouse?' he said.

'Yes,' said Kugo.

'Takegawara Onsen.' Kugo followed the man's finger to the end of the street. Sure enough, rising above the tiled rooftops in all its Meiji Period glory stood the great dame of Beppu's bathhouses.

'Hey, you got a cigarette?' the man asked.

But Kugo was already ten paces down the street, too far away to hear the curse word hurled after him. When he reached the entranceway, he stopped. He wanted to stand a moment and reflect on why he had travelled so far from home. He gazed up at the great arching veranda, handcrafted over a century ago by men skilled in their trade, roofed with decorative kiln-fired tiles, and welcoming with its lazily flapping blue noren entrance curtains. It was a bathhouse of immense proportions, weathered and aged, with traditional clay plaster walls and a vast sweeping roof. Through the open windows of the building's wings, Kugo glimpsed patrons moving about in crisp blue and white yukata. He pushed aside the entrance curtains into an enormous foyer. A ticket counter stood to one side, and above it were listed the bathhouse services and their prices. Kugo stepped up and said, 'One ticket for the hot sand bath, please.' The female attendant leaned forward. Her tanned forearms were huge.

'Have you been drinking?' she said.

'Drinking?'

'Yes, drinking alcohol.'

'Why?'

'I can smell it on your breath.'

'But I only had a couple of beers and that was thirty minutes ago.'

She pressed her palms on the counter and leaned further towards him. 'You can't enter the sand bath if you have been drinking within the hour,' she said flatly. 'You'll have to come back later.'

For a moment, Kugo couldn't quite comprehend the situation. He looked at the huge antique wall clock, then back at the woman. She smiled, and it caused him to release something like a whimper. With her gaze on his back, he slipped through the curtains and out onto the street.

On the seafront he found a small park bench overlooking a marina. Out to sea a flotilla of tiny sailboats were putting the breeze to good use, tacking back and forth across the harbour. Seagulls wheeled and cried, the tide sloshed against the breakwater, and when the breeze was blowing right, he thought he heard the laughter and cries of the sailors. He must have drifted off because when he roused himself, the sun had slipped behind the mountains of Oita in the distance and the breeze had turned chilly.

Kugo returned to the Takegawara Onsen bathhouse to find a different woman behind the ticket counter. She smiled warmly and said, 'There is one place left for the next sand bath, if you hurry.' She passed him a folded yukata and pointed to the male changing rooms. Kugo thanked her, paid, and made his way quickly across the vast lounge area where a few patrons sat mopping their flushed faces and drinking cups of chilled water from an antique dispenser. Having exchanged his clothes for the light cotton robe, he slipped through the curtain and slid back the door to the room housing the sand bath. It had the vague smell of a beach, and sulphur too. On each side of a narrow boardwalk, female staff gently shovelled heated sand across the bodies of patrons lying in rows, to the uninitiated looking like corpses at a mass burial. Kugo noticed that all of the female staff had large forearms. One of them directed him to a ready-made depression at the very end of one of the rows. There he lay down and, surprised at the heat of the sand, allowed the staff to cover his body with smooth, rhythmic motions. The heat soon penetrated his body and a deep sense of wellbeing began to fill him. It was a moment when life's worries dissolved, and when one came to fully appreciate the time-honoured tradition that had been soothing the souls of weary travellers for thousands of years. Kugo released a long sigh. Cocking his head to one side, he wondered if there were others sharing the same sense of euphoria. His gaze roamed the restful forms of other sand bathers in their neat rows with their eyes closed before coming to rest on the person beside him, a young man just like himself.

Kugo's eyes widened.

***

He sat alone in the male bath. His pulse rate had subsided, but he felt light-headed. A new mood had overcome him. He was angry. But was he angry with himself? Or was he angry at his pursuer? He didn't know, and the confusion only made him more irritable.

The male bath was located in one of the pavilion's wings. It was large and airy and carried a whiff of olden times; there were no faucets, no shampoo or soap, and only a small bamboo stool to perch on while one sluiced oneself with scoops of scalding hot water. The bath itself looked more like a dirty, sunken pond, its murky water sulphurous and slimy on account of a heavy mineral infusion.

Kugo released an exasperated sigh. He stared out of the window at the darkening sky. A swallow came and went from its nest beneath the pavilion's eaves, and for a moment he admired its unwavering dedication to raising its young. He thought of his own parents and how they had done the same for him. He wondered what they were doing at that moment; the thought made him suddenly homesick.

Kugo sat quite still, eyes closed, and composed himself. The sound of footsteps descending the stairway towards the bath reached him, then the sound of another bather taking a stool and sluicing his body.

Kugo swivelled and when he spoke, it was with a harshness

that surprised even himself. 'Why are you following me?'

The naked man froze. His eyes widened. 'You! Following you? You're following me!'

Kugo wondered if he had heard right.

'All the way from Kobe you've been on my tail,' the man continued. 'I saw you watching me on the ferry, in the cafeteria, on the train to Beppu, the hot spring tour, and now here! Who the hell are you and why are you pursuing me?'

'But …' said Kugo. He felt suddenly dizzy again. 'You've been following me!'

'Are you a nutcase?' The naked man was indignant. 'I'm going to call the police.'

Kugo rose from the bath, dripping and naked. He faced the man, his muscles taught as piano wires. 'Not before I call the police on you!' he shouted.

The two men glared at one another, and the only sound was of the swallow hatchlings peeping from their nest, high in the bathhouse's eaves outside the window.

The man spoke first. 'So you're not a private detective?'

'Hell no!'

'Wait a moment. You look familiar.'

'You do too.'

'You work in Kobe?'

'Yes …'

'Whereabouts?'

'Setouchi Shipping.'

'You're kidding me.'

'Public affairs. Fifth floor.'

The man rose from his stool and took a step closer to the bath. 'I'm in sales. Second floor.'

'But what are you doing here?'

The man slipped into the water opposite Kugo. 'I saw an advertisement—'

'A billboard?

'Yes.'

'A billboard with a bathhouse, some yukata girls and a night ferry?'

'Yes!'

'When I saw you on the train, and then again at the hot springs, I thought my boss had sent someone after me.'

'You're a freshman?'

Kugo nodded.

'Me too. I couldn't stand it anymore. I had to get out. I needed a—'

'Holiday,' said Kugo. He smiled.

***

Later in the changing rooms, as the men dressed themselves, a card dropped from Kugo's pocket. The man stooped to pick it up and he read the lettering slowly, 'Candy-Candy? I have the same card!'

'Impossible,' said Kugo.

The man fumbled from his wallet an identical pink business card.

'Where did you get that?' Kugo asked.

'From my tour guide. She said her sister runs this bar downtown.'

'Mine too. Your tour guide sang?'

'And she had big things ahead of her.'

Kugo said nothing, his mind working overtime. He glanced at his watch. 'Come on, we've got three hours before the ferry leaves.'

It was dark as the two men made their way along a narrow street in Beppu's small but compact nightlife precinct. A simple map on the reverse side of the business card brought them to a block of apartments. Smoke wafted from a ground-floor yakitori joint on one side, a small standing bar on the other. The men's gaze fell to the vertical signboard above them. At the very top, a pink neon sign pulsed the words 'Candy-Candy'. A rattling elevator delivered the men to the fifth-floor landing, at the end of which they found a door painted in pink gloss.

Kugo pulled on the handle.

'Irasshaimase!' came a shrill welcome greeting. As if by echo, and even more shrill, it sounded again. Two women advanced on them, and when they reached the door their smiles gave way to surprise. Kugo and his companion traded glances. The women were of the same height and body shape and their faces were near identical. Both wore yukata in subtle floral designs with hems reaching all the way to their small, sandalled feet.

'Twins,' murmured Kugo.

'Twins,' his companion confirmed.

'I'm Candy after five p.m.,' Kugo's tour guide said.

'But I'm the *original* Candy,' said the other, edging in front of her sister.

Into the evening the two men drank while the women sang karaoke ballads about springtime and unrequited love in the port towns of Kyushu. Then the women drank, and the two men sang ballads about Kobe and the harbour lights, and the beautiful women in yukata who strode the streets of the old port precinct in summer, when fireworks exploded high over the city and turned the night into day. Then together the four of them sang, so loudly and so cheerfully that no one heard the far-off sound of a ship's horn signalling its departure from port.

Twenty Kilometres to Wombat Flat

The screen door slammed shut, its flywire flapping loose behind her. She'd get Mick to take a look. Ask him to cut the high grass in the top garden while he was at it; warmer weather meant brown snakes on the move. Chicken coop would have to go too; useless without chickens. Damn foxes. She'd bake Mick a meatloaf in thanks. Good neighbours were hard to find. Meatloaf. She hardly ate it these days; it was her husband's favourite.

She descended the stone path to the carport and stopped to peer beneath the bottom step, her gaze meeting with the eyes of a huge blue-tongue lizard.

'Morning, Rodgie.'

The reptile stared back as if it hadn't blinked in a thousand years. She snipped at the bottlebrush, yellow roses, a little gardenia from beside the carport, enough for a small bouquet, which she wrapped in newspaper and tied with twine. She rested it on the back seat of the blue Valiant Charger, climbed in and gunned the engine, like her husband used to.

Warm, dry air rushed in through the window, vague with the smell of a distant grassfire. She drove down quiet streets of rural town homes, old miners' cottages with white picket fences and neat English gardens, roses nodding drunkenly in the hot breeze, jasmine fighting for life. Miners' cottages were the new gold, Mick reckoned. City folk just kept on coming, fleeing the urban crush, returning to work in it every day ...

The mournful wail of a steam locomotive carried over the rooftops and belltowers of the town—the weekly 'bush run' for the tourists between Bendigo and Melbourne.

She passed the old fire station, now a cafe, with patrons slouched at outside tables, dogs at heel, thumbing broadsheets and scribbling in notepads, looking clever. Was she the only one with two jobs and a mortgage to service? She drove on, past the war memorial with its forlorn German field gun, the BI-LO supermarket, and the Canning Hotel with its morning happy-hour beers and the old diggers with strawberry noses who nursed them. They would forever be there. She would forever be here.

She stopped outside the Chinese fish and chippery, crossed the road to the bakeshop and ordered two veggie pasties, one to eat in, the other to go. She took a corner table and, with *The Sun* as a tablecloth, ate hungrily and read disinterestedly stories about cricket clubroom break-ins, stolen pie warmers, grassfires and truck tyre blowouts. She turned to the footy pages: the Saints were back at the top of the league after a long dry spell. She wondered when her own dry spell would end.

Back in the Charger, takeout pastie on the hot vinyl next to the wilting flowers, she pulled a U-turn that set tyres screeching, heads turning, and headed south out of town. Elm trees stood sentinel along the highway, and the long shadows they cast offered momentary respite from the mid-morning glare.

She had almost passed the last tree when someone stepped out from of its shade, a small, slightly built figure with long dark hair in denim shorts and a t-shirt. It held out a piece of cardboard scrawled on in black marker pen, the destination a blur as she barrelled past.

She squinted in the rear-view mirror, through the dust and glare, and caught the hitchhiker's gaze, devoid of expression or emotion; it made her think of Rodgie. She eased off the pedal, braked and pulled over in a cloud of dust devils.

The figure grabbed a backpack and shuffled quickly toward her, smooth brown face in her window a moment later.

'Melbourne?' he said.

'Wombat Flat,' she answered, concealing her surprise at the young Asian man.

'Is that far?'

''Bout twenty kay. You can pick up a lift at the roadhouse there.'

He hesitated, considering this detail.

'Up to you,' she said, waiting.

'Okay.'

She popped the boot, he dropped in his backpack and then climbed in beside her. A new smell now filled the car: old sweat and something spicy; not unpleasant, just different. The

Charger's tyres found traction, spat gravel and clawed at the blacktop.

'Thought you were a woman.'

He forced a laugh.

'I mean, I don't normally pick up guys out here. I'm Fiona, anyway.'

'Manabe.'

'Mana-bay?'

'Man.'

'Okay, Man.' She chuckled. 'You're the first *man* I've picked up today. Where you from?'

'Japan.'

'On holiday?'

'Working holiday.'

She glanced quickly at his t-shirt, once white with 'I Love Cairns' barely discernible across the chest.

'Been on the road long?'

'Six months.'

'Big country, isn't it.'

'Big.'

They drove on in silence, her passenger shifting his feet now and again, venturing nothing but watching the landscape, noting its details: the startled cockatoos lifting off dried-up dams, the rusted car wrecks, the endless, featureless paddocks, save for a precious few livestock sheltering beneath a solitary tree.

She held the wheel with one hand, commanding it into curves, easing it down the straights, eyeing on each side the glades of red gums, rivergums and stringybarks, until the forest thinned and clusters of stone cottages appeared. A township with rainwater tanks half-full, inhabitants hunkered down, watching cricket, drinking beer, quietly surviving. That's what you did out here—you quietly survived.

Beyond the town the road straightened. A car had pulled over on its verge while its driver, all butt crack and beer belly, wrestled a dead animal into the opened boot.

'Roo,' she said, noting her passenger's interest. He craned his neck as they passed.

'Kangaroo?'

'Yup.'

'What will he do with it?'

'Probably feed it to his dogs. Free meat. Some people round here eat it themselves.' She glanced in the rear-view mirror, recognising the vehicle.

'Have you ever hit one?' he asked.

They mounted a rise and entered another long stretch of undulating road. Forest reappeared, growing almost to the verge. She slowed the car as a kangaroo warning sign flashed by.

'No.' She breathed out. 'Look, I've got to stop up here for a minute. Won't take long.'

Halfway along the straight she pulled over. She got out, took the flowers and the pastie and stepped into the forest. At a small clearing she stooped to a cairn of rocks, tossed away the old flowers and laid the bouquet and the pastie in front of it. She stood for a moment, whispering something, feeling his gaze on her back, then returned to the car.

He said nothing. Out of respect, perhaps. She couldn't tell.

'What's waiting in Melbourne?' she asked, fending off the creep of an uncomfortable silence.

'I'm meeting a friend.'

'Gunna look for a job?'

'I have one.'

'Really?'

'Yes.'

'Sushi bar?'

'No.'

'Okay …'

'Someone died back there, didn't they?'

She glanced at him quickly and his face was earnest.

'My husband.'

She gripped the wheel with both hands, felt it slippery beneath her palms.

'I'm sorry,' he said. 'How?'

'Roo hit him. He was on a motorbike, early morning, misty. Died instantly.'

'You think his spirit lives there?'

'You mean, like his ghost?' She laughed. 'Hell, I doubt it. He never was one for hanging around. Why?'

'In Japan the spirits of our ancestors return once a year. In August. We pray to them, present offerings, like you did.'

'Well, he loved veggie pasties.'

'My father loved beer. We place a can on the family altar and drink together every year.'

'I'm sorry to hear that. I mean, that's a nice a tradition.'

'You believe in ghosts?'

'Sorry?'

'Ghosts.'

She shifted in her seat, felt her pants damp with perspiration. With the forest behind them, farmland rolled out on each side, parched golden hills, desolate as dunes in the Sahara. A pall of smoke smudged the horizon, the grassfire she'd smelled earlier perhaps. She drew a breath quickly and exhaled with a puff.

'God, I dunno. Never thought about it. You a travelling mystic or something?'

'I'm a tattoo artist.'

She threw him a surprised glance, long enough to linger on his smooth, sun-browned legs and hairless, gleaming arms.

'You're not much of an advertisement.'

'I'm sorry?'

'Tattoo artists usually wear their art, don't they?'

'My family owns a hot spring hotel. Tattoos are no good for business. People with tattoos scare away customers. It's a yakuza thing. Y'know, mafia.'

'Don't care for them much myself. Tattoos, that is. Every man, woman and child's got one these days.'

'My friend says Melbourne people love Japanese tattoos.'

'Yeah, well, they are all very arty-farty down there.'

'Arty-farty?'

'They like art.'

'How about you?'

Her gaze remained on the road's undulations. She'd never thought about art; never had time to with a mortgage, night shift at the bacon factory, day shift at the roadhouse, a little kip, a quick shower and a mouthful of tea and toast in between. Art? Hell, she couldn't pen a pauper's portrait for peanuts.

'It's alright,' she lied.

They drove on, and the silence grew strangely comfortable; the rush of hot air, the empty road winding its way through

land that melded into itself, intense in depth and colour—
reassuring. Then the grasslands fell away and the road descended into a gully where a slow-moving stream cut through
a glade of river gum trees.

'Got a favourite?' she asked, easing onto the brake.

'Favourite what?'

'Tattoo.'

'Do you know yokai?'

'I know yokel.' She chuckled, adding quickly, 'Nup, no
idea.'

'Yokai are creatures—monsters, ghosts, fairies, that kind of
thing. They're part of Japanese spirit world. They live in our
imaginations.'

'You tattoo them?'

'I *interpret* them, then draw them on paper. My friend
does the tattooing. She likes my designs. She says Melbourne
people will too.'

He slumped back in his seat and looked out the window
at the rivergums and the light-dappled stream that writhed
through them. She glanced at her watch; at a bend in the road
she slowed, then made a quick manoeuvre. She pulled the
Charger onto a rutted track and descended into the glade. Her
passenger straightened up, looked back at the highway, then
at her.

'Don't worry,' she said. 'Got something to show you, won't
take a minute.'

The big blue muscle car drew up beside a small oxbow
lake. Water from the stream rotated in a wide eddy at its mouth
before moving gently on downriver. She got out and stomped
through the long grass to the water's edge. Tentatively, her

passenger followed.

'What is this place?' he said.

'You're keen on monsters, right?'

His gaze ranged over the still, tea-coloured water, the lush reeds crowding the bank, the fallen gum tree half-submerged, and the driftwood hanging like bleached bones in the low branches.

'This is what we call a billabong. They appear after the winter floods.' From somewhere upstream a kookaburra concurred and the stream gurgled. 'City folk find them creepy.'

He crouched down on his haunches, forearms resting on knees, looking out across the still water, waiting.

'Ever heard of a bunyip?' she said.

'No.'

'It's a kind of water monster, part of our folklore.'

'What does it look like?'

'Some say it's half-bird, half-crocodile with feathers or fur. Others say it looks like a huge dog with claws and a horse's tail that swims like a frog and stands two metres high on its back legs.'

'What do you think?'

She stepped closer to the water's edge. In the cool stillness of the lake, far from the town and its opinionated inhabitants, she suddenly felt self-conscious of her own voice. 'Well, I reckon it's just a yarn, a story that's gotten bigger over the years. The first settlers used to see seals and sea lions in the rivers round here. Said they'd swum up all the way from the coast. The Aborigines reckon bunyips are evil spirits that like water and only come out at night. Over time, maybe the two stories just became one. I dunno.'

'But what do *you* think it looks like?'

She laughed. 'Me? I imagine a big hairy purple lizard with sad green eyes, not ugly, just lonely, like someone with no mates who everyone steers clear of because he's … he's different.'

'Like kappa.'

She turned to look at him.

'A water sprite,' he said, watching the water. 'In Japanese we call them *kappa*. They make mischief, trick children into drowning themselves …'

'Sounds terrible.'

'Yes, and no. They are part of Japanese culture. They're imaginary, but if you tell children about them, they won't go near a river or lake by themselves. That is a good thing.'

She turned back to the lake and watched small fish leaping for nymphs, ripples spreading out across the dark, glassy surface.

'I suppose it is …' She looked at her watch. 'Shit!' She climbed the bank and hurried back to the car. 'I'm late for work.' She revved the engine and before her passenger had even time to close his door, the Charger launched back up the track.

'Thank you,' he said.

'For what?'

'For taking time to tell me about bunyips.'

They reached the sealed road and she dropped her foot. The engine growled and the car leaped forward. She felt strangely refreshed.

'No worries,' she said, and smiled.

Once out of the gully, the land rolled over and over like

brassy pots and pans upturned and gleaming in the midday sun. Then the winding road straightened and a small settlement floated ahead of them on the horizon. 'Welcome to Wombat Flat' announced a bullet hole–riddled sign.

Soon she was pulling into a dusty forecourt outside a building with a long tin roof and a wooden deck lined with chairs and tables. Placards advertised wayfarers' favourites— Mr Whippy and Mrs Mac's pies—while the sign on the roof spelled out to one and all in large, faded blue letters 'Swordfish Cafe'.

She heard him pronounce the name.

'Yup, not a swordfish for a hundred kays in any direction.'

'You work here?'

'Here, and a bacon factory. But that's another story. Come in and I'll get you a Coke.'

A handful of travellers sat at tables inside, red-faced and haggard, coaxing life back with cold drinks and hot pies. The hitchhiker took his Coke outside. She glimpsed him through the window, sitting at a table on the terrace, sipping from the bottle and scribbling something into a notebook he'd pulled from his backpack.

An articulated truck pulled off the road and into the forecourt—a big metallic-blue cab and trailer—all dust and diesel and rolling thunder. A tour bus followed in after it, pulling in beside the truck and disgorging its cargo of interstate travellers, who kept her and the cafe staff bustling from pie warmer and fridge to till and back again for the next quarter of an hour. When the commotion had died and the last passenger had climbed back on board, she glanced at the window. The truck had gone. The hitchhiker too.

She pushed through the flyscreen door, past the tables of empty bottles and plates, to where the hitchhiker had sat. Beneath the empty Coke bottle a note lay folded. She opened it, mouthed the two words every hitchhiker says before parting ways, and looked back at the bottle. A small paper figurine balanced on the glass lip. She picked it up and placed it in the palm of her hand, eyeing the small green lizard-like frog creature that sat with its legs crossed. On its back, the word 'kappa'.

***

The Swordfish Cafe was reborn a year later. 'Under new management' read the sign on the door, and in small letters, 'Licensees: Mick and Fiona Noonan'. The building sported a fresh sky-blue paint job with navy trim, while an industrial-sized pie warmer sat on the counter filled with bacon-and-egg and veggie pasties, and a new deck overlooked the sealed car park.

Inside, bluegrass music played and two ceiling fans shifted the delicious aromas of fresh-baked pastries from the kitchen to the front door and back again.

A TV set mounted high in the corner played the latest sports news from around the state. Mick sat at a table beneath it with a coffee beside him, a box of roofing nails rolling about in his hand.

'Jeez, would you look at the tatts on this guy. Like a human art gallery,' he said. He lifted the cup to his lips and slurped. She looked up from the fridge, Coke bottles in hand, and watched as the captain of the Saints—a tall, muscular young man with red hair—stepped up to the microphone.

'Congratulations on the big win in Melbourne today,' said the reporter.

'Yeah-nah, all credit to the boys for puddin' in such a strong effort,' said the captain.

She turned back to the fridge, half-listening to the unimaginative questions and answers that followed. Then the reporter remarked, 'A rather impressive tattoo on your shoulder there. Would you tell us about that one?'

'This one?' said the captain, turning his back to the camera and hoisting his jersey above his shoulders. Inked in deep purple and flecked with bright greens and yellows, a fearsome lizard-monster wrapped itself across his muscular back, the emerald eyes vivid and sharp, yet somehow sad-looking.

'This 'ere's a bunyip,' he said.

A Coke bottle exploded onto the cafe floor. The sound carried to the edge of the highway, where a blue-tongue lizard hissed and scurried away.

The Gem Polishing Unit

'English for Repeating Students' was assigned to part-time language instructors because none of the full-timers wanted to teach a bunch of teenaged misfits whose love of English grammar rivalled their affection for the dentist's drill.

They were restless young men and women, not clever in the academic sense—most wouldn't have known the past-perfect tense if it had punched them on the jaw—but on the sports fields and judo mats of our university, they were royalty.

They came from farmsteads and fishing villages, construction families, truck driving and carnival clans, sent by parents who knew the market value of blood and bone but also knew that you didn't need a pass in English I-A to get a job with the police department or the Self-Defense Force, which is where most of us assumed we'd end up.

So it was that in the summer of '97, due to a mix-up by student administration, I joined the English haters. For the record, I disliked English as much as the next kid and would have been happier for the entire judo team to sit on my face after a summer training session than to have to spend summer afternoons listening to a blustery, overweight American verse me in adverbs of frequency, or whatever they were. At least in judo you learned to take a fall, and in this town, that could be of real use.

What intrigues me now is that every single member of the class of '97 is today a successful businessperson. Kenta Kayama runs his own organic farm upcountry, supplying apples, nashi pears, figs and strawberries to boutique restaurants all over the Kansai region. Mako Tanaka has a busy downtown restaurant right here in Himeji; I see her sometimes after drinking on Friday nights. Issei Funagi started a racehorse transporting company in Nishinomiya and Yuta Nakajima owns half the oyster farms between here and Ako city along the western seaboard. The other class members are also doing well, I hear.

But the really big surprise has been Jiro Takeda. The toughest, meanest kid who ever swaggered the halls of Himeko University is now a florist! He runs a chain of stores stretching from Hokkaido to Okinawa—even has a branch in Tokyo's Ginza ward, supplying flowers to politicians, rockstars and sumo wrestlers' girlfriends. Someone told me he won the contract for the Tokyo Motor Show.

And me? Well, I guess you could say I'm the exception. You see, I never left this place. My business card says 'Chief of University Maintenance and Security'. It's a living, I'm not complaining. So then why am I telling you all of this? Well, if it weren't for those jackhammers on the ninth floor drowning out my coffee break right now, I would not have remembered the repeaters' English class of '97.

When the American quit halfway through the first term, the university was desperate for a replacement. After advertising the position they received only one response. They didn't even bother to interview and just gave the job to the sole applicant.

This new teacher had a special request. He wanted his own office, separate from the other two part-time instructors who shared the staffroom. Back then, part-timers did not qualify for such a privilege, and still don't, but since the university was in a tight spot, administration quietly acquiesced. They requisitioned a storeroom on the ninth floor, threw in a table and a chair and slapped a number on its door: Room 910.

The other English teachers in the Faculty of Foreign Languages sneered. Who was this upstart? A few days before he was due to begin, a sign mysteriously appeared on the door of 910. In hand-scrawled marker pen it read 'Gem Polishing Unit'. None of us understood the meaning of those words back then—but we do now.

Goto was his name. Not Mister Goto, or Goto-sensei. 'Just Goto,' he told us. I will never forget the first time I saw his face. He had a scar on his jaw like a vein of silver, a moustache covering a bent out of shape lip, and a piece of his left ear was missing. He looked like he'd lived more than one life. Apart from his face, there was no other defining characteristic. Everything else about him—his height, his body shape, his hairstyle, his eye colour—was unremarkable. He wore long-sleeved shirts, buttoned at the collar, and through the entire rainy season and into July, never once did he roll up his sleeves or wear a summer business shirt.

Ah, the jackhammers have stopped. Now, let me think. On the first day of June we drifted in, bellies full from lunch and heads primed for dozing. The sports jocks arrived first, slumping over their desks as the judo boys and girls dribbled in, all cauliflower ears and sweat-soaked t-shirts. After them came the 'yunkees' in their low-slung jeans, spiky orange hairdos and thin, sneering lips.

None of us knew what to make of this stranger in our midst. None of us cared. But soon a feeling of unease spread through the room. It was not just his appearance but what he *did*. He had rearranged the classroom so that the desks and chairs, instead of facing the whiteboard, now faced the window. This forced us to squint into mid-afternoon sun. It was like you read in those World War II manga comics about the Zero fighter pilots who attacked the Americans from out of the sun. It had an oddly subduing effect on us.

That first day, he never used the whiteboard, never touched a CD player or a textbook. He simply asked us to write our names on a card and place it on our desks. We traded glances with each other and shrugged. The American had not even bothered to learn our names, treating us as a single entity to be painfully herded towards summer holidays.

The yunkees tested the water first. They ignored his instructions, took out their phones, drew penises on the desktops and, when that began to bore them, slept.

Then all at once, from out of the sun came a voice that said, 'Issun no mushi ni mo, gobu no tamashii.'

Eyes opened. Heads lifted. Gazes fixed on the silhouetted

man at the front of the class. Had Goto just said that? And what kind of accent was that—Tohoku? Satsuma? Tosa? No one knew.

Goto repeated, but this time in English, 'Even a worm an inch long has a soul half an inch long.'

At first there was silence, then from the back of the room someone murmured, 'Fucking crackpot.' Goto showed no reaction. Not that we could see anyway, because he was completely silhouetted by the sun. From behind his lectern he produced a small woven cane basket and asked everyone to place their phone inside. Anyone who did not, he said, would receive an instant fail. The class complied.

All except Jiro Takeda. He was a big, brawny kid with a crew cut and wire-thin eyebrows. He was from Takasago, a steel town on the other side of the Ichi River where they told the seasons by which way the smokestacks billowed. Jiro looked up and grunted in the negative. The class held its breath.

When Goto turned sideways into the sunlight, his face was as passive as a temple pillar. He advanced on Jiro, giving him time to reconsider. But Jiro's calloused knuckles only tightened around his phone. A snarl rose from inside him. What happened next I cannot explain. From Goto's pocket a black furoshiki cloth, the kind used to carry goods in olden times, appeared. It seemed to fly by itself through the air and landed over Jiro's clenched fist. He gave a loud yelp and flinched, rubbing his hand as if it had been burned. Goto whipped away the cloth. When he held it up, the shape of a phone was clearly visible inside. Then he shook the cloth, and the phone was gone.

Jiro leaped up and lunged.

'Masao-san has it,' said Goto quickly.

Jiro froze. 'What?' he said.

'Masao-san has your phone. It will be returned after class. Now, please take your seat.'

Jiro looked like he'd just been walloped with a baseball bat. He hung there in the sunlight, dumbstruck. There was no 'face' to lose because Jiro didn't have one—it was completely blank. He returned to his desk, to sit in silence and brood.

None of us knew who Masao-san was, nor what Goto had meant by his comment, but I later found out that Masao was the name of Jiro's father. He'd died in a factory accident when Jiro was a high school student. How could Goto have possibly known his name? When the lesson ended and our phones were returned, Jiro's was among them.

We awaited our next lesson with a mixture of curiosity and loathing, but mostly curiosity. Even the often absent yunkee Nakajima-san showed up. He was a tall, thin, bleached-hair kid whose dropout friends were all motorbike gang members and who were constantly pressuring him to join them. Nakajima swaggered in late, headphones on, and slumped into a chair at the back of the room. He glanced warily at Goto, but Goto barely noticed him as he instructed the class on the task ahead. Nakajima lay his head on the desk and closed his eyes.

'Baka mo ichi-gei,' said a voice. It caused Nakajima to leap up and violently pull the headphones from his head, as if someone had increased the volume tenfold.

'Even a fool has one talent,' Goto repeated.

Nakajima rubbed his ears and glared back at him.

'Your father is a fisherman, isn't he?' asked Goto.

Nakajima scowled.

'And he has taught you how to fish, hasn't he?'

Nakajima looked about furtively.

'And you are good at it.'

A look of discomfort crept into Nakajima's face.

'You know *why* you are a good fisherman? Because you watched, listened and learned.' Goto smiled and his lip curled oddly. 'You are not a fool, Nakajima-san. You have a talent.'

The lesson continued, and for the half-dozen lessons that followed, Nakajima, who was sometimes late, never wore his headphones in class again.

July arrived and the summer heat set in. The humidity rose and the whine of cicadas in the cherry trees outside the windows only made us feel more listless. It was around this time that English for repeaters took a new direction. Instead of listening to CDs of native speakers talking about sports, weather, food and shopping, Goto instructed us to listen to ourselves. He explained first in English, then in his strange Japanese, how to write a personal profile: easy stuff at first, like our age, birthdates, hobbies, pets and so on. Then he asked us to write about our families and our home life, and next, about our hopes, dreams, fears and ambitions. It was as if he were asking us to mine our own lives, to split the ore and sift the muck for nuggets and gems, experiences that had changed us, for better or for worse. This might sound grandiose but I believe now he was sending us to the depths of our souls to find out who we really were, what we were really worth not just to ourselves or our families and friends but to society and, perhaps, the world.

If we finished a task early and Goto was satisfied, we could leave the classroom. A strange thing began to happen, however. Instead of leaving, we stayed. We stayed and we wrote. I can't speak for others but I found myself writing things that I could never say in class, things that I was ashamed of, like the time I stole a tortoise from my neighbour's pond, or the time my teenage sister got caught dating a married man, or my parents' divorce. And though my vocabulary was poor, my grammar terrible, I felt a sense of relief as my words filled the paper.

The dog days of summer continued and gave us no respite from the heat and humidity. One afternoon, an electrical storm struck the city. Lightning needled the hills above the university and thunder boomed so loud that it shook the windowpanes. An almighty crack sounded and the entire campus was thrown into darkness. All except our class, where the lights continued to glow and Goto continued to instruct us in his strange mixture of English and Japanese, seemingly unaware that our third-floor classroom must have looked like a lighthouse on that dark and stormy afternoon.

As August approached and other teachers began their ritual of scaring us with reminders of test dates and grading systems, Goto said nothing. Then one day he made an announcement that shocked us all. There would be no test, he said. Instead, our final assessment would be an interview in Room 910. One student at a time.

To decide the order, we drew tickets and my name was pulled last. We had questions. What was the scope of the test? What kind of questions would we be asked? Goto replied that we would have to give a presentation about ourselves.

Then Kayama-san, who was seated on the far edge of the front row of desks, asked, 'Is that a tattoo on your back?' The class looked at Kayama-san, then back at Goto. For the first time since we had known him, he showed surprise. None of us could see any tattoo from our seats because the sunlight made it difficult to see anything at all.

'It's a scar,' said Goto quickly.

'It looks like a kid's face.'

'No one chooses his scars, Kayama-san. Finish your stories for homework, everyone, and bring them to class next week. That's all. Thank you.' We left with our minds working overtime.

The night before the test, I was hit by a motor scooter and knocked off my bicycle while returning from my part-time job. The doctor looked at the X-rays of my shattered elbow and hairline fracture on my pelvis and said I'd be in hospital for two weeks. University administration said that so long as I could produce a doctor's certificate, I would receive special consideration for the term's assessments.

The days passed slowly, painfully, eased by painkillers and the visits of my friends who brought gifts of manga comics and snacks. When my thoughts turned to the repeaters' class, it dawned on me that I had no friends because we were all drawn from different faculties. I had no news about Goto's 'interview'.

Halfway through August, and a few days after leaving hospital, I met Tanaka-san in the video rental shop. She had been my writing partner in Goto's class. She was a big-breasted girl with a thick black pigtail and a judo swagger, but she was also soft-spoken and shy.

'How did the interview go?' I asked.

'What interview?'

'Room 910. You know, Goto's interview.'

She looked surprised, then suddenly self-conscious.

She drew me into an aisle and said, 'You didn't hear?'

'Hear what?'

She looked over my shoulder. 'Goto's not a teacher.'

'What?'

'He's a medium.'

'What the hell are you talking about?'

'He talks to the dead.' She looked pained, but continued. 'Goto asked us to talk about ourselves, our lives. Then he asked us about the future, where did we think we'd be in ten years' time. After we'd answered him, his voice changed. He sounded very old and used many strange words I'd never heard.'

A mother with two young children stepped into the aisle, thumbing her phone while her kids ran amok. She stooped, picked out three or four DVDs and dragged her children to the counter. I turned back to Tanaka.

'And?' I asked.

'I was speaking to my ancestors. They were trying to help me, to tell me what I should do in my life.'

'Holy shit.'

'I asked my grandmother some questions later, about our family history. She said that we are descendants of court chefs, that my ancestors even cooked for the daimyo Honda Tadamasa.'

'What did Goto say? I mean, his voice.'

'He said that I should focus on what I'm good at and never give up because success will come eventually.'

'What do *you* think?'

'I don't know what to think. It's funny, I like cooking but my parents want me to get a job at city hall. It's stable and safe, they say.'

'Where's Goto now?'

'That's the really strange thing. He disappeared after the interviews. No one knows a thing.'

I visited the campus the next day, limping through the empty corridors to the teachers' office building and took the elevator to the ninth floor, where Room 910 was at the end of a darkened hallway. The door was locked, the 'Gem Polishing Unit' sign gone, and only a single waiting chair sat against the wall outside. I sat down and rested, pondering what Tanaka had said about Goto's 'direct line' to her ancestors, about their advice. A chill shot through me and I shivered. I got to my feet and left.

**

As chief of maintenance and security, my job is to keep this campus running smoothly and safely for all students and staff. From time to time, or whenever I'm visiting the ninth floor of this building, I think about what happened back in the summer of '97. I have even been to city hall and to my family's Buddhist temple to investigate my own ancestry. It seems my forebears were engineers. Centuries ago they had helped lay the stone foundations of the majestic White Heron Castle, which rises at our city's centre and attracts so many foreign visitors today.

As for Goto, there is one last piece of information I've managed to find out. I haven't told anyone—not even Tanaka-san—but in 1998, a story appeared in the papers about a body that had been found beside the highway on the Sea of Japan coast. The police had not been able to identify it, except to say that its chest and torso were covered in tattoos. Not of the yakuza variety but, strangely, with the faces of twelve children.

Now, this might be all one huge coincidence, but one year earlier on that exact day, on that same highway, a school bus overturned killing its driver and all of the students on board. Only a female trainee teacher survived. The news story quoted her as saying that she had seen the driver using a mobile phone just before the accident.

For What It's Worth

The second-floor lounge of the Foreign Correspondents' Club had not been Heng's meeting place of choice. Although it afforded a spectacular view of the Mekong and Tonlé Sap rivers merging in the distance, it was one mostly enjoyed by foreigners. For this reason, the FCC was also expensive; a coffee cost three times more than at the Hour Hak Cafe on Street 82, where Heng usually met with other Phnom Penh tuk-tuk drivers between fares.

On this occasion the client had arranged the rendezvous place, so there was little for Heng to do but sit and wait, shifting restlessly in the deep leather armchair. He looked about at the foreigners who sat at the balcony tables, their puffy cheeks like ripe mangoes, their linen shirts and skirts clinging like wet tissue paper to their pale skin. They hardly smiled at the small Cambodian staff who flitted between the tables delivering burgers and beer.

Despite the heat—it was thirty-seven degrees—Heng barely broke a sweat. The dry season, with its languid afternoons and warm fragrant evenings, agreed far more with him than the crushing humidity of the wet season. He checked his watch: quarter to four.

A waitress approached and asked in Khmer for his order. He gave a nervous smile and said he would wait. Resting his head back on the armchair, he breathed deeply and gazed up at the slow-turning ceiling fan, wondering if the next thirty minutes of his life would go according to plan.

A loud crack startled him. He turned to find two young European men facing off over a billiard table at the rear of the lounge. One of them waved to the staff and called for more gin and tonics.

The foreignness of the lounge began to irk him. He sought reassurance in the sounds beyond the long reed sunblinds: the hoots and honks of tuk-tuks shuttling along Sisowath Quay, the putt-putt of passing sampans on the Tonlé Sap, and the eerie singsong call of a steamed snail vendor working the sidewalks.

He glanced at his watch. Ten minutes to four.

On the iodine-coloured walls of the lounge hung photographs of the city's inglorious past: images of monsoon-flooded streets, Khmer Rouge child soldiers marching through rain, landmine victims waving their stumps at passing personnel carriers … Nothing but darkness and misery. He wondered why such photos were on display. His thoughts returned to the meeting ahead and he touched the small backpack at his feet instinctively.

At five minutes to four, a Panama hat appeared at the top of the stairway. The man wearing it was small and slim like Heng, only older. He wore beige cotton pants and a pink polo shirt. His gaze ranged the room and, sighting Heng, he moved lightly through the tables towards him. 'Thank you for coming,' he said, offering a short bow.

He was Japanese, that much Heng knew. He'd picked him up on the city limits three days earlier and at first glance had thought he might be Korean or Chinese; the city was full of contractors working on new riverside hotel developments. After small talk, the passenger had enquired about chann crassna, the agarwood whose fragrance is highly sought after by the Japanese, and whether Heng might know how he could procure some. Heng had said no, but later, as he passed by the National Museum, a brain wave had hit him. His tuk-tuk registration was up for renewal in a few weeks, which would require palm-greasing at the Department of Transportation. There was also the matter of replacing his three balding tyres ... By the time they had reached the Central Market in the heart of downtown, Heng was ready with his proposition.

'Shall we?' the Japanese said, indicating a balcony alcove beyond the billiard players. After a waiter had taken their orders, he produced a packet of Marlboro Gold and offered a cigarette to Heng. They smoked for a while, and Heng felt the man's gaze shift back and forth between him and the National Museum, which lay beyond the garden behind the FCC.

'Have you visited the museum yet?' Heng asked.

The Japanese glanced back at the museum, its tapered eaves rearing up like the delicate necks of waterbirds, graceful and glinting in the afternoon sun. 'No,' he said.

The waiter returned and placed two small cups of black coffee on the table in front of them. They drank slowly, the Japanese slurping, Heng sipping. They smoked another cigarette. When they had finished, the Japanese asked, 'So you have the item?'

'Yes,' Heng said, a little too quickly.

'Then would you accompany me to my room?'

Heng nodded and the Japanese called for the bill and paid. Under the waiter's gaze, they descended the stairway to the street. The Sisowath Quay traffic was light. Beneath the plane trees, tuk-tuk drivers reclined like drowsy cats in their cabs, awaiting a customer or the onset of the cooler evening, whichever would come earlier. Heng avoided their gaze as he followed the Japanese around a corner and into a side street. A noodle cart stood on the sidewalk. The vendor, with her child asleep on a filthy mat beside her, looked up hopefully as the two men passed by. At the end of the street Heng glimpsed the corner cafe where he had parked his tuk-tuk. In the shade of its cascading bougainvillea, two uniformed police sat watching the passing traffic. Heng's gaze did not linger; he followed the Japanese up a stairway and came to a halt on the first-floor landing. A key was inserted, the door opened and Heng ushered inside.

The room was large and cool. An air conditioner hummed in the corner. Pamphlets and business cards with the FCC motif lay untouched on the sideboard. In fact, there was little to say that the Japanese had ever stayed there: the bed covers were trimmed, the amenities undisturbed, and except for a small travel bag resting on a corner chair, there were no clothes or personal effects anywhere. The Japanese turned on the side-board lamp and stood waiting.

Heng took this as his cue. He unzipped his backpack and drew out an object the size of a large cucumber. He passed it to the Japanese and watched him remove the brown paper wrapping. But instead of the smile Heng had been hoping for, deep furrows creased the man's brow.

'This is a buddha,' he said darkly.

'Yes.'

'This is bad. This is *very* bad.'

'What do you mean? It's from Pursat,' Heng said, suddenly anxious.

'Wat Pursat? The Buddhist temple?'

'The supplier said only Pursat.'

'What is this? You think I'm a fool? It is against the law to take a religious artefact out of the country!'

'But it's chann crassna, one hundred percent. It's what you wanted.'

The Japanese shook his head. Murmuring and mumbling, he crossed the room to his travel bag and pulled out a small leather case and a pair of rubber gloves. Beneath the sideboard lamp, he slipped on the gloves and took a scalpel from the case. Heng craned his neck, watching curiously as the man lifted the buddha and shaved a slither from its base. Using tweezers, he held the morsel of wood beneath the light and scrutinised it intently. He then took out his cigarette lighter and ran its flame lightly beneath it until the wood began to smoulder. A thin tail of purple smoke rose into the air. Heng watched the man's face hover over it, his eyes closed, drawing the fragrant air into his nostrils.

'We call it kyara,' the Japanese said, exhaling with a loud sigh.

Heng nodded, hearing but not comprehending.

'Kyara means precious.'

Heng smiled hopefully.

'You are right. It *is* from Pursat. The fragrance says so,' said the Japanese. He returned to the bag and took out a small device with a stainless steel plate on top. Carefully, he balanced the buddha on top and pressed a button.

'Five hundred and eighty-six grams …' He produced a pocket calculator and his slender fingers danced over the keys. He held it up for Heng to see.

'No!' Heng cried. 'We agreed—one thousand US dollars!'

'Yes, but this is a religious statue. It complicates matters.'

'You can cut it up.'

'Cut it up? Are you joking? The wood will dry. The oil quality will be lost!' Irritation crept into his voice, as if he were explaining all of this to a child.

Indeed, Heng was not knowledgeable in such matters. To him, incense was incense. But there was something mysterious in the manner of Japanese people. They seemed to place great value on the simplest of things. They were willing to pay far more for a piece of chann crassna—an old piece of smelly wood—than anyone else.

'Five hundred is my final offer,' said the Japanese.

Heng forced a laugh. 'No, no, no. I cannot do that.' He advanced on the effigy. But the Japanese made an evasive movement at the last moment, putting it beyond Heng's grasp.

'Alright, seven hundred,' the Japanese said quickly.

'No.'

'There is risk involved in taking it out of the country.'

'I have to pay my supplier,' Heng lied. 'One thousand.'

'Eight hundred and I must have a certificate for Japanese customs.'

'I have prepared one.' Heng pulled from his backpack a badly typed letter stating, in English, that the item was neither an artefact nor made from any species of endangered plant, and that it had been 'fumugated' to WHO standards.

The man took the letter and squinted. He frowned at the wording.

'You must pay me one thousand,' said Heng, barely able to hide his desperation.

But the Japanese simply stood there, staring at the letter. 'Kyara is worth more than gold to some people. But not to my customers. Nine hundred is my final offer,' he said.

'Pay me one thousand and I will drive you anywhere for the rest of your stay.'

'That's a fine offer, but I leave tomorrow. Nine hundred— or nothing.'

Heng's gaze fell to the scalpel that lay on the sideboard and his mind raced with possibilities.

'Nine hundred or nothing,' the Japanese repeated. He picked up the scalpel and put it back inside the case.

Heng's gaze returned to the figurine and it suddenly occurred to him how much trouble this piece of wood had caused him. He was not an overly religious man, nor was he superstitious, but he began to wonder if a greater force was now conspiring against him. He sighed. Then, with a solemn nod he said,

'Alright.'

The Japanese beamed. He reached into his pocket, drew out his wallet and counted nine hundred-dollar bills in American currency. He fanned the money across the bed.

Heng scooped up the notes and stuffed them into his chest pocket. 'Thank you,' he said, and moved quickly towards the door.

'Do you have a business card?' asked the Japanese.

'A what?'

'A business card.'

'No, no, I don't,' Heng said, placing a hand on the door.

'Well, here is mine,' the Japanese said, pulling from his wallet a card embossed in English and Japanese lettering. 'Perhaps we might do business again in the future?'

Heng took the card and hurriedly slipped it into his pocket with the cash. 'Goodbye,' he said, and descended the stairway at a trot. When he reached the bottom, he turned in the direction of the corner cafe and gave a short wave. The two policemen rose from their seats and walked towards him. 'Room one A,' Heng said as they passed. When he reached the cafe, he glanced back in time to see the officers step onto the first-floor landing and rap their knuckles against the door.

Heng's tuk-tuk lay parked in the shade of the sprawling bougainvillea vine. There was a passenger seated inside, a man in his fifties wearing polished black shoes and a beige uniform with epaulettes. A pair of Ray-Ban flier's glasses hid his gaze, and between his thick brown fingers a cigarette smouldered.

'Business good?' the man enquired.

Heng slid onto the driver's seat and passed the roll of banknotes discreetly through the rails of the cabin. 'Nine hundred,' he said.

'Nine?'

'He wouldn't go higher.'

'You see,' said the man, thumbing the notes. 'You see what happens when you steal? Life becomes complicated. When someone steals from the National Museum, it's a problem for me. It means I have to find the thief and punish him. If I don't, I look weak.' He stuffed the cash into his chest pocket and resumed smoking. 'Fortunately for you, I am a clever man. I've given you a chance to make amends. Now the museum will be happy. They will get back their buddha. My men will be happy, they will make the foreigner pay for his misdeed. And you, you must be happy too. I will tell the museum that the buddha has been returned anonymously.' He threw the unfinished cigarette to the ground. 'Which leaves the question of the remaining one hundred dollars ...'

Heng stared grimly ahead.

'Let me think about it while you drive,' the man said. He patted Heng on the shoulder, who gave the ignition key a sharp twist. The tuk-tuk coughed to life and pulled out and into the side street. Passing the hopeful noodle vendor, Heng glimpsed the open door on the landing. He wondered how much the Japanese was being shaken down for.

Sisowath Quay was stirring from its slumber. The sleepy tuk-tuk drivers were gone and the tourists had crept back, filling the cafes and restaurants along the riverside esplanade. Heng heard the horn blast of a ferry. He felt the moist, turgid air of the river wash over him, and with it a sense of relief came quietly creeping back.

He turned off the quay and entered a long boulevard lined with plane trees. Hidden behind them stood the ancient abodes of the French colonial merchants and public officials. Their decrepit facades, sullied by tropical rot and pock-marked by bullet holes from another era, still exuded an air of power and influence. Heng brought the tuk-tuk to a stop outside a sprawling two-storied residence whose brass plaque announced 'Royal Gendarmerie of Phnom Penh'.

He cut the engine and waited.

His passenger leaned forward, so close that Heng could smell the tobacco on his breath and the spiciness of his shaving cologne. 'About the one hundred dollars—let's call it a retainer's fee, shall we?'

'What do you mean?' said Heng.

'You seem like someone who knows how to get things. Sometimes I need things. Perhaps we might do business again in the future?'

Heng felt the man's large paw press down on his shoulder, heard him chuckle, then watched as he stepped through the gates, saluted the duty officer, and disappeared inside the gaping doorway of the building.

Heng fished out a half-finished cigarette and lit it. For a few moments he sat and smoked, squinting into the waning sunlight, trying to make sense of the day's events. Try as he might, he couldn't decide whether his fate had taken a turn for the better or for the worse. He recalled a proverb that the owner of the Hour Hak Cafe liked to tell her customers. Whenever the tuk-tuk drivers complained about their customers, she would say, 'The tiger depends on the forest and the forest depends on the tiger.'

What Heng wanted to know was this: what did the forest receive in return for hiding the tiger? He resolved to ask the cafe owner the next morning. He finished his cigarette, twisted the ignition key and gunned the engine loudly. With the duty officer of the gendarmerie looking on, he pulled out into the traffic and set off in search of a customer.

The Tooth Collector

Wondering when this rain will stop? Another hour, maybe longer. You can set your watch by these afternoon thunderstorms. You picked a good place to wait—best kopi in all of Kota Kinabalu right here. This cafe is run by an old friend of mine. That's his sister, May, over there behind the counter. Say, mind if I join you? Thanks. Another cup? It's on me.

Don't mind me asking but are you British? How did I know? Well, your accent, I suppose. And your skin—you look like you've never seen daylight. Ha! I'm joking of course. To tell the truth, and this might sound strange, but you look just like a young man I met right here twenty years ago. He was also from England. A student from London. Took a year off to have a young man's adventure—you know, climb Mount

Kinabalu, see the Sepilok orangutans, the nest collectors of Gomantong caves …

Adventure. A funny word, don't you think? Some people travel halfway around the world to see something new, try something different, and spend a lot of money doing it. Me, I come to this port cafe every afternoon and have an adventure, and it costs me only a few ringgit! As a matter of fact, I had an adventure last night with the woman who runs the durian stand down the street. She's a wild one, I can tell you. But that's another story.

Ah, here's my coffee now. Terima kasih. You're a student too? Biology? Of course. Plants and animals, Borneo has it all. The exotic, the colourful, the dangerous … What do I mean by dangerous? Well now, that all depends on what *you* call danger. Say you travel upriver, into the heart of the jungle, a jungle filled with deadly snakes, poisonous spiders, man-eating crocodiles, crazed elephants. Dangerous, right?

Not to me.

I spent ten years in the logging camps of the mighty Kinabatangan River. Snakes in the roof, scorpions under the bed, leeches on my testicles. Got used to it. Had to. I had a family to feed.

But the jungle can be dangerous in another way that you might not think of. It can mess with your mind. Far from home, family and friends, it crowds in on you, clouds your sense of what is right and wrong, it beguiles and confuses you, like river mist. I've seen men lose their minds. I've seen a grudge turn to a squabble, a squabble to a fight, then one man kills another because he believes that man was trying to do the same to him. Sure, you might have money, you might have God, but neither will save you when all others have lost their minds.

Sorry. I'm rambling. What do I know? I'm just an old boatman. Ashok is my name. And you? Andy?

By god! That's the very same name as the young man I met here all those years ago. Ask my friend Min Tan, the owner of this cafe.

I guess we're stuck here while this rain falls, so let us drink coffee and I'll tell you a story. A story, I'm sorry to say, with no happy ending.

Sticky rice cake? May makes them herself. Here, try one.

Ah yes, Andy, the young adventurer. He was studying to be a dentist. Min Tan met him right here, as I have done with you now. Min Tan was a river trader back then, dealing in rubber, pots and pans, gasoline, sandalwood and birds' nests. See that long boat tied up over there? It was Min Tan's once and I was its pilot. I owe a lot to that man. He got me out of the camps.

You can't see because of this rain but across that gulf there is a river. The Sungai Sugut, it's called, a winding brown torrent that begins in the mountains and pushes all the way to the Sulu Sea. Twenty years ago, only orang sungai, river people, lived there. That's when I first met Min Tan.

He was in trouble. The rubber trade was collapsing, world prices had crashed and he was almost washed up. But Min Tan loved the trader's life and he knew that if he could help the river people then the river people might help him. He had an idea.

Wow, see that lightning! Reminds me of nights on the Kinabatangan …

River tours. That was Min Tan's big idea. Show tourists the true Borneo, the orangutans, monkeys, elephants and crocodiles, roaming free in the wild. And the river people? Well, they didn't need radios, alcohol or cigarettes because the loggers brought them in to barter for access to their land. No, Min Tan wanted to give them something meaningful, something that might actually help them, in return for access to their waterways.

And that's where Andy came in. When Min Tan discovered that Andy was a dental student at a famous college in London, he made him an offer. If Andy would agree to come with him upriver on a field clinic expedition, then Min Tan would guarantee him the experience of a lifetime. Best of all, it would be free of charge. Two Malaysian doctors would be coming, and together they would help the river people. All Andy had to do was help out.

Help out how? Andy asked.

Hand out basic medicines, take notes, offer some dental advice, that kind of thing, Min Tan said.

Well, naturally this excited Andy. Perhaps he saw it as a chance to prove himself, to have a story to tell his friends and family when he returned to England—to have an adventure!

Min Tan told Andy to be at the cafe in two days' time. They would leave early and if Andy was not there, well, Min Tan would leave without him—no hard feelings, no problem at all.

You can guess Andy's choice or I wouldn't be telling you this story.

We took that longboat, *Garuda II*, with her small cabin, outboard engine and shallow draft for the journey. We filled her with tinned food, rice and bottled water, and trunks of medical supplies, as much as we could carry. My job would be to pilot her up the Sungai Sugut, and with my assistant, a young

Bajau sea gypsy named Ali, keep her running smoothly.

We crossed the Gulf of Sulu at dawn and the going was perfect—calm seas, turtles and dolphins diving off our bow, all the way to Terusan, a fishing village at the mouth of the Sungai Sugut. This was to be our rendezvous point with the two Malaysian doctors, who would be coming by boat from Brunei.

But when we arrived, bad news was waiting. The doctors wouldn't be coming. They had telephoned to say that family members of the King of Brunei had fallen ill and officials were keeping their best medical staff in the country. Well, this surprised Andy. But an even bigger shock came when Min Tan informed him that he would now be the sole medical expert on the trip. You see, it was too late to turn back. Supplies had been paid for, fuel ordered along the route, and headmen of four upriver villages were expecting them. Min Tan had invested every last ringgit in this venture. To him, one doctor was better than none.

Did I say 'doctor'? Andy insisted he was not a doctor, not even a dentist. He was a *dental student*. But he could provide medicine and basic first aid, couldn't he, asked Min Tan. What kind of medicine, asked Andy. I'll never forget his face when he opened the medical chests filled with packets of aspirin, bottles of iodine, bandages, malaria tablets, mosquito nets, brandy! Now, I'm no expert, but even a poor old boatman like myself could see that this was playing a little amateur.

Andy looked downcast. He hardly spoke. He spent the entire afternoon down on the jetty looking out to sea in the direction of Kota Kinabalu. Min Tan went down to talk to him and I remember Andy throwing up his hands and shouting. But there was little time for argument because the village headman soon sent for them. They had a patient. A fisherman had been hit on the head by a coconut while bringing his nets ashore. The two of them hurried back to the village and sure enough, there in the hut sat the fisherman with blood streaming down his face and the most miserable expression I'd ever seen. They cleaned the wound and Andy somehow stitched the skin together. Min Tan handed the fisherman a bottle of brandy and sent him on his way.

The headman was impressed. He threw a small party. Min Tan looked happy. I think he saw this as a small victory. Even Andy seemed pleased with himself. He was getting 'hands-on' experience, and for the time being, he forgot his problems.

That night, as we drank arak and smoked local tobacco on the headman's porch, I witnessed the most dramatic sunset I had ever seen. It was as if the whole western sky was on fire. Perhaps it was an omen.

The next day, my assistant and I woke early. After we had changed the propeller to a smaller size for the journey upriver, we arrived back in the village to a big surprise. A line of people stood outside the headman's hut. The story of the fisherman and the coconut had spread quickly. Inside an old schoolhouse, Min Tan and Andy were hard at work, passing out painkillers to people with fevers, applying iodine and ointment to those with skin cuts and infections, and noting down the names of the most serious cases that would have to be sent to Kota Kinabalu.

When Andy received his first toothache case, he asked for the dental kit. On seeing its contents, he flew into a rage. He told Min Tan that this was the twenty-first century and that no one used antique instruments like these for modern dentistry. What could Min Tan do? He'd borrowed the kit from his eighty-year-old cousin, a retired dentist in Sandakan.

In quiet tones, Min Tan persuaded Andy to start with the worst cases. The first was an elderly woman with an abscess. They gave her a small glass of rum, then while Min Tan held her down, Andy pulled the bad tooth. And so it began. The village people left the schoolroom holding their mouths and jaws and looking miserable. But not one of them complained. Again, the headman was happy. He threw another party. And as word spread along the coast to other fishing communities, more cases began to arrive, and it might have continued that way if Min Tan hadn't pressed on with his plan.

Under a dawn mist, we left Terusan with its fisherfolk holding their swollen jaws and watching us from the shore, perhaps wondering where their teeth had gone. When Min Tan asked this very question to Andy, he pulled an old coffee tin from his bag and gave it a shake. The sound carried across the water like a witchdoctor's rattle. One hundred and three teeth—almost three per person! Why was he collecting them, asked Min Tan.

For research, said Andy.

Odd behaviour, don't you think? Certainly, but my concern was to pilot the boat safely upstream to the village of Sungai-Sungai, not to worry about a tin full of teeth. We travelled for five hours under the hot sun, up that great slow-moving mass of muddy water and debris, and every twist and turn, every riverbank and towering tree looked the same as the last. Once, Andy shouted and pointed at movement on the far bank. We turned to see a crocodile thrashing among the reeds, a baby pig in its mouth.

The jungle captivated Andy with its sights and sounds: the hornbills that glided over the treetops, the howler monkeys, bearded pigs and monitor lizards that roamed the shore. Later there were elephants, and Andy clapped his hands and laughed like a child, watching them trample the muddy bank and disappear into the forest as we motored past.

When Min Tan spotted a fisherman in a wooden skiff, he directed me to cut the engine so he could buy river prawns. While we waited under the hot sun for the two men to do their business, a sudden splashing sound came from the bow of the boat. My assistant shouted that Andy was swimming! The fisherman looked up. He too shouted and waved his arms wildly. Min Tan dropped the prawns. He rushed to haul Andy back inside the boat and I will never forget the sight of that young Englishman, lying there like a big, stupid, pale catfish, smiling while Min Tan glowered down at him. The old fisherman shook his head. He said his own son had been taken by a crocodile while swimming in this same river eight years ago.

What it is about youth that make them so fearless? Do they really think they can cheat death? Or are they just stupid? You may laugh at my questions but I'll tell you, there are things a young man will learn the hard way, and not without regret.

Ready for another coffee? May! Kopi dua lagi!

We reached the village of Sungai-Sungai on sunset and a man with a gun was waiting. He sat on the jetty, bloodshot eyes watching us, until the headman arrived and explained that pirates were active in the area. Two outboard motors had been stolen a week before and Kota Kinabalu had sent a 'policeman' to keep watch.

Andy became an instant hit—the younger villagers had never seen a European. The older ones remembered them vaguely from the time of the Borneo Trading Company, before Sabah gained its independence, they said.

That night a stormed rolled in. Like a deaf orchestra playing on a tin roof, it crashed and bashed all night. I'd never heard anything like it. None of us could speak for the noise. So we ate and drank until midnight, and when we awoke the next morning there was a line outside of sick and injured that stretched all the way from the headman's house to the jetty.

They came with heartburn, hookworm, chest pains, back pains, burns and breast infections, and at the end of the line, a young girl stood holding a stillborn baby goat in her arms. The blood pressure measurer we had brought stopped working after a few minutes. Min Tan said it was the humidity, but Andy found that the batteries were old. While my assistant and I helped hand out medicines as best we could, Andy seemed to be in another world. He asked the villagers about their teeth, inspected their mouths, and soon he'd set up a chair inside the headman's house and was pestering Min Tan to make an announcement. Min Tan gave in and a second line quickly formed. The headman and his 'policeman' looked on, watching the villagers enter one by one—some who'd walked for hours through the jungle, barefoot with babies on their backs—and watching them leave with jaws held in their bony hands, faces tight with pain and misery.

Ah, here's the coffee now. Terima kasih, May.

When we left Sungai-Sungai at dawn, Andy and Min Tan were arguing. I heard nothing over the roar of the engine but watched Andy move to the bow of the boat and stay there, with the coffee tin and dental kit between his knees, all the way to Lingkabau.

Min Tan sat slumped in the stern, frowning and scratching his belly. He pretended to read the old newspapers that our food and supplies had been wrapped in. When it rained he moved inside the cabin. But Andy never budged, and just as well—he hadn't bathed since we left Terusan. He just sat unflinching as the torrents fell on him, while I did my best to navigate through the dancing water.

Lingkabau came and went; another village, another clinic. And all the while Andy's coffee tin grew heavier. The river grew narrower, the current faster, the eddies more dangerous and demanding my total concentration. We reached the village of Salulgong exhausted and, after tending to the sick and injured, ate dinner and bedded down in a longhouse. Sometime in the night I was woken by the sound of men arguing outside. Through the gaps in the bamboo wall I saw Min Tan in a real state. I heard him accuse Andy of endangering the entire trip with his behaviour.

Duties, cried Andy, standing half-naked in the moonlight. He accused Min Tan of not listening to him when he'd insisted he wasn't a doctor, that he was a *student*!

Then why was he pulling so many teeth, Min Tan shot back. The headmen in the last two villages had pressed him with the same question.

A student must learn by experience, shouted Andy. Besides, he'd been promised an experience of a lifetime, hadn't he?

Min Tan growled. He withdrew to brood and again the longhouse fell silent.

In the early afternoon of the fifth day we arrived at Kaingaran, near the headwaters of the Sungai Sugut. The headman was eager to see us as a man had appeared from the jungle that morning to say his pregnant wife had become ill. It would take five hours on foot to reach her and bring her back.

Andy was not feeling well—diarrhoea, he said—so Min Tan, myself and my assistant set off with the husband and a team of village men. But something was bothering Min Tan, and though he didn't say, I believe he was worried about leaving Andy in the village alone. When we reached the woman, she was feverish and weak, but still breathing.

It was on sunset when we arrived back in Kaingaran. Save for the gas lamps that glowed like fireflies against the darkness of the jungle, the village appeared deserted. Then a boy hurried towards us, breathless.

Come! Hurry, he cried.

Min Tan rushed forward, following him to a small building that served as a schoolhouse on the jungle's edge. A single lamp glowed within. At its threshold, Min Tan hesitated. Then came a sound I hope never again to hear in my life.

Shouts and screams and crashing noises came from within the schoolhouse. Min Tan dived inside with the village men close behind. All went dark and more crashing sounded. Soon the village men emerged and in their arms they carried their headman, his jaw bandaged, his face bleeding and swollen.

Min Tan appeared in the doorway, his face grim, his gaze dark. In one hand he clutched Andy's coffee can, and in the other a set of bloodied dental tools. He marched quickly to the river, hurried to the end of the jetty, and with the villagers looking curiously on, he flung the blood-soaked instruments into the water. Then he held out the can and emptied it.

Look! The rain has stopped. I should go. My lady friend, the durian seller, she's expecting me. Oh dear, it seems I've left my wallet behind. I'm ashamed to ask, but would you mind? I'm so sorry. You're very kind …

And Min Tan, you ask? Well, let me say this—he sold his boat, bought this cafe and never returned to the Sungai Sugut. As for Andy, well, you might say that he never left. A boy from the village said he saw him hunched naked at the river's edge that night, talking to himself, clawing the mud, searching for something.

The next morning they found only footprints. The Kota Kinabalu police said Andy had drowned. They always say that. But you know what I think? I believe a bigger set of teeth collected him.

Thanks for the coffee.

Tenderloin

The Picaroon Club stood on a hill at the Paris end of the city. Its salmon pink facade rose eight stories between a diamond jeweller and a florist, and its corniced entranceway, half-hidden by plane trees, was guarded by a retired Royal Marine named Colin.

Through this door stepped the city's elite: men of means and influence, men who still toasted the Queen before dinnertime and turned out once a year in their tuxedos to celebrate Yuletide. It was one of the few places where a private school old boy could dine on marbled steak and mash without his wife or surgeon knowing.

To oversee the smooth running of this exclusive establishment, its five hundred strong membership had elected an Englishman by the name of E. W. Combes.

To the daytime staff he was Mr Combes, secretary of the club, a man who could sense a mislaid fork a mile away, a blemished wineglass at a hundred paces, a gravy stain at ten. His directives struck like velvet thunderbolts: he would sack the good, the bad and the lazy in a whisper if he thought the club's standards were in peril. The evening shift called him Tombs.

Although his taste in cars was generally appreciated—he drove a Jaguar in British racing green—his monthly meetings, held on Friday afternoons following lunch service, were to the chagrin of all. Then, the entire staff, including the room maids, waiting staff, kitchen hands, line chefs and sous-chef, would assemble wearily in the grand dining room to receive their 'pep talk'.

So it was one Friday afternoon in mid-December that E.W. Combes called a meeting. The staff stood about in a state of listlessness and languor until the ancient walnut grandfather clock in the foyer struck three and in strode the catering manager, bowtie flapping like a morpho butterfly at his neck.

'The secretary has been called away on sudden business,' he said.

The waiting staff took to the dining chairs as if the music had stopped, leaving only the kitchen hands standing. When the commotion had settled, the catering manager cleared his throat.

'We have a thief in the house,' he said grimly.

His gaze ranged the room searching for telltale signs—a nervous twitch, a bead of sweat, a buttock shift—but found none. The staff returned his gaze, unimpressed. Antonio, the head waiter, suppressed a belch, Dot studied her nails, and Gwen glanced at the half glass of sherry beside her purse on the waiter's stand. Only Marina the Polish sous-chef caught the catering manager's eye with a sudden effort to scratch between her broad shoulder blades.

The kitchen hands shifted uneasily; with their backs to portraits of Winston Churchill and Queen Elizabeth II, they looked like partisans before a firing squad. There was Dev, the small Sri Lankan with big flashing teeth, Dimitri the young Romanian, lanky and sniffing, and Pan from China, older, calm, all-seeing. Only Youssef the Moroccan bartender was absent. He worked evenings.

The catering manager turned to the head chef. 'Over to you, Ray.'

A large man in black and whites with soup-splattered clogs and a clipped beard stepped forward. In a thick Galway accent, he said, 'I'm very disappointed to report that some Wagyu Angus fillet steak has disappeared.'

'Disappeared—poof!' said the catering manager, snapping his fingers.

The head chef continued. 'These tenderloin fillets were ordered in specially for a dinner party tonight and—'

'Mr Combes,' interrupted the catering manager, 'Mr Combes would like to know what happened to them. The secretary has given the person involved twenty-four hours to step forward—in confidence.'

The effect was instantaneous: Marina resumed her scratching, Gwen stifled a yawn and Dimitri made a passing run at his nostrils with his jacket cuff. Of all the staff in the grand dining room, only Pan nodded solemnly.

Then Antonio spoke. 'Like an am'sty, you mean?'

The entire room turned on the stout middle-aged man with the smooth olive pate, Mafioso midriff and black bow tie dangling from his crisp white collar.

'A what?' said the catering manager.

'An am'sty. Y'know, like a pardon for steppin' forward.'

'Mr Combes will be the judge.'

'And executioner,' Gwen murmured.

The catering manager felt compelled to then to impress how lucky they all were to work in such a fine establishment, which paid its staff above the award rate, provided meals and even taxis home.

'Twenty-four hours,' he said.

The meeting was over. The servers, room cleaners and kitchen staff dispersed. Only the Ukrainian laundry ladies lingered, looking to Marina for a translation, which she gave with a flip-flap of her fat hand that made their eyes widen. I felt sorry for them, and for the kitchen staff. They weren't thieves; they were hardworking and honest. They didn't give two hangs for the rich and powerful. They only wanted a working week with a pay cheque at the end of it.

The birdcage lift rattled quietly to the tenth-floor locker rooms, disgorged its cargo of mumbling, grumbling waiting staff. Antonio kicked open the emergency exit door and stepped onto the rooftop. He pulled a pack of Camel Lights from under his cummerbund, slipped one between his lips and flicked his Zippo. He watched the city bustle below him.

'Who's the *tonto*?' he said, sensing my presence behind him.

'The what?'

'The idiot—the steak thief.'

I shrugged and joined him at the roof railing. 'I guess someone got sloppy.'

'Damn right they did.' He drew on his cigarette. 'The chefs aren't that dumb.'

'I saw Marina walking out with a half-dozen fresh oysters the other day.'

'Oysters are a dime a dozen, they're always on the menu. They all do it.'

'The kitchen hands don't.'

'That's 'cos they've got something to lose.'

'Dot says it's a gratuity because we don't get tips.'

'For what? Drinking coffee and smoking on the job?' He laughed dryly. 'She means a liberty.' He drew on his cigarette, letting the smoke slide from the corner of his mouth. 'No, this time the thief got greedy. They took a whole box when they should've just taken one or two steaks.'

'How do you know that?'

'Ray told me.'

'Well, don't look at me.'

'No one's lookin' at anyone and it's better left that way.'

Our gaze returned to the city and the river that cut a wide muddy swathe towards the bay. I could see stockbrokers drumming away at their office computers, construction workers chinwagging with coffee and cigarettes in hands, a crane driver napping in his cabin.

Antonio dropped his cigarette into a rusted Nescafé tin.

'Don't you get sloppy now.' He winked, then walked back to the exit door.

I left the club with Colin's gaze on my back and crossed the city gardens, where end-of-week drinks had begun early for a group of office workers, then entered the inner suburbs. I had an assignment to finish, a creative writing piece overdue since November. I still had no idea what to write, but as I paced the warm asphalt, a seed began to germinate, a tale of mystery and intrigue whose possible title pushed to the surface like mushrooms under moonlight: 'The Wayward Wagyu', 'The Flyaway Fillet', 'A Tenderloin Tale' … 'Steak Out!'

I passed the Old Burma Hotel and caught a whiff of stale beer through its opened doors. I turned around and went inside. Ordering a beer, I asked the tattooed barmaid if she had tenderloin fillet on the menu. She said no and asked if I was hungry. I said no, drained my beer and ordered another. Who could be so dumb? Who would have the gall to upset the working harmony of the club by stealing an entire box of prime fillet steak?

True, the Picaroon Club was a den of thieves: Normandy brie, Belgian chocolates, a Margaret River red, a Marlborough white or sometimes a half-kilo of Costa Rican coffee travelled out the door in our collective purses and rucksacks. But it was incremental, discreet, like a tunneller taking spoonfuls of soil from beneath a prison wall. No one got harmed because no one noticed.

As a junior waiter I was guilty by association, but I was a reluctant thief. If I worked private functions with the senior staff then by default I was party to the spoils, taking my 'gratuity' without remark or remorse. What else could I do? Refuse and be ostracised for *not* stealing? Antonio would say,

'Fuggedaboutit!'

I returned to my flat, slept a half-hour, took a shower and

returned to the club in time for the staff meal at half past five. Dot was in the staffroom, leafing through *The Sun*, a plate of cod and chips on the table in front of her with a ginger ale.

'Dinner for ten in the President's Suite,' she said without looking up.

'Business meeting?'

'A ninetieth.'

'I like birthdays. Any sparklers?'

'The old lady gets asthma.'

'Steak?'

Dot stopped chewing and looked up. Her eyes narrowed.

'As a matter of fact, it's chateaubriand. From the Hastings Club,' she said.

'The Hastings Club sent us their meat?'

'Ours was stolen—or did you forget today's riveting announcement?'

'I thought we were rivals?'

'They owe us for the Christmas decorations we lent them this year.' She returned to the paper and added, 'You know what they say—keep your friends close and your enemies closer.'

I laughed. Not because she was right but because Dot was the last person I'd have imagined to quote Sun Tzu while reading *The Sun*.

The dinner was held in a small private room, low lit and plush with vermillion carpet and a chandelier that hung over an oval-shaped mahogany dining table. The birthday girl arrived at six-thirty, a red love heart balloon trailing her wheelchair, with sons, daughters-in-law and teenage grandchildren in attendance.

I took the drinks orders while Dot passed around a tray of hors d'oeuvres—'horses' doovers', she called them. Gran ordered a Pimms and soda, the rest of the party Japanese Slippers. I made a call to the fifth-floor bar and in a short while Youssef sent the dumb waiter down with a yellow plastic bucket filled with a frog green cocktail and eight glasses. The note attached said 'No more Jap slippa'. I ladled the glasses, drank one and served the rest.

We served the pumpkin soup from terrines, following it with a dollop of King Island cream and a sprinkle of chives, then retreated to the waiters' annex. Dot left me to top up the wineglasses while she disappeared for a smoke.

A fifty-something mother of two from the western suburbs, smoke and drink had turned Dot's voice husky. The harder she worked, the more she drank, and the more she drank, the more she talked.

She wore her dyed blonde hair in a tight bun and her uniform a half-size too small, which helped her breasts defy gravity. She had a cabin attendant's gait and a smile that turned off and on like a seatbelt sign. Her make-up was a little too thick, but in the dimness of the club's salons, bars and dining rooms, it must have looked just right. The older members loved her. Some of the younger ones had even asked her out.

Dot was the kind of woman who could turn a dreary board meeting dinner into a Christmas party. She wore nice perfume, she was polite and tactful, and she knew how to handle the younger, cheekier club members in a way that amused the older ones. She was the kind of woman they all yearned for but could never have. She was their forbidden fruit, a fallen angel from the south side of the tracks.

Dot thought I was a smart-arse. She called me a 'clever little dick from the eastern burbs' because I went to university and studied creative writing. But she liked me because I listened. It was hard not to listen: hers were tragedies that would have made Aristotle weep. Some nights she'd laugh, others she'd cry. The catharsis flowed faster with red wine, and the more we worked together, the harder it became to finish a night sober.

Dot's sister had committed suicide three years earlier and left a twelve-year-old girl in her care. Dot had two daughters of her own: the eldest was an on-again off-again alcoholic, barely holding down a job in a roadhouse on the state border; the youngest was a long-haul truck driver who'd bought her own rig with money saved from three years as a FIFO in Papua New Guinea, and of this feat Dot was immensely proud. Which was more than she felt for her husband. He'd gone to work in the outback goldmines, had met a Vietnamese hooker named Lily—'a real gold-digger'—and they'd eloped with his savings to the tropical north coast. That was two years ago and Dot had heard nothing since.

'So who do reckon did it?' I asked, when she returned.

'Did what?'

'Stole the steak.'

'I dunno. One of the kitchen hands probably.' She busied herself with the plate warmer.

'I doubt it.'

'Why? They get paid less and have to feed their wives and kids.'

'That's mean.'

'That's life.'

The phone sounded. I picked it up and heard the clash and

bang of the kitchen hands' orchestra, then Marina's heavy breathing.

'Da chateaubriand, it come now,' she said. 'Two sauces, y'know?'

'Yes, I know. Bernaise and red wine.'

'*Tak, tak*. Okay, bye-bye.'

The dumb waiter delivered a tray of the Hasting Club's tenderloin fillet, seared to perfection with its blood juices oozing. I placed the sauce terrines on the platter and, while Dot laid warm crested plates in front of the guests, served two thick slices of fillet with a sauce of their choice. Dot followed with the roast potatoes, beans and stuffed mushrooms. It was a dinner fit for a British cabinet, not a ninetieth birthday party, but that was our specialty and no one complained.

The evening wore on, until the host signalled to us and we dimmed the lights. I lit nine candles on the birthday cake and delivered it with applause to the table, whereupon Gran gave the nine flaming decades her best shot and her tipsy grandkids snuffed out the rest. Dot sliced and I served. Cheese and coffee followed. Then, when Gran began to yawn, it was all over.

The birthday had been a success; it always was when the guest of honour was a nonagenarian. We dispatched the dumb waiter filled with dirty plates and glassware to another floor, to become another person's problem, then we collapsed in the dining chairs and poured ourselves the leftover Shiraz. Dot had had her first glass of wine before we'd served the cake. Now, it was strange seeing her sitting in the guest of honour's seat, a woman of somewhat similar appearance but decades younger, smoking a cigarette while she massaged her feet.

'Thieves, liars and scoundrels, the lot of them,' she slurred.

'Who?'

'The kitchen staff.'

'They work hard.'

'And we don't?'

'I'm just saying.'

She reached for the bottle and topped me up, then drained the rest into her own glass. She quaffed the lot and said, 'I bet it was that Asian guy.'

'Dev?'

'No, the one with the buddha eyes.'

'Pan?'

'Pan, Pan, the kitchen hand. What kind of name's that?'

'His family name.'

'Bet he changed it to get the job.'

'He was a doctor back in China.'

'Trees?'

'Traditional medicine.'

'Same difference.'

'He's got a family, wife cleans at a high school, kids ...'

'There you go, what did I say—he's got to put food on the table.'

'He's just not that kind of guy.'

'We'll see what Teddy's got to say about that.'

'Who?'

'I mean, Mr Combes ...'

If the light in the room had been brighter I was sure I would have just seen Dot's cheeks redden. She took the cheese knife and cut a slither of King Island cheddar from the leftover cheese board. She placed it on a water cracker, pushed it past her red lips and crushed it in slow, deliberate movements.

After we had arranged the chairs for the cleaning staff and extinguished the chandelier in the President's Suite, Dot took the birdcage lift to the locker rooms and I ventured to the kitchen.

They were hard at work; they always were. Dev operated the industrial dishwasher like a one-armed bandit, shoving in the trays of dirty plates and cutlery, yanking them out amidst billows of steam. Then he'd push them on to Dimitri, who jingle-jangled it all onto sorting mats beneath the blazing lights of the bain-marie. On the far side of the kitchen, Pan wrestled huge pots from the stovetops to the tubs, scrubbing them as if they were Howitzer muzzles. The humidity of the kitchen rivalled the tropics.

They said very little. Like all of us, the kitchen hands just wanted to get the job done and go home.

I pushed through the swing doors and into the bar where Youssef was mixing a final order for two businessmen who sat smoking cigars at a corner table.

'Hey, where you go with these?' he said, watching me take three bottles of beer from the bar fridge.

'For the kitchen staff.'

His gaze held mine momentarily. Then he grunted, shrugging in a way that said he wasn't watching, which was the way we all conducted ourselves at the Picaroon Club.

Dev and Dimitri took the beer, snapping off the caps with their tea towels and gulping it gratefully. Pan nodded his thanks but left his bottle unopened on the counter and kept on with his pots.

'So who do you reckon took the steak?' I asked Dev.

He pretended not to hear, took another swig of beer then

shook his head.

'C'mon, you guys see everything,' I said.

He finished the bottle and handed it back to me.

'Thank you,' he said.

I took the hint, poured myself a coffee and made for the swing doors.

'He knows,' Dev said quickly, jerking his head. 'He saw her take it.'

'Who?'

Over the thrum of the dishwasher, it was as though he had heard. Pan's head emerged from the gaping maw of a soup pot. He looked in our direction, his gaze steady, his expression unreadable. I knew then that I'd overstepped the mark. It was a given that Pan would never speak; no one would.

The weekend arrived with a low-pressure system delivered up from the Southern Ocean. The city braced itself against the elements, hunkering down over caffe latte and weekend papers while I sat at my writing desk, shivering, watching the rain drum pointlessly against the window. The harder I tried, the gloomier I became. By Sunday evening I had five pages of a half-baked mystery with no 'big bang' ending—no closure. The deadline was the following day.

The rain persisted into Monday and the morning city streets were filled with umbrellas and spraying tyre wash. I made my way sullenly to the club for the lunch shift. Colin, wearing a top hat and grey tails, met me at the door.

'They got him,' he said.

'Got who?'

'The thief.'

'Who, for Chrissake?'

'The Chinaman.'

'Pan?'

'Dot caught him drinking on the job, reported him to Mr Combes.'

'What? What about the steak?'

'Says he doesn't know anything.'

'You can't sack someone with no evidence!'

'Drinking on the job.'

'But we all—'

'You know what they say, mate, where there's smoke ... Oi, you stepping in or what?'

Dot didn't say much that day. She kept to herself; all the staff did. It was as if everyone was taking stock of the situation, considering who their allies and enemies might be.

When lunch had finished, I took the lift to the locker rooms. But rather than enter I stepped onto the rooftop. Drizzle fell, veiling the tall buildings in a fine mist and obscuring the river beyond. At the rail I look downwards, watching the umbrellas twist and twirl along the footpath below. I glimpsed a blonde-haired woman leave the club and make her way along the street to the corner, then turn. I crossed to the other side of the roof and leaned across the rail. Through the canopy of plane trees, I glimpsed her climb into a green Jaguar, watched as it pulled away from the curb and joined the afternoon traffic heading south.

I stood there puzzled, drizzle-soaked, and for a moment couldn't make sense of what I'd just seen. Didn't want to.

But just as Dot did, on nights when something was bothering her and she'd tell it out in a story, I hurried home through the rain, sat down at my desk and began to write.

The Picaroon Club stood on a hill at the Paris end of the city. Its salmon pink facade rose eight stories between a diamond jeweller and a florist, and its corniced entranceway, half-hidden by plane trees ...